Jake's Girl

AND

A Touch of Spring Fever

Jake's Girl

JEAN CURZON

— AND —

A Touch of Spring Fever

GRACE GOODWIN

WORDSWORTH EDITIONS

The paper in this book is produced from pure wood pulp, without the use of chlorine or any other substance harmful to the environment. The energy used in its production consists almost entirely of hydroelectricity and heat generated from waste materials, thereby conserving fossil fuels and contributing little to the greenhouse effect.

First published by Robert Hale Limited

This edition published 1994 by
Wordsworth Editions Limited
Cumberland House, Crib Street, Ware,
Hertfordshire SG12 9ET

ISBN 1 85326 503 9

Printed and bound in Denmark by Nørhaven

Jake's Girl

One

Samantha flicked an enquiring eyebrow at the tall figure lounging against the window frame.

'Things can't be that bad, surely?'

'Maybe not.' But she noticed a disquieting gleam in the solicitor's keen grey eyes. 'However, in many respects a business partnership is as binding an agreement as a marriage.' His mouth curved in the merest suggestion of a smile. 'More so in some ways.'

Samantha frowned as her mind turned to her errant partner.

Men! she thought crossly. Never around when you need them. Jake had certainly chosen a fine time to disappear from the face of the earth!

But, despite her annoyance, she felt a little surge of affection as his image danced before her. She and Jake had been through too much together for something like this – serious though it seemed – to come between them.

The man moved slightly and a shaft of hazy April sunshine darted past his shoulder to burnish Samantha's copper hair with fiery lights. She blinked and raised a slender hand to shield her eyes. An intricately carved seal-ring glinted on a silver-tipped finger and, for a long moment, his eyes rested on it speculatively.

'You have understood, haven't you?' She heard the

warning note beneath the urbane professional concern. 'Or would you like me to go over it again?'

'I understand, thanks.' Her face was rueful. 'It rather looks as if all Jake Matheson's debts are now mine.'

'Not quite as bad as that – only the ones incurred in your company's name.' He smiled and she saw his face came alive with an easy charm.

Too easy! Samantha thought warily. But that smile made him look oddly familiar. Just where had she seen it before?

Searching her memory at first produced a blank. Then she recalled the recent research she had been doing for that Moulin Rouge documentary for Channel 9 and the old publicity photographs she had seen of Edith Piaf and the young Yves Montand.

That must be it, she told herself uncertainly. With that shock of dark wavy hair, expressive mouth and those incredible quicksilver eyes, she had to admit that this man had a certain appeal.

Then she noticed the conjecture lurking in those eyes and remembered that he was Jake's solicitor, not hers. Her own interests were not his concern. She revised her assessment hastily. Attractive certainly but definitely not be trusted!

He's not levelling with me for one thing. It's as if he knows something that I don't. Something he's made up his mind not to tell me! Or – she had a flash of insight – maybe he just doesn't trust me either! The idea diverted her. A game of cat and mouse with neither knowing who was which! But her amusement was short-lived as the seriousness of her predicament hit home.

The solicitor's smile disappeared and was replaced by an air of cool briskness. Playtime is over, she thought uneasily.

'However, those bills do need to be paid, Ms James.'

He's going straight for the jugular, she told herself and her mind turned to the envelope in her handbag. When she'd opened it that morning she'd felt there'd been some mistake. But the invoice stated quite clearly that Jake had purchased a car in the company's name. And not just any old car: this was an expensive vintage model. Damn you Jake! she thought annoyed. How could you do this to us?

'But surely I'm not responsible for this?' She produced the offending document with a flourish.

With whiplash grace, he closed the gap between them. 'May I?'

Samantha nodded and saw his eyes narrow as he rapidly scrutinized it. Then they flicked towards her with perfect equanamity.

'Seventy thousand pounds?' One eyebrow arched into his forehead quizzically. 'But surely your partner must have consulted you about this purchase?'

Samantha's cheeks flamed.

He's deliberately trying to make me feel like a complete idiot, she thought. He's succeeding too! Her hands tightened over the wooden arms of her chair and she took a deep breath to calm herself.

'He did mention that he was thinking of buying a vintage car. It's his hobby, you see. But he certainly didn't say that he was buying it in the company's name.'

'Didn't you ask?'

'Well, no. But I assumed that....' Her voice trailed

off as she saw the faintly pitying look that flitted across his face. He must think that I'm just a stupid, gullible woman, she thought irritated. Perhaps he's right and that's exactly what I am! Her head jerked up defiantly.

'Just how well do you know him yourself, Mr Sinclair?' she challenged. 'Has he paid your own bill yet? Or will I find that I'm responsible for that, too?'

For the briefest of moments he appeared taken aback. Then he answered smoothly.

'My client's affairs – financial or otherwise – are not the subject of discussion here.'

Samantha looked at him sharply. He had definitely emphasized that word 'affairs'. I do believe he thinks that Jake and I are lovers! For a fleeting second the idea amused her. It would certainly have amused Jake.

'But he does seem to have put you in rather a tricky situation.'

Samantha remained silent whilst she tried to marshal her thoughts. It had been nearly three weeks since she'd last seen Jake. Not unusual really as they'd decided when they'd set up their company *Scene-Setters* that they should pursue their commissions independently. As their work took them to various places both in the UK and further afield, they were seldom both in London at the same time.

She herself had just returned from two weeks in Paris and had been horrified to discover that bill amongst the others lying on her mat. When she'd opened the letter from Jake's solicitor asking her to get in touch, she'd lost no time in making this appointment with him.

On the way here, she'd clung to the hope that he'd tell her that there'd been some mistake. But it was becoming increasingly obvious that he was going to do no such thing.

'I should have been more careful,' she said at length. It certainly wasn't in Samantha's nature to be bitter, but she was beginning to feel very much like it now.

'Perhaps. But most people trust their friends.' He went to sit opposite her. 'And you are – er – good friends, I take it, not merely business partners?'

His tone was studiedly casual but, to her intense embarrassment, she again felt a wave of colour sweep over her face.

'I really don't think that's any of your business!' she flashed, indignation lending a steely glint to her smoky-blue eyes. There was no way that she was going to discuss her relationship with Jake with this man! He wouldn't understand anyway. If he wanted to believe that they were having an affair, let him!

He showed no surprise at her reply but merely glanced at the file that lay open in front of him.

'I see that you're living in Mr Matheson's flat.'

'No. I'm not,' she corrected him brusquely. What made him think that?

'Really? I seem to have the same address for you both.'

'Perhaps you have. But the flat belongs to me, not Mr Matheson.'

One brow raised slightly in surprise.

'I see,' he said softly, making a brief note. But his look had been frankly disbelieving. She was right, she thought, he didn't trust her!

'Then it seems I've been misinformed. I must apologize.'

She heard a hint of cynicism in his voice. He obviously thinks I am lying, she thought exasperated. She stared across at him. But his expression was perfectly composed.

'What I'm wondering now, is just how far your partner has taken you into his confidence. As you know, he asked me to draw up your partnership agreement. I assume you are familiar with its contents.'

'Of course!' Samantha bristled. Did he think her a complete moron?

'I take it you have your own solicitor?'

'I most certainly do.'

'In that case I would strongly suggest' – he leaned forward as if to emphasize his words – 'that you consult him about this matter as soon as possible. Then perhaps he could get in touch with me and we can work out the best course of action together.'

Samantha's head came up defiantly.

'It wouldn't occur to you that I would prefer to deal with the situation myself.'

'I wouldn't advise you to do that, Ms James. It's very difficult for those closely involved to get a true picture of _'

'– the mess they're in,' Samantha finished for him.

'Well, I wouldn't have put it exactly like that.' Again the smile. 'But you do need somebody to advise you on how to _' The insistent shrilling of the telephone interrupted him and he returned to his desk. 'Excuse me a moment.'

For a moment Samantha listened idly. Then she

turned her mind to the question of whether she
wanted her father's solicitor to act on her behalf.

A picture of him immediately flashed before her
eyes – silver-haired, fatherly and infinitely reassuring.
That's exactly how a solicitor ought to be. Not looking
as if he'd just stepped out of some television law series
like this one did.

Her father's solicitor had been a friend of the family
ever since she could remember. Instinctively she
shuddered at the thought of him learning about the
predicament that she had unwittingly found herself
in. The last thing she wanted was to see his expression
of kindly concern as he attempted to make some sense
of the situation. What's more he would almost certainly
convey his anxiety to her parents, whatever
professional ethics might decree.

Both her parents had met and had liked Jake. But
her father had gently warned her about being
financially involved with anyone quite as
unpredictable as he'd judged him to be. And it rather
looks as if he'd been right, she thought wryly. If this
Sinclair man was to be believed, it looked as if she had
just become the proud owner of debts totalling well
over eighty thousand pounds!

There was a decisive click as the receiver was
replaced. Then he pressed the intercom button.

'Hold my calls, Elizabeth. I don't want to be
interrupted.'

As his attention returned to her, Samantha came to
a decision. 'I'd like to know exactly where I stand
before I contact my own solicitor.'

'As you wish,' he said evenly. 'But first, I'd like to
know something more about your company. *Scene-*

Setters, isn't it? Your partner wasn't very forthcoming about it, I'm afraid.' He sat back in his chair, linked his hands behind his head, and regarded her in a leisurely way. 'What do you do exactly?'

Samantha took a deep breath before she spoke. *He probably knows perfectly well what we do. He just wants to see how much I know about it myself! I bet he thinks I just gallivant around the country having a good time at Jake's expense!*

'You may know that my partner and I were at university together.' He nodded briefly. 'Whilst there, we became very involved in the college theatrical productions and came to realize how important the background details are. Things like the settings, costumes and historical accuracy generally. So we talked it over and decided to form *Scene-Setters* to research and advise film, television and theatrical producers on these aspects.'

'I see.' He looked at her reflectively. 'But don't film and television companies generally employ their own people to do this sort of thing?'

'The bigger ones do, yes. But quite a number of the smaller, independent companies find it less costly to use freelance consultants for this.'

'It appears that you both travel a good deal.'

'We do. We need to spend a lot of time searching for suitable settings. Both here and abroad.'

'Which is where your partner is at the moment?'

'Yes. In the States. Somewhere,' she added ruefully.

She had only missed him by a day. She thought of the message that Jake had left taped to the refrigerator door. *Sammy, love. I'm off Stateside for a few weeks. Bit of business and pleasure combined. Tell you all about it when I return. Keep smiling. Jake.* Several kisses had been scrawled underneath, but no address.

'Quite. Your work sounds fascinating, I must say.' Then his amiable expression was replaced by a frown. 'However, from what I can see, it appears that, quite apart from the purchase of the car, *Scene-Setters* has amassed a considerable number of debts.' He paused whilst he leafed through a number of papers.

Our accounts! thought Samantha, annoyed. What is he doing with those?

He anticipated her question.

'Your partner took the step of asking your accountant to pass these on to me. I understand that you were abroad at the time and that there was some difficulty in contacting you direct.'

Samantha nodded. She had been so engrossed in her research that it hadn't occurred to her that anything would be other than normal back in London.

'Perhaps you would care to take a look at these.'

He passed over a sheaf of bills and Samantha's spirits sank as she saw the amounts involved. Smothering an exclamation of dismay, she passed the papers back across the desk.

'I haven't seen most of these before. May I ask why my partner sent these to you rather than wait until I returned?'

'He asked me to settle these bills on his behalf in his absence.'

'Why on earth should he do that?' she asked bewildered.

'Ah. I see that he hasn't confided in you in this respect.' He hesitated. 'However, I feel that you are entitled to an explanation.' Again he hesitated.

Samantha waited expectantly. Despite the circumstances, she felt intrigued. Jake had always been very mysterious about his personal life. She could never even remember him mentioning his family. Samantha was never one to pry into things that didn't concern her. There were certainly things that she herself would prefer to remain private. But she had sometimes wondered where Jake had got the money to live on in the early days of their venture.

'Mr Matheson suggested that these bills could be settled by drawing against his trust fund.'

'His trust find?' she echoed obligingly as he appeared to expect some response.

'He is expecting to inherit a certain sum from a family trust on attaining the age of twenty-seven which, as you may know, is still several years away.'

Samantha nodded. Jake, like herself, was still only twenty-three.

'And can't this be arranged?' she asked hopefully, all at once glimpsing some light at the end of the darkened tunnel in which she now found herself.

He shook his head and a lock of dark hair fell forwards to shadow his eyes. He brushed it back impatiently.

'It's not quite as easy as that. Unfortunately, he has already drawn several large sums of money against the fund and the trustees have refused to advance further amounts. I'm afraid he doesn't yet know of this decision. However, I understand that it was never his intention for you personally to be responsible for his debts.'

Samantha, who had begun to anticipate that he was going to suggest a way out of her dilemma, gave a sharp exclamation of disappointment.

'That's not really much consolation to me, Mr Sinclair!'

But even as she spoke, Samantha realized that this was not quite true. In fact she was reassured to find that she had not so completely misjudged Jake after all these years.

Despite the present circumstances, she was sure that Jake would never intentionally hurt her. Deep down she still couldn't help clinging to the feeling that all this was a mistake. One that Jake himself could easily resolve if he were here.

Then suddenly, a suspicion reared its ugly head and wormed its way into her consciousness. She sat bolt upright in her chair and fixed him with a wary look.

'Are you one of the trustees yourself, Mr Sinclair?'

He looked a little disconcerted but the cool eyes held hers.

'Yes. I am. My uncle is the other.'

Immediately Samantha sprang to her feet.

'In that case, you will obviously be biased concerning the outcome of this matter. I really don't feel that there is anything to be gained in continuing this conversation.'

Unexpectedly he moved to bar her way.

'Please sit down again, Ms James. I can understand that you must find this very distressing. But we really should discuss this matter further and try to come to some decision about how to proceed.'

Samantha shook her head vehemently.

'Let me pass, Mr Sinclair!

A wave of hostility swept through her as she looked up at him, her eyes ablaze, not bothering now to conceal the fact that she was furiously angry.

Impassively, he stared back.

For a long moment their eyes locked. Then, mesmerized, she saw his pupils widen until only a rim of lighter colour bordered the dark centres. Like ripples from ancient millstones ... cast into some deep, dark pool ... one moonlit midsummer night ... she thought confusedly.

Despite her anger, a current as powerful as the undertow of a river in flood swept through her body. Immediately she saw her own feelings of shock and surprise mirrored in his own. But she also saw something else – hostility? Wariness? Something that she couldn't put a name to. But I think that's how I feel too, she told herself distractedly!

With an effort she tore her eyes away and stepped to one side, only to collide with him in the process.

As his hand shot out to steady her, Samantha felt her eyes drawn to the strong left hand, with a noticeably crooked little finger, encircling her narrow wrist. She could feel the warmth from his fingers steal up her arm like an unexpected caress and wondered what it would feel like if ... if....

She pulled herself up with a jolt and rapidly channelled her confused emotions back into anger. That feeling, at least, she understood! Once more in control, Samantha gave her arm a little shake.

'If you'd kindly stop doing an imitation of a heavy in a fourth-rate television movie, I'd be very much obliged if you'd let me pass!' she said scathingly, amazing herself that she could speak so coolly after the turmoil she had just been through. Immediately the slight pressure on her wrist was released.

'We really shouldn't let this matter rest here, Ms James.'

Samantha heard the calmness in his voice and wondered whether she could have misread the look she had seen only moments ago. 'All I'm asking is that you note down your solicitor's address before you leave.'

His hand dropped to his side and he took a step backwards, leaving her free to go. But Samantha made no move.

Help! she thought dismayed. A choice between the devil and the deep blue sea!

Samantha sat for a moment staring at his empty chair. Despite her protests, he had insisted on going to organize some coffee. She realized that he was deliberately giving her time to regain her composure. His own, too, maybe.

She recalled the moment of confusion she had felt when their eyes had locked together. Odd! But I'm not going to let a moment of attraction influence me, she resolved. I know perfectly well where that can lead!

Then her mind turned to someone who had never been far from her thoughts these past few years. To Tim. To the irresistibly charming and amusing Tim. She frowned. To the faithless and treacherously two-timing Tim!

She and Tim, Jake and Becky had met that first week at university and for nearly three years the four of them had remained inseparable. Until she had discovered Tim – her Tim – and Becky locked in a passionate embrace and realized that it was Becky he loved, not her.

Deep in thought, she wandered over to the window.
Despite the sunshine, it had been snowing quite hard
when she had arrived. It was late for snow, especially
after such a mild winter. From her vantage point she
could see the wrought-iron gates of the cemetery
opposite, their ornate black curlicues standing in
sharp relief against the whiteness of the snow. Just
like the writings of some ancient Sanskrit manuscript,
she mused.

The scene reminded her that she must confirm the
shooting schedules for the programme on the
supernatural she was commissioned to research. It
rather looked as if that particular cemetery could
make a good location. She would make a point of
checking it out on the way back.

When she again heard the sounds of his footsteps on the stairs, Samantha was quite ready to do
battle.

'Here we are,' he said brightly, setting the tray
down between them.

She watched covertly as he busied himself pouring
out the coffee. It would certainly be in her own best
interests to engage another solicitor to represent her
personally. However, in the meantime, she would see
what approach this man was going to take.

He stirred his coffee thoughtfully, tapping his pen
rhythmically on the table. The sound irritated
Samantha. It made her think of the sound that the
death-watch beetles made in church buildings. It
seemed to be an evil omen.

As his eyes met hers, Samantha instinctively knew
that she wasn't going to like what he was about to say.
His first words confirmed her guess.

'Could you give me some idea of the market value of your flat?'

'My flat?' Samantha stared at him. 'What on earth has that got to do with this situation?'

'Quite a lot, I'm afraid. If one of your creditors should decide to take proceedings against you, it might be necessary to _' He stopped at the look of horror that had flitted over her face, then continued hurriedly, '– but, of course, there's no need to cross our bridges before we come to them, Ms James.'

What he was implying struck Samantha as forcibly as a physical blow. At that instant a dark cloud moved across the sun and the room seemed to shrink. It was as if the walls had suddenly closed in both on her and on her world.

'Do you mean I could be made bankrupt?'

'As I've said, it may not come to that,' he replied soothingly, as if talking to a fractious child.

Then, for the second time that afternoon, Samantha shot to her feet. This time he made no attempt to stop her. But, despite her anger, she managed to swallow down the angry words that sprang to her lips and instead gave him her very sweetest smile.

'It may interest you to know, Mr Sinclair,' she said softly, 'that there is absolutely no way that I am going to sell my flat in order to pay for a car purchased by your client just because some penny-pinching trustees refuse to give him the money that is rightfully his!'

Then, head held high, she sailed out of the room, the heels of her boots beating an indignantly staccato tattoo on the polished floor.

It was with some satisfaction that she heard a half

smothered exclamation and the thud of an object being brought down heavily on the desk, just before the door slammed shut.

Two

Despite the harrowing hour she had just spent, Samantha felt her spirits rise as she walked back through the cemetery on her way to the car-park. It had been snowing and she had always found snow exhilarating. Only a week or two ago there had been a burst of unseasonably warm weather for late March. Now it had changed dramatically.

The snow had turned the scene into a setting from *Dr Zhivago*. As she walked, she noted how the hazed-over sun – a burning ember in a leaden sky – purpled the base of the yews and how the long shadow of the steeple on the little stone chapel pointed directly to the north like the needle of an enormous compass. Snow iced the trees and bushes with a delicate hand and drifts draped the sides of the tombstones. Samantha couldn't help thinking how at this precise moment in her life, her surroundings suited her mood perfectly.

As she had spent considerable time these last few years researching in surroundings such as these, she was somehow comforted by the scene. But she was not familiar with this particular cemetery and, as she hurried along, she cast a professional eye about her, noting some fine, Victorian gravestones. Very atmospheric, she decided. This might make a good setting for that programme she had in mind.

Her thoughts returned to Jake. If Jake were here now, they would probably be making light of this situation. They had been through worse experiences together. Yet again she recalled Tim.

She had felt badly betrayed, not only by him but by Becky. She and Becky had shared nearly everything of significance since their first days at university. She could still recall the numbness she had felt when she had first realized that they had apparently been sharing Tim, too!

She still couldn't think of Tim without a feeling of emptiness. There were days, she had to admit, when she didn't think of him at all but when she did the pain came back as if it were yesterday. She knew that Jake had felt exactly the same about Becky.

However, Jake must have seen the break with Becky coming and was there to offer sympathy. Together they had hammered out their plans for *Scene-Setters*. Once business had taken off, they had seldom found themselves in London together.

In the circumstances, it had seemed sensible for them to use her small flat as their base and their office. Jake seldom stayed in the flat when she herself was home. Samantha had never asked where he went at other times. He had always made friends effortlessly.

I do wish he were here now, she thought wistfully, then shut her eyes briefly as if to blot out an image. With a sense of shock she realized that the image that had come to mind was of the man she had just left. But let's hope, she told herself firmly, that our paths need never cross again!

The footpath widened as she passed the stone

chapel. Ahead of her, a small golden brown corgi with a bright red collar, skipped lamb-like in front of its elderly owner, barking ecstatically as it scattered the snow to all sides.

The woman glanced at Samantha as she passed.

'His first snow!' she said, looking at the dog fondly. The puppy sniffed at the air as if intoxicated by its unaccustomed crystal clarity. One ear drooped comically, enhancing the drunken effect.

Samantha laughed, slackening her pace to that of the woman, who was having some difficulty in keeping her footing. The sun had already begun to thaw the snow on the path and even Samantha, sensibly shod in boots with only a little heel, found the going treacherous.

'You'll want to be going on ahead now, dear,' the woman said as they reached the exit. 'I don't want to hold you back as I can see you're in a hurry. I need to take my time these days! And I'll be turning back soon.'

Samantha smiled goodbye and cut through a little alley into what she guessed would usually be a fairly busy street. Today it was deserted. The sense of euphoria that had lifted her spirits a few minutes ago now left her as fragments of her conversation with the solicitor insisted on returning to plague her.

She went over it again in her head. Despite her show of bravado and her absolute determination to fight against the odds, she already suspected that unless something of a miracle occurred she would need to sell her flat, and probably her little car, too.

Even if Jake were to make an appearance that very afternoon, it wouldn't alter the fact that his money wouldn't be forthcoming. She had a shrewd suspicion that Sinclair man could have done something about that if he had wanted to. But he obviously hadn't trusted her.

As she trudged along, the cold beginning to bite through her coat, she began to wish that she hadn't left her car in the car-park. The little cul-de-sac in which the solicitor's office was situated hadn't actually been shown on her map. As she was not familiar with the neighbourhood, she had felt it better to search it out on foot.

Samantha shivered. Apart from the elderly woman, she hadn't seen a soul since leaving the office. The wind had started to rise and she walked close to a long sheltering wall which was built to screen a children's playground from the road.

As she did so, a black limousine smoothly turned the corner ahead of her, slowly gliding by in the middle of the road with scarcely a sound except for the soft slushing of the snow.

In the back was a large coffin.

No flowers, she registered briefly. No mourners either by the look of things! The sight of the black hearse appearing so suddenly amidst the snowy whiteness of the steadily darkening afternoon struck a sinister chord in Samantha's already agitated state of mind.

'Hey! Stop! Stop!'

Suddenly a figure rounded the corner, waving wildly at the vehicle. Samantha watched fascinated as the newcomer panted after it. He was quite a plump man and by no means young. Despite the cold, beads of perspiration ran down his florid forehead.

He looks terribly upset, Samantha observed uneasily. But for someone so obviously out of condition, he certainly appeared to be sure-footed and she marvelled that he could keep his footing in such treacherous conditions.

The limousine suddenly accelerated and for a moment it seemed as if it would leave him. Far from being discouraged, the portly figure also began to pick up speed and actually appeared to be gaining ground. Then unexpectedly, the car glided smoothly to a halt.

Good! thought Samantha, watching this little scenario with avid curiosity, her own problems completely forgotten. It's waiting for him.

The man had slowed down to a trot. Samantha, from a distance of about ten yards, could hear him breathing stertorously. Then, horrified, she saw the vehicle roll backwards, knocking him down. After only a small, strangled cry of distress, the man lay face down in the snow, completely prostrate.

Oh God! she thought, standing motionless for a long moment before making a move towards the car. It must have been an accident, surely? Faulty brakes? But before she had gone more than a few steps, the doors of the limousine opened and its two occupants got out.

Both were dressed in funereal black, complete with hat. One of them went to look at the man lying in the road and the other opened the back of the car. Then seizing him unceremoniously by the arms and legs, the two hoisted him up and bundled him roughly into the back of the hearse.

Samantha suddenly found her voice. 'Hey! Be careful! You shouldn't move him! He may be...!'

But the words died in her throat. Both men had turned, seemingly noticing her for the first time. Then, in unison, they began to move towards her. Like great black vultures, she thought terrified, about to swoop on their prey.

As if in some nightmare, Samantha was rooted to the spot, unable to move. Then, breaking out of the spell with a tremendous effort, she turned and fled down the deserted street towards the newspaper shop on the corner.

No sound of pursuit reached her. She could hear only the noise of her pounding heart and of her boots crushing the snow beneath her feet. Then, just when it looked that she would gain the sanctuary of the corner shop, the ground appeared to slip from underneath her.

In a flash she seemed to visualize a strong hand with a crooked little finger appearing from nowhere to save her. But it was just a figment of her imagination. No one came to her aid and the world suddenly dissolved into a whirling white blur.

A tinkling sound stirred Samantha into consciousness of a throbbing headache and a feeling of nausea. She half-opened her eyes, then shut them again as the bright light threatened to split her head in two.

'— slipped and fell on the ice. That's the seventh today already,' she heard a voice float in and out.

'Ice,' thought Samantha hazily. 'Ice ... ice-cream ... ice ... rice ... eat up your rice pudding....' she mumbled.

'Hello, there. Are you awake?' This time a masculine voice, seemingly a bit closer.

Samantha again attempted to open her eyes, this time to see a hazy white figure bent over her. She wanted to sleep, but the waves of nausea threatened to engulf her.

'Badly concussed,' said the doctor. 'Send her to X-ray in case of a fracture then keep her in the ward overnight for observation.' There was a slight rustling as he consulted his notes. 'Any identification, nurse? There's no name or address here.'

'No positive identification, doctor. She was brought in by ambulance. There was someone with her. Not a relative or friend, I understand. But he'd seen her fall and wanted to make sure she was alright. She didn't have a handbag with her but a letter with an address was in her pocket.'

The doctor nodded. 'Good.'

'Oh, and reception took the name and address of the man with her. Quite a celebrity, it seems!' There was the sound of papers being turned and a muffled exclamation of surprise.

'I suppose someone's checking out the addresses on the letter?'

'Yes, doctor.'

Samantha made an effort to make herself heard.

'Police!' she murmured, trying to sit up but being restrained gently by the nurse. 'Murder!'

'What did she say?' asked the doctor, bending over her.

'It sounded like "murder", doctor.'

The doctor felt for Samantha's pulse.

'Can you tell us your name?'

'Jake,' muttered Samantha. 'Jake. Where's Jake?'

The young doctor looked at her thoughtfully and

switched off the light that had been focussed on her face.

'Keep her as quiet as possible, nurse. The police may need to be informed if we can't get an identification. She seems to be asking for someone called Jake. But it's hard to be certain.'

He scribbled rapidly on the notes and handed them to the nurse who immediately went about arranging for the X-ray and for Samantha's transfer to the wards.

It wasn't until the next morning that Samantha became fully aware of where she was. Her head still ached abominably but much of the fuzziness had disappeared. The night sister, who had been putting the final touches to her records before going off duty, came over.

'Feeling any better yet?' she asked sympathetically.

Samantha nodded. Then wished that she hadn't.

'We need to have your name, please.'

Samantha obediently recited her name and address and, in return was given an account of where she was and how she came to be there. She herself could remember nothing.

'A passer-by came with you in the ambulance. A young man.'

Samantha looked confused. A man? Jake? No, not possible! Jake was in the States. She felt too tired to think clearly. At the back of her mind was the feeling that there was something she needed to do urgently – but she couldn't think what. All she really wanted was to sleep. As the nurse tidied up her bed and busied herself with her charts, Samantha fell into an uneasy doze.

For most of the morning, she drifted in and out of sleep. She was aware that some of the patients had visitors and felt quite thankful that, as yet, nobody knew where she was. She really didn't feel up to seeing people at the moment. She was, therefore, surprised when a nurse came over to her bed accompanied by two men.

'Visitors for you, dear,' she said to Samantha, plumping up her pillows and smoothing the covers of an already immaculately made bed. Then she turned back with a smile to the men, eyeing the younger one with unmistakeable interest and fussing around them in what Samantha vaguely registered as a rather unnecessary way.

'Try not to stay too long, please,' she told them. 'The patient needs to rest.' She moved away but kept well within earshot.

Samantha, who had been drowsing, fully opened her eyes, blinked rapidly several times and suddenly recalled the scene she had witnessed immediately before her fall.

'How ...? What...?'

In her confused state words failed her. She could only lean back against her pillows and just stare. Then, with a rush, the events of the previous afternoon returned vividly to mind.

'We've brought you some flowers,' said the plump, little man, smiling at her benevolently and holding out an impressive bouquet of freesias and carnations and some magazines. 'How do you do. I'm Harry and this is Paul.'

Samantha continued to stare at him in bewilderment. She made no move to take the flowers.

'I don't understand,' she stammered at last. 'I saw you knocked down! You were lying in the road and....' She broke off shivering.

Her well-rounded visitor laughed boomingly.

'We're flattered, aren't we Paul! I must say, I felt I deserved at least an Olympic gold medal, if not an Oscar, for that run! It brings me out in a cold sweat just to think of it. What's more, I had to do it three times in all before we got a take.'

'An Oscar? A take?' Light suddenly dawned and Samantha smiled wanly, feeling incredibly foolish. 'Oh, you're an actor! And I thought you'd been run down on purpose!' She laughed shakily. 'I didn't see any cameras.'

'You wouldn't have. They hadn't arrived yet. Problems with the weather. So we decided to have a little run through whilst we were waiting.'

'But you were knocked down! Surely that was for real!'

Harry grimaced ruefully.

'My stand-in didn't turn up either. But, don't worry about it. I bounced off that hearse like the rubber ball that I am! Paul here tried to go after you to explain. But you were off like a rabbit!'

Samantha turned to the other side of the bed where the younger man stood. For the first time she got a good look at him. Even though she was certainly not at her most perceptive, she could hardly fail to notice that he was rather attractive. No wonder the nurse was hovering around!

He grinned at her disarmingly. With his light brown hair ruffled in a way that suggested he had just run his fingers through it, blue eyes that danced with

laughter and a boyish smile, she knew that she had
seen him somewhere before. Nevertheless, she really
couldn't identify him as one of the two black-clothed
men who had so terrified her yesterday.

'Looks familiar, doesn't he?' said Harry jovially,
reading her expression correctly. 'You might know
him better from *Stepney Mansions.*'

Of course! she remembered belatedly. They're Harry
Barrington and Paul Mitchell! She had rarely had
time to watch television in the last year or so. Despite
this, she knew that *Stepney Mansions*, featuring two
private investigators working in London's East End,
was one of the most popular programmes on the box.
Both she and Jake had actually worked on the locations of one episode set in Cambridge. But she had
never met the stars in person. Still, I should have
recognized them! she reproved herself. After all, I do
work in the business.

'Don't tell me you don't watch it!' Harry raised his
eyebrows in an expression of comic despair.

'I think Samantha's probably got far more
interesting things to do with her time than watching
us,' said Paul, pulling up a chair close to her bed.

Now that voice she certainly did remember,
immediately registering the interesting gravelly
quality that had so intrigued herself and her friends
when at school. She looked at him again more closely.
Probably quite a bit older than he looks. That boyish
air of his was deceptive.

'The nurse told me your name,' he added. 'I came
with you in the ambulance yesterday, although you
were still incognito then!'

'He couldn't take his eyes off you, dear! He's quite

accustomed to lovely ladies throwing themselves at him, but knocking themselves unconscious is something new!'

The next half an hour passed very pleasantly and Samantha found herself highly entertained by their joint account of all the things that had gone wrong at yesterday's filming. A catalogue of disasters that had apparently culminated with a little dog taking an instant liking to Harry and chasing after him playfully on his dramatic run.

'Then the dratted animal refused to let anyone get near Harry,' complained Paul. 'It caught hold of my trouser leg when I went up to him and absolutely refused to let go! In the end I had to take them off! It was the only way to get away from him!'

Samantha chuckled. A thought struck her. 'Was it a little corgi, by any chance?'

'It was indeed. Nothing to do with you, I hope!'

'I think I must have passed it earlier. With an elderly lady.'

'That's the one! She found the whole thing very amusing. Harry said we'd send her a copy of the video to show her friends. But it won't do my image any good, I bet!' he grumbled. But there was a grin on his face that was irresistible.

Samantha was amused to see that her bed had become quite a focus of attention as the news that two television celebrities were visiting swept through the wards like wildfire. A number of nurses and patients came up and shyly asked Paul and Harry for their autographs. One even asked for Samantha's, thinking that hers, too, might be worth having.

Then Harry looked at his watch.

'I'm afraid I must go,' he said regretfully. He planted a light kiss on her forehead. 'An old show business tradition, dear, as you must well know. Now make sure you don't let this rascal tire you out. I should warn you that his reputation is quite, quite scandalous! And he has a particular fondness for redheads!'

Before Paul left, he had determinedly extracted Samantha's telephone number, promising to ring. Maybe his kiss on the cheek lingered a little longer than necessary but Samantha quite enjoyed the envious expression of the nurses. She had met a number of attractive men during the course of her work. This one appeared nicer than most and seemed great fun.

But it crossed her mind to wonder why she hadn't felt that certain *frisson* she had experienced with that dreadful Sinclair man.

Despite the distractions of the afternoon, Samantha's head was feeling a good deal better. Settling back on her pillows, she began to flick through one of the magazines that had been left for her, so she didn't see the tall figure that had paused to have a word with the ward sister. Nor did she see him striding purposefully towards her bed. However, the eyes of the nurse followed the lithe figure with undisguised interest.

'Feeling better, I hope?' said a sympathetic voice.

Samantha's eyes widened as she raised her head.

'Mr Sinclair!' she said weakly. 'What are you doing here? Not another unpaid bill, I hope!'

He laughed pleasantly. I haven't heard him laugh before, she thought. The sound was surprisingly reassuring.

'For you,' he said, carefully extricating a plant from its elaborate wrappings. He placed it on top of her locker.

Samantha stared at it. It had delicate, almost transparent, heart-shaped leaves that were indigo in the centre shading through blue to a delicate pale lilac.

'It's really beautiful,' she said at length. 'I've never seen one like that before.' She put out her hand to touch one of its veined, silken leaves. 'It's just as if a swarm of tropical butterflies had settled on it. What's it called?' She searched in vain for a label.

He laughed again.

'I'm afraid I've no idea! But the colour reminded me of your eyes. I'm glad you like it.'

Samantha's eyes widened.

'Oh!' she said, astonished, recognizing the compliment. Was this the man who had interrogated her with such ruthless efficiency yesterday? The wary, speculative look that she had noticed then seemed to have completely disappeared. She wondered what had happened to change his attitude so markedly.

'Thank you,' she murmured, suddenly confused. 'But how did you know I was here?'

'The hospital contacted me early this morning.'

Samantha digested this information with surprise. 'Why on earth should they do that?'

'There was that letter from me in your pocket. They told me you'd had an accident and that you hadn't yet been able to identify yourself. They couldn't get any answer from your flat and wanted to know if I could give them the name of a relative. I couldn't but I came as soon as I could.'

'That was very kind of you,' said Samantha politely. If anyone had asked her a few minutes ago, she would have said that he was the last person she wanted to visit her. But suddenly seeing him again made her feel somehow comforted.

'Not at all,' he said casually. But there was a gleam of laughter in his eyes. 'You are my client, after all.'

Samantha felt that this was highly debatable in view of the way that their last meeting had ended but she had no inclination to dispute the point.

'That reminds me. I had a letter from your – er – partner this morning.' He sounded amused.

'You did?' Samantha's eyes lit up suddenly. Thank heavens for that! she thought. Maybe now they could make some sense of the situation.

He smiled genially at her obvious relief.

'The sister said you were asking for him before you regained consciousness.'

'I was? I don't remember.'

'It's sometimes surprising what the subconscious throws up!' he laughed. 'Although in the circumstances it was quite natural for you to do so!'

Samantha glanced up at him covertly. Yes, this was certainly a different man from the one she had met yesterday.

'Did he say where he could be contacted?'

'No. But I understand he's on the move.'

Samantha smiled faintly. 'Sounds like him.'

Her visitor draped himself in one of her chairs.

'Sounds like both of you! It must be difficult for the two of you being constantly on the move.' His voice was sympathetic. 'You can't get much time together.'

Then he sat back and smiled benevolently, shaking

his head at her in a mildly reproving manner.

'But why on earth didn't you tell me yesterday that the two of you are getting married?'

Three

Samantha sat bolt upright. 'Married?' she asked weakly. 'Married? Is that what Jake said?'

He leaned forward slightly and patted her on the hand.

'Don't look so startled. You didn't expect to keep it a secret for ever, surely?'

Samantha thought rapidly. Married? What on earth was Jake playing at? Was this just a ploy to elicit support for his cause with his trustees? She dismissed this notion immediately. Jake didn't even know that he wasn't getting the money he wanted. Besides, it didn't sound like Jake to be so devious.

'What exactly did he say?' she asked warily.

'Just that he'd been doing some serious thinking these past months and had finally decided to settle down with the most marvellous girl – and colleague – in the world. I must say my uncle – his other trustee, if you remember – will be greatly relieved.'

Colleague? she wondered, thinking hard about the jobs Jake had done recently. She drew a blank.

'Will it make any difference about the fund?'

'Most probably. It's unlikely that we will put any obstacle in the way of what appears to be such a suitable marriage.' He smiled at Samantha and once again patted her hand.

I wish he'd stop doing that! she thought. It makes

me feel about six years old.

'He sends you his love, by the way.'

'Oh.' Samantha, bewildered as she was, was finding it hard to make much sense of this visit. She suddenly felt desperately in need of some peace and quiet in order to think over this latest development.

It was certainly true that they badly needed Jake's trust money if they were to clear their debts. Jake's debts mostly, she thought wryly. On the other hand, all her instincts told her to tell this man that he was mistaken. That she and Jake had absolutely no intention of getting married.

'I think,' she began hesitantly, then gave herself a mental shake. 'I know,' she said firmly, 'that there's been some mistake. Jake and I have never discussed marriage.'

Her visitor suddenly looked astonished, his dark brows peaking into his forehead comically.

'Ah!' he said at last, looking curiously abashed.

Despite herself, Samantha couldn't help being amused at the look on his face. Like a naughty schoolboy caught out in a misdemeanour. It was strangely familiar, however. Her own brow wrinkled in concentration. But in a moment his expression had changed.

'I really must apologize! I think I may have been rather indiscreet in mentioning it. It seems that he hasn't yet spoken to you about it.' He looked contrite. 'I really don't know what to say!'

He smiled disarmingly.

'I'm so sorry. Will you forget this conversation. I certainly won't mention it to another soul. Not before you and Jake....' Again his voice trailed off. But he shrugged expressively.

'Mr Sinclair,' she began as firmly as she could manage, 'I must assure you once again that there is absolutely no question of my marrying Jake. We are just very good friends – and business partners as you already know.'

Instantly his eyebrows drew together in a single implacable line.

'I see.'

She saw his mouth harden a fraction. No, you don't see at all, she thought dismayed. Oh lord! Wasn't she in enough trouble as it was without this sort of complication.

Again he smiled. But this time his eyes held a guarded look.

'Many couples prefer not to marry these days. It's obviously a commitment that shouldn't be entered into lightly. You're both young and if you're not absolutely sure _'

'You misunderstand the situation,' she broke in sharply. Her head was beginning to ache abominably. How was it, she asked herself, that she was so unexpectedly discussing marriage with this man.

'I think not,' he said quietly. But there was a disquieting undertone in his voice. Suddenly he reached out his hand and, encircling her wrist with one long finger, stared down at her right hand searchingly.

'That's a very unusual ring,' he murmured, looking at the delicately carved silver seal-ring on her finger. 'I couldn't help noticing it yesterday. A present from Jake, I assume.'

'That's right.'

'Unless there are two identical rings in existence, which I doubt, this ring once belonged to his grandmother. His gift marked a special occasion, perhaps?'

'Yes. Very special.'

As their eyes met she found herself blushing.

This is silly, she thought crossly. I know what he's thinking and he's completely wrong. True, Jake had given her the ring. But it had been a perfectly friendly little exchange of gifts to celebrate the end of their first year in business. He hadn't told her that it was a family heirloom!

'I quite understand,' he said briefly. But there was a gleam in his eye that unsettled her.

For a moment there was silence. Although the finger held her wrist with the lightest of touches, Samantha was uncomfortably conscious of the curious feeling of intimacy this had on her. How easy it would be, she thought, to fall in love with this man. Instantly she recalled Tim. There was no way she wanted a repeat performance of that! She withdrew her hand from his.

When he spoke again it was in the same polite, formal tone that he had used in his office yesterday.

'I'm glad to see that you're on the way to recovery. Now that I know you're in safe hands, I'll trouble you no longer. You must be very tired.'

Samantha made a little sound of assent.

'Will you be in here long?' he queried politely, looking around the packed ward.

'The doctor said that I shall probably be able to go home tomorrow morning. Thank you for visiting me. The plant is really lovely.'

As he stood looking down at her, Samantha was suddenly acutely conscious of her appearance. Clad in the less than dignified hospital nightie and with her hair tussled from her pillows, she knew that she wasn't looking the way she would want to appear to this man. She wished that she had been able to run a comb through her hair and perhaps apply a touch of lipstick.

Lipstick! The word stirred her consciousness and she had a dreadful thought. 'Oh God!' she said feelingly.

Her visitor, feeling himself dismissed, had been on the point of leaving but now turned sharply. 'Something wrong?'

'My handbag!' Samantha turned to her locker and franctically searched for it. But apart from a red plastic bag provided by the hospital for her clothes and a comb and toothbrush that must have been hospital regulation issue, the locker was empty. 'I must have dropped my handbag. My keys were in it!'

He murmured an expression of sympathy.

'No spare ones? With friends? Under the mat?' he added, good-humouredly. But she detected an ironic edge to the deep voice.

'I'm not a complete idiot, Mr Sinclair,' she said with as much dignity as she could summon up. Her headache had returned with a vengeance.

'I'm sure you're not.' He moved closer and now she could see genuine sympathy in his eyes. 'I'm sorry. I know it's no joke to lose your keys. I've done it myself more than once. Have you somewhere you can stay whilst you get the lock changed? The ward sister told me you'd had visitors earlier this afternoon. With them, perhaps?'

'No. I hardly know them.'

He raised his eyebrows slightly as if waiting for her to elaborate, but Samantha remained silent.

Thank heavens he didn't know the full story! What a fool he would think her. Mistaking a scene in a film for reality. Even that elderly lady with her dog hadn't done that!

With a jolt her thoughts returned to her present predicament.

She could, of course, go home but the thought of explaining the situation to her parents was too much to bear. Jake ... her job ... the little flat she'd been so proud of.... She raised an arm to dash away a treacherous tear. What a fool he must think her, she told herself yet again. Weeping over a lost key!

Hearing her mattress creak, she looked up suddenly to see him sitting on her bed, the grey eyes watching her commiseratingly. Then, reaching into the pocket of his jacket, he took out a handkerchief. Quite unselfconsciously, he leaned forward and wiped away her tears in the manner of a parent with a small child.

She made an involuntary movement of surprise and as she did so his arm brushed against hers. The touch burned through the thin fabric of her nightdress and she flinched at the contact, as if from a red-hot iron. Their eyes met and, as in his office, she began to feel herself drawn inexplicably towards him. An irrational desire for him to wrap his arms around her and to comfort her swept through her.

This is stupid, she reproved herself unhappily. I don't really want this! I just want to be left in peace!

But, despite herself, the sounds of the ward receded. The over-bright chatter of visitors and the anxious murmur of worried relatives; the clink of cups from the tea trolley; the brisk steps of busy nurses on the polished floors and the distant drone of the television in the day room, all faded from her consciousness as she stared at him. Miraculously, the busy ward became a desert island on which they alone existed.

With an effort she lowered her eyes, endeavouring to escape the web of conflicting emotions that threatened to enmesh her. His lips were very close and she saw the line of his mouth soften. For a brief moment she wondered what it would be like if he were to kiss her and when his hand came up to gently brush away a strand of hair that had fallen across her mouth, she felt sure he was about to do so. The unbodied kiss hovered between them perilously like a soul still waiting to be born.

Then suddenly he stood up and the spell was broken. 'I'll make some enquiries about your handbag,' he said equably and Samantha wondered if she only imagined a huskiness in his voice. But the slight curving of his lips was certainly real.

I do believe he's laughing at me, she thought, her feelings of a moment ago already banished as her confusion turned to something approaching anger.

'Please don't bother!' she retaliated briskly, recovering her composure with an effort.

He looked surprised as he stood there. For a second Samantha saw a hurt look pass across his face. Then a curtain seemed to come down over his eyes and his expression hardened.

'It's no trouble at all,' he said formally.

Once again he was the man who had so aggravated her in his office. Samantha stared back and wondered why she had ever thought of him as anything else.

'I'll be in touch.' Then he whirled on his heel and strode down the ward.

Samantha watched him go with a mixture of relief and exasperation. But she was aware that these feelings were tinged with something infinitely more disturbing. She picked up the discarded handkerchief and looked at it frowning. It's just that bang on the head, she told herself firmly, giving the hankie a little shake. When I'm out of here, I probably won't give him a second thought!

Determinedly, she shoved the offending object under her pillow and picked up one of her magazines. The first thing I'll do when I get home, she decided, will be to find myself another solicitor – she took a sip of water from the glass at her bedside – and that will definitely be the last I see of you, Mr Brett Sinclair! She raised her glass in a toast.

'My! You have been having a busy afternoon!' declared the nurse, who had been observing the scene with as avid an interest as her duties allowed.

Her patient made no reply.

Samantha sat in the dayroom and glanced at her watch yet again. Still only eleven o'clock! She couldn't believe a morning could last so long!

'Someone called Brett Sinclair rang and asked how you were', a smiling nurse had informed her earlier. 'He said you were to wait for him and that he'd pick you up some time before twelve. He sounded really nice. Lovely voice. Is he your boyfriend?'

'No.' Samantha had replied shortly. 'He's my solicitor.'

The little nurse had looked surprised.

'Really? Well if he's as dishy as his voice, I wouldn't mind getting into a spot of bother myself!'

Samantha recalled the nurse's remark, a slight smile hovering around her lips. But her smile disappeared as she remembered her lost handbag. Probably gone for ever, she told herself. Heaven knows how she was going to get in when she got home! But she found the thought of that Sinclair man being there surprisingly comforting.

'Ready, Samantha?'

Samantha started as he entered the dayroom as if on cue. It was the first time that he had used her name, she noticed. The resonant voice gave it a pleasantly rhythmic sound.

She nodded. Then catching a glimpse of what he was carrying over his arm, gave a little gasp of surprise.

'My handbag. How on earth did you manage to find it?'

'Without much difficulty, luckily. The police said that a handbag with credit cards in your name had recently been brought in by a woman with a little dog.'

'That was a stroke of luck!' she said, privately reflecting that the elderly lady had had a very eventful walk yesterday.

'She said that she'd seen a pretty redhead carrying one just like it only a few minutes before and hoped that "nothing untoward" had happened to you. In the circumstances, I managed to persuade them to release it into my custody.' He presented it to Samantha with a boyishly triumphant air.

Samantha rummaged through it feverishly.

'My door and car keys are still here. Thank goodness for that! I hadn't much fancied doing a breaking and entering job!' She looked up at him, feeling unaccountably shy. 'Thank you very much, Brett. I really don't know what I'd have done without it!'

His name had come easily to her lips and she saw a slight smile play around the corners of his mouth, as if he tacitly acknowledged that they had entered a new, less formal stage in their relationship.

Outside, the snow had cleared completely. Samantha saw that the weather, which had been very cold for late April, had now turned warm, with fleecy, lamb-like clouds gently grazing their way across the watered-blue meadow of the sky.

She took a deep breath. Despite some fumes from the traffic, the air seemed fresh and invigorating and cleared away the antiseptic smell of the hospital that had been so pervasive.

Her companion ushered her to a dark blue estate.

'If you could drop me at the car-park by the station, Brett, I'll be able to pick up my car.'

'Later,' he replied, his eyes still on the road. 'I think I'd better make sure you get something to eat first.' He shot her a quick glance. 'That is if you are feeling up to it.'

He pulled up smoothly at a crossing and looked across at her, searching her face keenly.

'I must say, you're still looking very pale. Are you sure you wouldn't prefer to go straight home?'

Samantha, in fact, would have preferred to have gone straight home. Her head was quite clear now but she hadn't had a restful night and this was beginning to make itself felt. But he had put himself out a good deal on her behalf and it seemed impolite to refuse. Besides, a little voice whispered treacherously, another hour or so in his company won't exactly be an ordeal! But she pushed that line of thought firmly out of her mind.

He noticed her hesitation. 'If you are not feeling well enough,' he began.

'No, a meal would be lovely,' she murmured politely, her eyes looking straight ahead at several children crossing the road on their way to the park.

She was aware that he was still looking at her. The coat she had worn when she had slipped on the ice had been thrown in the back of the car. Now she could sense him scrutinizing her as she sat bolt upright in her seat and steeled herself to resist the unaccountably warm feeling that shot through her.

Turning suddenly, she saw that he was staring at a bruise on her bare right leg, just below the knee. A relic from her recent fall.

'That looks nasty,' he said sympathetically, and she saw genuine concern written on his face.

'Just a bruise,' she heard herself saying. But his look had seemed like a caress to her wound.

For a fraction of a second their eyes met. Then he turned back to the road, waited until the last little girl had scooted across and started up. Samantha felt curiously shaken.

After circling around the adjoining streets, Brett found a parking spot reasonably close to The Local, a busy little pub very near her flat. She and Jake frequently used it together when they were both in town.

'Hi, Sammy! How're you doing?'

The pretty, self-assured girl behind the bar looked up smiling as they entered and Samantha noticed the look of frank appraisal she gave Brett.

'Fine thanks, Liz.' She slipped on to a vacant stool alongside the bar. Brett went to stand beside her. 'How are the studies going?'

The girl pulled a face.

'Could be better. A lot better, I'm afraid. I'm going to have to get down to some serious work if I'm to pass my exams next month. I've just told Bob that I'll have to give this up for a bit.' She grinned. 'You or Jake don't want my job by any chance, I suppose?'

'It may come to that,' Samantha smiled wryly.

'I haven't seen Jake in here recently. Is he away?'

'Abroad for a while.'

'I thought he might be. There was someone in here this morning asking about him.'

'Oh? Did he say who he was?'

'No. Seemed very keen to get in touch, though.'

Samantha looked at her sharply, alerted by an unusually serious note in Liz's voice.

'He looked a bit of a thug to me. One of those characters who look as if they've just stepped out of an old gangster movie. I certainly wouldn't fancy rubbing him up the wrong way!'

Samantha laughed. But she found the idea oddly perturbing. Her eyes met Brett's and when he spoke he echoed her own disquiet.

'It looks as if we aren't the only ones anxious to get in touch with Jake.' His brow furrowed. 'I don't want to alarm you, Samantha. But I must say, I don't like the thought of that at all!'

Four

They ordered their food and took their drinks upstairs to the cheerful, oak-panelled dining-room, sitting at a table by the window. Again, it was Brett who gave voice to Samantha's anxiety.

'Whoever was looking for Jake must have gone to the flat first before coming here on the off-chance someone would know him.'

'It certainly looks like it.' The implications made her feel uneasy.

Their food arrived, breaking the somewhat awkward silence that had arisen. Samantha had little appetite for the hearty meal that had been ordered. Someone looking for Jake could quite easily mean that he had other large debtors whom she knew nothing at all about. Involuntarily, she sighed. Brett glanced at her sharply.

'It might be a good idea if you were to go home for a few days. That was a nasty knock on the head and you should rest. You have parents?'

'Yes. I have. But no, I don't think it would be a good idea to go home. I have commissions to carry out. Despite what you may think to the contrary, I do work for my living, you know.'

They ate in silence for a while. When he spoke, he again echoed her own misgivings.

'I don't like the idea of you staying alone at the flat.'

He touched her arm comfortingly. 'I don't want to worry you unnecessarily, but whoever was looking for Jake might well return.'

'But it's Jake he's looking for, not me!' she protested, sounding far more confident than she felt.

'Hmm!' His disapproving tone sounded exactly like her father. She suppressed a smile with difficulty.

'I promise that I'll be very careful about opening the door to strangers,' she said, deliberately demure. 'In any case, he could well be a friend of Jake. He does have them, you know!'

'His description hardly inspired confidence.'

'Maybe. But Jake, like myself, knows quite a lot of people in show business. Curious though it may seem, there's quite a demand for really villainous-looking characters. He was most probably one of Jake's actor friends.' But even to herself her voice lacked conviction.

Brett reached across and covered her hand with his.

'I see a lot of this sort of thing in my work, Samantha,' he said obliquely. 'You may be right, he could be quite harmless. But debt collectors can have some unorthodox methods. Just occasionally things can get out of hand.'

Samantha looked askance, but he didn't elaborate further.

'You must promise to ring me at the slightest thing that makes you feel uneasy.'

Help! she thought amused. He's putting me in the role of the defenceless little woman. Well, if that's what he likes....

An imp of mischief decided her to play along. She looked up at him from beneath her lashes and gave him one of her most beguiling smiles. The one she usually reserved for her father's friends.

'Thank you, Brett,' she murmured and lowered her eyes demurely. 'I won't forget.' To be honest, she told herself, it was rather nice having a guardian angel!

But she saw him frown and for a few moments there was silence.

'Samantha.'

'Yes, Brett?' She looked up to find his eyes fixed on her sternly.

'You're not in love with him, are you?'

She stared at him astonished. His statement had sounded like an accusation.

'In love with whom?' she heard herself saying inanely.

'Don't play games, Samantha. You know perfectly well whom I mean. Or is Jake not the only man in your life?'

She met his eyes steadily. 'I've already told you once that there's nothing between us.' Why was it, she asked herself curiously, that this man seemed so interested in her love life?

'On your side, maybe. But what about Jake? Judging from his letter, he's head-over-heels in love.'

'Possibly. But not with me.'

'But you live with him,' he said flatly. 'Or are you the kind of woman who thinks nothing of that?'

Samantha remained silent. Her headache had returned with a vengeance. There seemed no point in arguing with this man. He had obviously made up his mind that she was some kind of a Jezebel. Nothing she could say would alter that.

Then to her consternation, he reached across the

table and took her hand. Instantly her face flamed as a vibrant current sparked between them.

'I thought so.' His voice was quiet and devoid of any triumph. 'You have a passionate nature. You're a woman who needs a man in her bed.'

Samantha stared at him.

Passionate? Her? The suggestion was almost laughable. Since her fiasco with Tim, she had virtually led the life of a nun!

Admittedly, there had been occasions when she'd thought seriously about letting a new relationship develop further than just friendship. But just the memory of what had happened before had sent her firmly to bed with a book and a mug of hot milk. There would be time for men, later, she'd assured herself. Besides, just for the moment, she'd wanted to concentrate on her career.

The pressure on her hand increased. To her consternation she felt it tremble beneath his touch.

'You don't deny you feel something?'

Samantha sat speechless.

No! she couldn't deny the disturbingly strong feelings that were coursing through her body at the mere touch of his hand. But that didn't mean she always reacted this way!

She had a definite feeling that this was a situation where a girl should protest vehemently. Maybe a righteous slap was in order! But deep down she felt a little flattered that this attractive – but infuriating – man should have come to such an outrageous conclusion.

Abruptly, he withdrew his hand and rose to his feet. 'Shall we go?' he asked.

Then as she made no move, he laughed. But there seemed to be little humour in the sound.

'Don't worry, Samantha.' His hand rested on her shoulder in an almost fatherly manner. 'I'm not about to take advantage of the situation. I'm not the kind of man who moves in on a girl when her lover is away. Especially when that man is his – um – client.'

But he had hesitated before saying 'client', she noticed. Not for the first time she observed that the relationship between him and Jake seemed too emotionally charged to be accounted for by a client-solicitor relationship alone. She tucked the thought away in the back of her mind. She would think about it later. When she wasn't so tired.

Purposefully, she wriggled from his grasp and stood up.

'I'm quite ready to go now.'

He took her arm firmly and marched her down the stairs and through the bar.

Help! thought Samantha, shooting a startled look at Liz as she did so. I do believe I'm under arrest!

Liz glanced over and waved and Samantha could have sworn she saw a look of envy on her young face.

On her direction, Brett drew up outside a Georgian end-terrace house. After the trauma of the last few days, Samantha felt a sense of relief as she looked up at the familiar building, its window balconies ablaze welcomingly with spring flowers.

The house had only recently been converted and Samantha had been given the choice between the first floor flat and the basement. She had chosen the latter, mainly because of the small but much appreciated garden at the back of the house.

'Would you like some coffee, Brett?' she asked hesitantly, wondering whether he would construe this simple invitation as something far more meaningful.

She half-hoped he would refuse for she badly needed some time and space in which to work out the best way of tackling the problems which had loomed up so unexpectedly. And I think that he is going to be one of them, she thought with a sidelong glance at her companion.

Samantha was aware that a curious sense of intimacy had grown up between her and this man, who a few days ago had been a complete stranger. Now she knew that she had to distance herself from him for a while to get her life back into perspective.

On the one hand he and his uncle seemed to be the source of her problems by refusing to allow Jake to draw money from his trust fund. On the other, there was no doubt that his support during the past few days had been very welcome. And that's as far as I'm going for the moment, she reflected, firmly refusing to think about the more personal feelings that he stirred in her.

So busy was she rationalizing her situation that she almost forgot that the subject of her analysis was still sitting beside her. She saw that he was watching her with an oddly obscure expression.

'Look, why don't you put the kettle on,' he said at length, 'and I'll pop back and fetch your car. You don't want to leave it in the car-park longer than necessary. So if you could let me have the keys I'll be back in a few minutes.'

'But your own car?' she interrupted. 'What will you do with that?'

'I'll leave it where yours is now and pick it up later. It's not far from here at all.'

'That really is most kind of you,' she said, unfastening her seat belt. He leaned across her in order to release the car door at precisely the same moment that she did so herself and his hand closed over hers.

His body was so close to hers that Samantha could feel the warmth of his breath and smell the spicy tang of his skin. The door catch sprang open and he withdrew his arm, but not before Samantha had felt the pressure of his fingers instinctively increase and seen a tightening of the muscles at the corner of his mouth.

'Thanks,' she managed coolly and swung her legs out of the door in one deft movement. She sensed that his eyes were upon her as she ran down the stone steps to the door of her flat. It was not until she had put the key in the lock that she heard the car drive away.

As she pushed open her front door, she was seized by an overwhelming feeling of strangeness. As if she had entered the wrong flat. But it took only a glance to register the truth.

She'd been burgled!

As she surveyed the room from the vantage point of the door it looked as if she had entered a war-zone. The cushions had been hurled from the chairs to the floor, books had been tossed from her bookshelves and her few pictures hung lopsided on their hooks.

Automatically she left her front door open, her brain registering the possibility that her intruder might still be on the premises. Hesitantly, she walked across the small hall leading to the two bedrooms. The door to her own room was open and, gingerly, Samantha went inside.

The mattress had been pulled from the bed on to the floor and the contents of her chest of drawers had been tipped on top of it. The doors of the built-in wardrobe were swinging open and most of her clothes had been pulled out and thrown on to the floor. Jake's room was in a similar state.

Samantha passed through a whole gamut of emotions. The first sense of shock being quickly followed by a feeling of outrage and anger that someone had violated her home in this way.

Now as she entered her living-room and surveyed the chaos there, her spirits drooped. She subsided on to the heap of cushions on the floor despondently and was still there a few minutes later when Brett returned.

'Samantha?' His voice was urgent. 'What's happened?'

In a glance he took in the scene. Then, with another quick look at her to make sure she was not injured, he disappeared into the hall. Samantha heard him moving rapidly around the apartment. On his return he went straight to the telephone and dialled.

'What are you doing?'

'The police....' In a few short sentences he explained the situation. Then he turned back to Samantha, who had been watching him through wide, pain-filled eyes.

Now as he approached her, he stretched out both his hands. She took them and he very gently pulled her to her feet and into his arms, cradling her reassuringly.

Samantha clung to him soundlessly, her head against his chest. Very gradually she became aware of the power in the arms holding her and allowed herself to slowly relax against him. As the tension seeped out of her body, she felt another, unnervingly pleasant, sensation taking its place.

For the briefest of moments she abandoned herself to the feeling of safety that being in his arms gave her. Safety, she told herself, but excitement too. Not for the first time in the past few days, alarm bells began to ring.

But it was Brett who disentangled himself from her embrace.

'I've put the kettle on,' he said softly, holding her at arm's length. 'Let's have that cup of tea, shall we?'

Whilst she was busily making tea – not the easiest of jobs as the intruder had looked into every canister in his search for cash, sometimes tipping out the contents to make sure he had missed nothing – Samantha could hear Brett dealing with the young constable who had just arrived.

'It could have been a lot worse, sir!' he said cheerfully, surveying the scene. 'At least he wasn't a grafitti artist, like some! And he's even left the telly! Quite often they're only after things that they can easily carry and easily get rid of. Like jewellery, videos and computers. Money too, of course, if there's any hanging around. He was probably in and out of here in about ten minutes flat.'

The two men joined Samantha in the kitchen.

'Not too bad in here, either,' he went on chattily. 'That's where he must have got in.' He indicated a broken pane of glass which had permitted the intruder to unfasten the catch. 'You would be safer having security locks installed here, sir.'

He looked out into the small garden. The brick wall surrounding it was at least six feet high. In one corner a rainwater butt had been upended. 'That's where he got back over the wall. If I were you, sir, I'd put a nice bit of trellis on top of that for a bit of extra height.' He accepted a cup of tea and helped himself to biscuits. 'Let's have a list of what's missing. You'd be surprised at what turns up eventually.'

They found that the chaos, which originally had looked horrific, was relatively easy to put to rights. Cushions were dusted and returned to their chairs; books were replaced tidily on the shelves. The dishes were washed and returned to their places on the dresser: the rooms were thoroughly vacuumed.

Samantha, unwilling to wear her clothes after they had been handled by the intruder, gathered them into a plastic bag for washing. Others were set aside to be taken to the cleaners.

She couldn't yet be sure but it looked as if, apart from a few pieces of jewellery, the video, her answering machine and a sum of cash she had in a jug in the kitchen for emergencies, relatively little had been taken.

Brett had been a great help, she reflected. He had looked up the name of a glazier who, after some haggling had agreed to come in the next day to replace the glass. In the meantime, Brett had made a respectable looking repair to the broken window.

Now, after all the frenzied activity, they were sitting companionably in Samantha's pretty blue and white painted kitchen.

'If you give me the name of your insurance company, I'll get in touch with them first thing Monday morning.'

'Thanks. I'd really appreciate that.'

'And I'd better have a copy of that list when you make it.'

'Sure. But I'm not really certain exactly what might be missing from Jake's room. He has several cameras, I know, but he might have taken them with him.'

'Just note what you can. We can straighten the details out later.'

'I only wish he were here now,' she said.

She saw his eyes gleam for a moment and she knew that the mention of Jake had caused this. But when he spoke his voice was thoughtful.

'I'm sure you do. This coming on top of your accident is very tough luck.' He stirred his tea absently. 'Do you have friends you could go to for tonight? You won't want to sleep here alone until things have been fixed.'

Privately, she had been thinking the same thing. There were the people upstairs, of course. When she was at home one or another of the tenants would often borrow something or join her for coffee in the garden. But she had no wish to impose on them and the flats were not really large. She did have several friends whom she could at a pinch ask but –

'What about your family?' he asked interrupting her thoughts.

'No. They would be worried if I told them what had happened.'

He was silent for a moment.

'Brett,' she began tentatively. 'That man who was looking for Jake. You don't think he had anything to do with it, do you?'

'It's impossible to say. But it's best you don't stay here tonight in any case. Certainly not before the flat has been made secure.'

He took a biscuit from the tin and munched it thoughtfully. 'All things considered,' he said at last, 'by far the best thing for you to do would be to come home with me.'

'With you? But I hardly know you!' The implication of what she had just said brought colour to her cheeks.

He looked at her, his mouth curving in amusement. 'I'm asking you to be my guest for the night, Samantha, not to share my bed. I have a perfectly good spare room. And I promise faithfully not to seduce you. Unless of course....'

He left the sentence unfinished, but the smile on his face was enough to deepen her confusion. Wretched man! she thought in annoyance. He was teasing her. Just when she was beginning to feel comfortable with him! She stood up and began loading the dishes into the sink.

He brought over his empty cup.

'Of course, if you'd rather not!'

Samantha let the silence between them deepen whilst she considered his offer. Why not? she asked herself. If she accepted his invitation she wouldn't have all the bother of explaining the break-in to someone else and to go through the trauma yet again. But she hesitated.

'Will we be alone?' She turned around to see that he was grinning disarmingly. Again something about his expression was vaguely familiar.

'Does that worry you, Samantha?' She liked the deeply musical way he said her name. It made it sound like a gentle breeze murmuring through the trees. Most of her friends abbreviated it to Sammy.

He moved a little closer and she saw that there were little blue flecks in his eyes that she hadn't noticed before. 'You've just heard me promise _'

'Not to seduce me,' she finished for him, smiling too. But he hadn't answered her question, she thought. This is just a game to him.

He placed both hands on her shoulders and looked down at her, a grin still tugging irrepressibly at the corners of his mouth.

'I can assure you that you'll be well chaperoned. Or rather' – he paused, choosing his words with care – 'that I myself will be properly chaperoned!'

'Meaning?' She looked up at him from beneath her lashes in a way that she knew was provocative. Jake had teased her about what he called her "siren" look – the one she usually reserved for over-pedantic officials.

She, too, could play games!

The fingers on her shoulders tightened appreciably and she felt herself sway towards him, her head tilting back even more. For a long moment, as in the hospital, she was sure that he was going to kiss her. Then abruptly he released her.

'Nothing you need worry about, I assure you! Do you need to pack some things?'

'I've put everything away for washing. I don't fancy wearing clothes that have been ... have been....'

'I understand.' This time the grey eyes gleamed in sympathy. 'No problem. I can find you anything you need at the flat. Don't look so woebegone! In a few days time you'll have forgotten that all this ever happened.

In the meantime, you'll be perfectly safe with me.'
Samantha wasn't so sure.

Five

Brett opened the door and stood aside.

Samantha looked with pleasure at the long, open-plan living-room with its large expanse of polished wooden floors. One long wall consisted entirely of uncurtained windows. In front of these were ranged wide glass shelves carrying a multitude of exotic looking plants. She was amazed by their variety and lushness. It was not yet dark and the last rays of a dying sun filtered through the leaves projecting a psychedelic display of shape and movement on the opposite wall.

He noticed her staring at them. 'I have no garden,' he murmured.

'They're really gorgeous, Brett.'

As she continued to look around, her eyes were drawn to a fine, free-standing open stove with a wide, brick hearth centred at the far end of the living area. Behind this, Samantha could just catch a glimpse of what appeared to be a kitchen area opening on to a balcony.

She crossed the room to stand in front of the stove, admiring its clean-cut lines. Brett came to stand beside her.

'It also fires the central heating,' he explained. 'It can get chilly in here with all that glass.' He nodded towards the windows.

He settled her on one of the very long pale leather sofas.

'Put your feet up,' he ordered.

Samantha did so. Despite the warmth of the room, the leather felt cool against her skin and she shivered slightly.

'Still chilly?' he enquired solicitously. 'I think you'd better have a brandy to warm you up a bit. Then I'll show you around.'

'Thanks.' Samantha didn't really like brandy, but now she accepted the drink gratefully, cupping her hands around the outsize glass. She watched the pale amber liquid swirl gently. What a long day it's been, she reflected lazily, already lulled into a sense of langour by the blessed peacefulness of her surroundings.

For a while they sat in a companionable silence, punctuated only by the reassuring sound of the hopper quietly feeding the stove with fuel.

Samantha relaxed, letting her mind wander over the curious chain of events that had led to her being here in this beautiful room with someone whom only two days ago she had considered her worst enemy. And how do you feel about him now, an insidious little voice whispered. Her eyes closed as she banished the question from her mind. I'll think about that later. Maybe. When I'm not so tired.

Through strangely heavy lids she looked across at Brett, who was sitting bathed in the soft light of a lamp. His face was in half profile and a wing of dark hair had fallen across his cheek. Her eyes rested on him sleepily. He looks much younger like that, she reflected drowsily. More vulnerable, somehow.

Then, as she watched, another face seemed to dance before her and she sat bolt upright. What had started as an embryonic inkling now grew into a fully fledged suspicion. She must be right. What an idiot she was not to have realized it before! Things were now beginning to make a little more sense.

Brett turned sharply. 'Anything wrong?'

'Not at all.'

'Something on your mind, then?' he insisted. 'Problems, perhaps?'

'Not really, Brett.' She smiled at him sweetly. But there was no softness in her eyes. 'However, there is something I'd like to ask you.'

'And that is?' he prompted, raising an amused brow.

'Just what relation are you to Jake.'

This time both eyebrows went up simultaneously.

'My word!' he exclaimed in mock horror. 'We are bright this evening aren't we. You're right, of course, Miss Holmes. Or should I say Ms Holmes. Jake is a relative. My cousin in fact.'

Samantha frowned. 'But why the secrecy? You should have told me instead of letting me....' She broke off.

'Instead of letting you what, Samantha?' he queried softly.

It had been on the tip of her tongue to say, 'Instead of letting me believe it was me you were interested in.' Instead, she said annoyed, 'Instead of treating me like some sort of an idiot.'

Instantly, he looked contrite.

'I'm sorry. That wasn't my intention at all. I just felt that it would be better for you not to feel too overpowered by the family connection ... me being both Jake's cousin and one of his trustees.'

Family money, she thought bitterly. No wonder he was so keen on letting me shoulder responsibility for Jake's debts! And no wonder, too, that he has been keeping an eye on me now. For if I am responsible for Jake's debts, he is also responsible for mine!

'You had no right keeping me in the dark about your personal interest in Jake's finances. It was downright unethical, to say the least!'

He slanted her a silvery glance.

'Most solicitors represent their families, Samantha. There is nothing new in that. And I did try to persuade you to get in touch with your own solicitor.'

'But you didn't tell me why.'

'It didn't seem important for you to know,' he said simply. 'Surely it's not such a big issue.'

'Not to you, perhaps! But it's obvious, even now, that Jake's interests are your sole concern. Not mine!'

In a flash he was sitting beside her.

'That's not true,' he said quietly. 'I have always felt that we had a responsibility towards you. And now that you are practically family _'

'But I'm not "practically family" as you put it. How many times have I got to tell you?'

His eyes darkened.

'That will be for you and Jake to sort out,' he said coolly. 'In the meantime, the least I can do is to offer you my hospitality.'

'I don't want you damned hospitality, Brett Sinclair!'

'Maybe not. I can understand that. But in the circumstances....' He shrugged his shoulders significantly. Then suddenly he smiled so diffidently that Samantha was taken unawares. 'It rather looks as if we're stuck with one another. For tonight, at least.'

Samantha looked down at her glass, trying to get the anger she felt under control. He probably didn't like this situation any more than she did, she concluded grudgingly. He just felt under some sort of obligation to her. For Jake's sake. The thought gave her no consolation. On the other hand, she certainly didn't fancy going back to her flat. Not yet.

When she looked up, she had made up her mind to make the best of the situation. As he'd said, it was only for tonight.

'Why is it, d'you think, that Jake has never mentioned his family to me?'

She saw that he looked relieved at the change of subject.

'I'm not sure. His parents – our mothers are sisters – split up when Jake was about twelve. His mother married again and now lives in Australia so he very rarely sees her. As for his father, he just disappeared completely.'

Samantha looked askance.

'Disappeared?' Despite her annoyance, she was curious to hear about Jake's mysterious background. She'd often wondered.

'Nothing sinister, I understand. It's just that he didn't seem to want anything to do with his family after the divorce. My father and uncle have tried to fill the gap but Jake is very sensitive about it under all that apparent confidence. His trust fund was set up by his grandfather but he feels very badly about his father's lack of interest in him.'

Samantha remembered Becky and Tim. It must

have hurt Jake just as much as it had hurt her.

'We are all very fond of Jake and my mother thinks the world of him,' he added.

Despite her little gesture of protest, he got up and refilled her glass. She sipped at it thoughtfully.

'I suppose you know why I am telling you all this?'

Surprised, she heard the warning note in his voice.

'I think I get your drift,' she said coolly.

He was telling her that he didn't want Jake to be hurt again. Neither did she. But she knew that whatever romantic liaison Jake had entered into, there was nothing she could do to either help or hinder it. Only Jake himself could resolve that situation.

For a while they sat in silence. Then Brett took her now empty glass and stood up.

'You're still looking very pale,' he said. 'Would you like to see your room, now.'

Samantha followed him through an arched opening on the wall opposite the long windows. This led to a narrow hallway running the entire length of the apartment. Several rooms opened up off this and Brett paused in front of one.

'I hope you'll be comfortable here.'

'I'm sure I shall,' she murmured.

The room was simply furnished and, apart from the comfortable-looking bed, the only other items of furniture were an elegant mahogany dressing-table and a bedside table with an exquisite Tiffany lamp. A full-length framed mirror on one wall reflected back their images and the delicate colours of the fabric draping both the bed and windows. A very feminine room, she decided.

Their eyes met in the mirror and he touched her

elbow lightly. 'I'll be back directly.'

He disappeared but returned almost immediately carrying a pair of jeans and a plaid shirt over his arm.

'You might like a change of clothes. These are my young nephew's and should fit reasonably well, so please use them if you want to. The bathroom's over there.'

Samantha looked down at her crumpled skirt and sweater. Back home she hadn't wanted to change and to put on the clothes that had been so rudely disturbed and handled.

She smiled, now beginning to feel the brandy warming her in a rather pleasant way, her previous irritation almost forgotten.

'Thanks,' she said and hiccupped loudly.

'You OK?'

She nodded and hiccupped again.

'Maybe I shouldn't have given you that brandy. Not so soon after coming out of hospital.'

Samantha shook her head, still smiling. There was no mistaking the concern in his eyes. What a pity, she thought impassively, that his concern was for Jake's girl – not for her.

'The brandy was lovely,' she said. 'Just what I needed.' This time she hiccupped twice.

As he stared down at her, Samantha saw the hint of laughter in the silvery gaze.

'I'll leave you to get changed then. Call me if you need anything.' The door closed behind him.

Slipping out of her clothes, Samantha stepped under the steaming hot water. As she let the water play over her, she felt the tension in her body gradually easing away. Soaping herself with the exquisitely perfumed soap – whose choice? she wondered – she watched the gushing water rinse away the bubbles. If only her worries could be washed away so easily.

The shower curtain was patterned with exotic birds and ferny plants and as the light filtered through it, throwing shadows on the tiles, it seemed to Samantha that she was in some tropical paradise. Lost as she was in a world of her own, she was not aware of time passing. It was only when a slight chilliness suddenly wafted over her that she awoke from her reverie. Reluctantly, she turned off the water.

'Are you all right in there, Samantha?' Despite her objection to being so abruptly brought back to earth, Samantha was aware of the note of anxiety in the voice.

'Perfectly thanks, Brett.'

'I've made coffee. Join me in the kitchen when you're ready.'

Then from somewhere in the distance she heard a bell ring and wondered idly who it could be. Brett had certainly given her the impression that someone else lived here. A chaperone, he'd said. A housekeeper, perhaps?

Certainly the apartment seemed very well run, she mused, slipping into the denims. They fitted rather well, she observed, slinging her own leather belt around her hips and checking her image briefly in the mirror. Combing back her shoulder-length, still damp hair, she pulled it up into a pony-tail. A dab of lipstick and she was ready.

As she approached the kitchen, she could hear voices. Brett's sounded apologetic but it was the second voice that made her pause before entering the room.

'... it seemed to be the least I could do.'

'What a nuisance, Brett!' Samantha heard the exasperation in the huskily low voice. 'But I can well see that you wouldn't want to leave her alone here!'

They're talking about me! she thought indignantly. I don't know who she is, but she sounds as if she expects me to steal the silver!

'Sorry, Gina! There wasn't really anything else I could do in the circumstances. I'll try to make it up to you some other time. I promise!'

There was a sound of subdued laughter. Then the voices ceased. Samantha paused for a second before she went through the arch into the room.

The occupants stood in the middle of the kitchen area, their arms wrapped around each other. The woman's back was towards her and Samantha could see Brett's lips against her hair, his hands moving down her body with every indication of familiarity.

Samantha stood transfixed, automatically registering what a picturesque couple they made. Exactly like the cover of a romantic novel. But although she knew that he was still virtually a stranger, it somehow seemed like discovering Tim and Becky all over again.

She was just on the point of drawing back, when Brett raised his head and gazed directly at her. Samantha looked away hurriedly feeling for all the world like a peeping Tom.

Unruffled, he released his companion but kept one arm over her shoulders as he pivoted her around to face Samantha.

'Don't go, Samantha,' he said, seeing her poised for

flight. 'Come and meet Gina.'

My chaperone! she thought suddenly – or rather his! The wretched man seemed intent on disconcerting her!

Gina stood regarding Samantha completely unabashed, a speculative look in her lively hazel eyes.

Samantha stared back at her. She appeared to be a few years older than herself, tall, slender and elegantly dressed in a silky sheath of a bronze colour that perfectly complemented the deep mahogany hair that clung to the contours of her head like a burnished helmet.

She makes me feel like a hoyden, she reflected, unhappily conscious of her borrowed jeans and damp hair.

'Hello, Samantha. Brett has been telling me about you. What a perfectly dreadful thing to happen!' The pleasantly husky voice sounded genuinely concerned but Samantha was conscious of the woman's eyes rapidly assessing her.

'I must say, from what Brett said, I'd imagined you'd be much older,' she continued frankly. 'Usually poor Brett has the most boring clients in the entire world. Don't you darling?' Suddenly, the throaty voice tipped over into bubbling laughter.

Samantha smiled uncertainly and drew back slightly. She hadn't been prepared for this.

'But, of course,' the woman went on, 'I'm forgetting that you're a friend of Jake. And any friend of Jake's...!' She left the sentence unfinished but smiled and shrugged her slim shoulders eloquently.

'You know Jake?'

'Naturally! Who doesn't?' The voice managed to

give it an innuendo that relegated Samantha to just one of a series of insignificant bimbos who paraded without consequence through Jake's private life.

Brett looked up from the breakfast bar where he was intent on pouring coffee and Samantha noticed the look of wry amusement on his face. I do believe he's quite enjoying this, she thought annoyed.

'We were just about to make some omelettes, Samantha. How would you like yours?'

'Not for me, thanks. I think I'll get an early night. They got us up at the crack of dawn this morning!' She took the coffee with a painfully bright smile.

'Head OK?' The cool grey eyes studied her intently.

'Fine thanks.' But, under his penetrating gaze, Samantha felt the colour beginning to creep over her face. She was beginning to feel embarrassed by her intrusion on this cosy domestic scene.

'I must say you look a little flushed. Not setting in for a cold, I hope!' There was no mistake about it. Those eyes definitely held a hint of amusement. 'You'll find some aspirin in your bathroom cabinet. Unless, of course, you'd prefer another brandy.'

The teasing note in his voice was quite obvious now and Samantha could see a corner of his mouth curving in amusement.

'An early night will be enough,' she said shortly, annoyance beginning to replace her discomfiture.

Gina looked from one to the other quizzically. She noticed Samantha's heightened colour and moved over to sit on one of the stools in front of the breakfast bar, crossing her long legs elegantly.

'Have I missed something here?' she enquired lightly, directing her remark to Brett. But there was no mistaking her possessive look.

Then she turned back to Samantha.

'You mustn't let this dreadful man annoy you, Samantha. Make sure you put him in his place if he gets uppitty! He needs a very firm hand or he's absolutely impossible!'

Brett laughed affectionately.

'Take no notice of Gina. She runs an agency and is so used to throwing her weight around all day that she forgets we ordinary mortals don't play by the same rules!'

'You make me sound like a prison wardress!' Gina complained. But the smile she directed at him was amused. 'And since when, Brett my love, have you considered yourself to be an ordinary mortal?' Then her look became more intimate. 'And as for playing by the rules, you seem to make them up as you go along!'

Her next remark was directed to Samantha.

'Male chauvinist piggery runs in the family, I'm afraid! I suppose you've found that out already being a friend of Jake.' Again that speculative glance. 'But I'm sure you can handle him. I haven't seen Jake for ages! How is he, Samantha? Still as mercurial as ever?'

'I suppose you could say that,' she replied, smiling back. Thinking about it, Gina's description of her errant partner was an apt one. She guessed that Brett must have told Gina that she and Jake were friends – lovers even! No matter. It really wasn't important what Gina thought. What either of them thought for that matter.

Despite this, a traitorous voice from within told her that it certainly did matter. For some reason she couldn't yet explain, she found herself in the position of wanting to clarify the situation for once and for all.

She became aware that both pairs of eyes were now looking at her expectantly and feigned a half-yawn, covering her mouth with her hand.

'I'll say goodnight, then. Will you excuse me, please?'

'Sleep tight.' Brett smiled at her. 'I'll see you in the morning.'

'Goodnight Samantha.' Gina's voice was friendly but her eyes held a curiously hard look. 'We're sure to bump into one another again.'

With a quick answering smile, Samantha turned on her heel, closing the door softly behind her and retraced her footsteps along the passageway, her feet sinking into the thick carpeting, masking any sound she might make.

It took only a few minutes to prepare for bed and to pull a jade nightshirt over her head. The bed lived up to its promise of being a comfortable one and Samantha had had a very long day. Almost as soon as she closed her eyes, she was asleep.

She awoke with a start and a profound sense of disorientation. She put out her hand and fumbled for the switch on the bedside lamp. Immediately the room was bathed in a soft iridescent glow. Gradually her surroundings and the events of the past few days sorted themselves out.

Only one o'clock, she discovered. Far too early for a well-mannered guest to go roaming around. Immediately she recalled Brett's words. 'I can assure you that I myself will be properly chaperoned.' Her mind flashed back to the picture of him and Gina together in the kitchen, locked in one another's arms.

So that was what he'd meant! No wonder he was laughing at her. This was all just a game to him! She would be foolish to think otherwise!

She tried to settle back to sleep.

Once or twice she heard Gina's unmistakably infectious laugh and the deep, masculine tones of her companion. She drifted into an uneasy doze but awoke to the knowledge that she was suddenly incredibly thirsty.

She listened intently. No voices. No sound of any kind, in fact. Noiselessly she slipped out of bed. Gina might still be in the flat and she certainly didn't want to disturb anyone. Automatically her feet reached out for her slippers before she remembered that she hadn't brought them with her.

A dim light had been left in the hall and Samantha found her way to the kitchen area quite easily. She reached out her hand to switch on the light and blinked as the room was illuminated by a series of vivid stabs as the fluorescent lighting sprang into life.

She tiptoed over to the fridge, her bare toes curling inwards on contact with the coolness of the floor tiling. Taking a tall bottle from the door, she began to pour the aromatic juice into a glass. Its door still open, the fridge began to hum noisily.

'Samantha?'

The voice behind her was little more than a whisper but the unexpected noise caused her to start violently. She turned her head quickly. The bottle, already slightly slippery from condensation, slid through her fingers and shattered on the floor.

As she stood there, as immobile as an alabaster figurine, the splintered glass rising like miniature

icebergs from the slowly spreading orange pool, her
eyes took in the figure at the door.

Why isn't he wearing clothes? she thought, mildly
surprised that he should suddenly appear naked
before her. Well almost naked, she amended, noticing
the briefs. She took in the deep olive skin that stretched
tautly over the hard, muscular frame. I wish my body
were that colour, she reflected enviously.

For a moment the man stood motionless beneath
her frankly assessing stare.

He's giving me cold feet, she thought, and stifled an
impulse to giggle. Then, looking down, she saw the
broken glass and the orange juice lapping gently at
her soles and realised the predicament she was in.

'Oh!' she said. Her voice dropped softly into the
silence and the figure at the door moved.

'Stay exactly where you are and don't budge!' his
voice rapped out commandingly. A cupboard door
clicked and then he was standing there with a broom
in his hand.

Samantha lost her battle as the threatened giggles
began to shake her uncontrollably.

It must be hard to appear totally in control when
wearing virtually nothing but a broom! she thought
merrily, amused to see that Brett appeared completely
oblivious of the entertainment that he was affording
his guest.

She continued to chuckle as he efficiently swept
away the glass, creating a clear path. Another click
indicated the return of the broom to its cupboard.

'I said, don't move!' the voice again barked as
Samantha shifted position slightly. In two strides he
was standing in front of her and Samantha felt herself

swept off her feet like a child as he picked her up
bodily and marched with her out of the kitchen and
along the hall.

Instinctively, Samantha turned her face into his
chest. Is that his heart thudding or mine? she asked
herself. Her lips brushed against his skin. Smooth,
she thought. Not what I might have thought with all
that dark hair. Unthinkingly, her tongue lightly flicked
out. He tastes like ice-cream, she marvelled. She felt
his arms tighten in response to her touch, pulling her
closer. Involuntarily, her own arms snaked around
him.

Brett pushed her bedroom door open with his foot
and deposited her none too gently on the bed. In the
soft glow of the lamp, she could see his face bent over
her and could sense rather than see his eyes moving
over her body.

'Sit up, Samantha.'

The unexpected command caused her to stare at
him wide-eyed. He took her hands and pulled her into
a sitting position.

'Your feet,' he explained briefly. 'You may have
picked up some glass.' He knelt down and examined
the sole of each foot in turn, lightly running his hands
over the skin as he did so. 'They seem to be OK but
check again in the morning.'

His voice was completely matter-of-fact but
Samantha was acutely conscious that he still held her
foot and she knew that his touch had now become a
caress. Unsuccessfully, she attempted to stifle a sigh
as the warmth evoked by his touch sent little fires
flickering through her veins. She smiled down at him
through drowsy eyelids.

Abruptly the touch ceased and her eyes shot open. She watched, her eyes enormous in her pale face, as he lifted both her feet on to the bed and tucked her duvet chastely under her chin.

'Brett?' She heard the sound escape from her throat huskily and was surprised by the invitation it held.

But he was already at the door. She couldn't see the expression on his face but when he spoke she could hear the mixture of laughter, exasperation and something infinitely more disturbing in his voice.

'I can well imagine that Jake will never find life dull with you around!' Then the door closed behind him and he was gone.

'Wretched man!' she said out loud, banging her pillow into shape. But she found herself smiling.

She closed her eyes and, as an experiment, tried to conjure up Tim's image. But, surprisingly, the familiar face failed to appear.

'Tim?' she whispered into the darkness.

'Who?' her subconscious whispered back.

Six

Samantha awoke to the tantalizing smell of coffee wafting through the apartment. Despite all the mishaps of the previous few days, she felt refreshed and quite ready to tackle whatever the day might bring. She washed and dressed rapidly. Suddenly she felt ravenous.

Brett was in the kitchen, busily watching a sizzling frying pan. She was acutely conscious of the appraising glance that swept over her as she entered.

'You look much better this morning. I hope you like a fry-up for Sunday breakfast.'

'Lovely. Where's Gina?'

'Gina?' He sounded surprised. 'She went home last night.' His voice was matter-of-fact. 'Sit down at the table, Samantha. You'll be more comfortable there than at the breakfast bar. I'm about ready to serve up.'

Samantha took a seat at the table in one of the little alcoves. It was attractively set with a freshly laundered yellow gingham cloth, blue-banded crockery and matching blue-handled cutlery. A basket of warm, crusty rolls invited her attention.

'This looks lovely and I'm starving!'

'Good.' He dished up the food on a large serving plate. 'Help yourself. The coffee's already in the pot.'

Samantha needed no second bidding and filled her plate with little mounds of sausages, button mushrooms, and scrambled eggs.

Brett nodded approvingly and for a while they ate in silence. But Samantha caught herself sneaking covert glances at him. Now that she knew the relationship between him and Jake, she could see that there certainly was a resemblance and wondered why she had not seen it before.

He met her eyes. 'Penny for them,' he said, smiling.

'That's a curiously old-fashioned expression', she replied lightly. 'Do people still use it?'

'Only old fogies like myself.'

'Your words, not mine,' she murmured.

'Well then? You looked so serious. What was passing through that pretty head of yours?'

A compliment? But that was all part of his game. 'I was just thinking about Jake,' she said truthfully.

'Ah, that's it! I thought you had a certain sparkle in your eye.'

She ignored him. 'I was just thinking that you aren't the least alike,' she lied glibly.

'Really. I must say I'm a trifle disappointed.'

She looked mystified. 'Why?'

'Well, after last night's revealing little episode, here in this very room' – he paused for dramatic effect – 'I'd have imagined that those very observant eyes of yours might have singled out some distinctive family birthmark – or at least a mole – common to both of us.'

Samantha forced herself to reply casually.

'None that I could see. Though I wasn't really interested enough to make comparisons.'

But she only just managed to keep her face from flaming by concentrating very hard on the coffee she was pouring.

The wretched man had certainly got it into his head that she and Jake were lovers, she thought. Despite what he'd been told to the contrary. Well he could go on believing it so far as she was concerned. Why should it worry her? Then she recalled the way she had felt last night and couldn't help wondering what might have happened if he had stayed longer.

'I'm glad to hear it.'

But she could tell from his voice that he had been thinking along the same lines as herself. Then he smiled – the same one she'd seen in his office – quite charming but with that certain steeliness in his eyes.

'You realize, of course, that Jake's wellbeing means a lot to my family.'

Her eyes held his steadily.

'I must make it clear, Brett, that although I've every sympathy with Jake, I'm not his keeper. And he's not mine. We both have our own lives to lead!'

His face darkened visibly and she knew that her answer displeased him. There'd be no point in her telling him again that Jake's happiness didn't depend on her. He just wouldn't believe her!

'So I see.' She heard the reproach in his voice but controlled her temper with an effort.

'Meaning what, exactly?' She held his eyes challengingly.

'I think you know perfectly well what I mean.' His words were clipped, his mouth taut.

'I'd prefer you to make your meaning clear.'

'Last night!' he said quietly.

'What about last night?' She narrowed her eyes suddenly, quite unconsciously mimicking his expression.

'The little games you get up to when Jake's away may well be your own affair, Samantha. But don't you think you're playing a little too close to home for comfort?'

'You flatter yourself, Brett Sinclair!'

'But I was right, wasn't I?' His voice was composed, but she could sense the underlying cynicism.

'About what?' she countered, already knowing what was coming next.

'About you needing a man in your bed.'

In one swift movement he had risen to his feet and, taking both her hands in his, pulled her to face him.

'Tell me, Samantha.' His voice now was dangerously soft. 'Is it just the family resemblance? Or would any man do?'

She stared at him. Instantly, she replayed the scene of last night, recalling the way he had held her against his chest. She felt again the way his arms had tightened around her and she shivered.

Help! she thought distractedly. It's ten o'clock on a Sunday morning. The sun is shining and the bells are already ringing for morning service. Yet here am I with a man I scarcely know. And I desperately want him to make love to me!

'Samantha?'

She felt herself swaying towards him.

Then the image of Gina, so lively and elegant, with her arms wound around Brett's neck, intruded rudely into her thoughts. She recalled, too, the shock of finding Tim with Becky. Then she looked at the man scowling down at her. No, she decided resolutely. She certainly didn't want to be part of that kind of scene again.

'Well?' A brow lifted in enquiry. 'Do I get an answer. Will any man do?'

Samantha bit her lip hard.

Damn him! Jake's cousin he may be but he'd no right to question her in this way. She raised her head challengingly.

'That's for me to know and for you to find out!'

She heard the glib cliché emerge with a sense of dismay. And she knew then that she'd played right into his hands.

His eyes took on an icy brilliance. Then he dropped her hands and turned on his heel.

'Well then.' His manner was now perfectly controlled. 'I think we understand one another perfectly. So if you've quite finished here, we'd better get round to your place or that glazier of yours will have come and gone.'

The rest of April passed and they were into May.

Samantha had already had several postcards from the States and was pleased to be reassured that Jake was still as seemingly carefree and as ebullient as ever. But, as yet, no address for him.

So far as Jake knows, she thought, studying the picture of the Everglades in Florida that had dropped through her letterbox that lunchtime, everything is going on as normal. Or as normal as anything could be where the volatile Jake was concerned, she thought affectionately.

Jake had obviously assumed that his share of the bills was being paid out of the trust money. He would have had no idea that the trustees might refuse to pay out. Since meeting Brett, she had understood him better. Certainly she bore him no ill-will for what had occurred.

Thinking of Jake, as sometimes happened, made her recall Tim. She was surprised that she could now do so without any of the bitterness that had characterized her last few months at college or the hurt that had shadowed her life since. At least some good had come of the situation, she reflected.

Luckily, the owner of the car that Jake had bought had not yet taken any proceedings, although she had received a second demand for payment. Brett had told her to keep him up to date on the situation.

She had heard from him twice since that night at his flat. He had telephoned her once to ask how she was settling down after the burglary and again three days ago.

'Samantha?'

She had recognized his voice immediately. The little nurse had been right, she'd reflected, cradling the receiver in both hands as she'd stretched out on her sofa. His voice certainly did make him sound dishy. The telephone somehow gave it a warmth and friendliness that she hadn't noticed when speaking to him face to face. When she was with him she was always conscious of the facial expressions and gestures that sometimes ran counter to what he was actually saying. There was no doubt about it, he wasn't an easy man to get to know.

'Yes, Brett.'

'I thought you'd like to know that the insurance company have been in touch and they're paying your claim in full.'

'Great! Thanks a lot! I wasn't expecting to hear from

them for ages. What magic words did you use?'

He laughed. 'Well they certainly weren't "Open Sesame"! They were a bit touchy about your having no security locks. Rightly so, in my opinion! They insist on your installing them immediately.'

'I suppose it would be sensible.'

'Would you like me to arrange it for you. I happen to know of a reliable company who would probably do it quite reasonably for you. I could get in touch with them?'

'Thanks, Brett. I'd really appreciate it.'

'It's no trouble!' he said cheerfully. 'I'll get back to you when I've contacted them. Anytime this week OK for you? Or will you be off on your travels?'

'I'll be in London until the middle of next week so the sooner the better, I suppose. Tomorrow would be best if they could manage it.'

There was a short pause.

'Samantha?' His voice had lost some of its breeziness.

She waited, her mind already framing an answer to what she somehow knew he would ask next.

'Will you have dinner with me on Thursday? I think it would be a good idea for us to meet up again to talk.'

'That would be nice,' she replied politely, stalling for time. 'But I'm meeting my accountant one evening this week and I'm not yet sure which one he can make. May I ring you later to let you know?'

'Certainly,' a formal note had crept into his voice. 'I'll wait to hear from you then.' He waited for her to say goodbye before she heard him crisply replace the receiver.

The next morning, promptly at 8.30, two lugubrious men from the security company had arrived.

'Thieves' paradise here, miss!' said one gloomily, casting a jaundiced eye around her flat.

'Even a schoolkid could be in and away in two minutes flat,' added his companion. 'I bet you haven't had a good night's sleep since it happened.'

They had immediately got down to work and in a surprisingly short space of time Samantha had been informed that she would now be as safe as if she were in Alcatraz.

Samantha had telephoned Brett to thank him and to accept his invitation. She had been in two minds whether to do so or not. The idea that he was keeping in touch mainly in order to keep a watchful eye on her persisted.

The reasons for this had seemed painfully obvious to her. Firstly, he wanted to make sure that Jake's girl – as he firmly believed her to be – was behaving in a suitably decorous fashion. Secondly, he needed to reassure himself that she wasn't drawing unnecessary money from the business account and thereby putting both Jake and herself even further into debt.

But, now, as she stepped into a simple velvety sheath of midnight blue which showed off the alabaster smoothness of her skin to perfection, she had to admit that she was looking forward to seeing him again.

When he rang her bell at eight precisely, she was ready.

'Come in, Brett. I'll just get my handbag.'

He hesitated slightly as he entered and Samantha thought for a moment that he was about to shake hands. Instead he caught hold of her shoulders lightly and kissed her cheek. He uses the same aftershave as Jake, she observed. She knew this because she had bought it for him. He had professed to like it so much that he had used no other brand since.

The kiss was just a polite, perfunctory peck but Samantha was glad that he had set an informal note for the evening. It would be very pleasant to have a quiet, relaxed dinner. After the circumstances in which they had parted, she had half expected him to want to resume their purely professional relationship of client and legal adviser and she certainly didn't want to spend the entire evening talking about unpaid bills.

'That's a lovely perfume you're wearing, Samantha.'

'Thanks. Jake bought it for me in Paris.' The remark slipped out quickly without thought. She regretted it at once. Immediately, his expression hardened.

'He has good taste,' he said softly. But there was an edge to his voice that disturbed her.

He looks at me as if I'm Jake's property, she thought annoyed. This situation was becoming tiresome, like a game that has gone on too long.

But she heard herself saying blithely.

'And you wear the same after-shave as Jake. I know that because I gave him that brand at Christmas.'

She was rewarded for her temerity by a quiver of his eyebrows. I bet that's firmly put me into Jake's bed! she told herself wryly. No doubt whatsoever about that. But it's his fault. He provokes me!

'Jake and I certainly do seem to have a lot in common, don't we?' His brows arched into the thick hair.

'Gina certainly seemed to think so.'

'She did, indeed. Although I wasn't sure exactly to what she was referring. But she and Jake are great

pals, so you girls probably have the advantage of me
in that respect.'

'Aren't you worried that Jake might be upset at
your seeing Gina if he is such a good friend of hers?'
she retaliated waspishly.'After all, you did make a
point of emphasizing just how sensitive he is?'

'Gina?' he feigned surprise. 'Good lord no! Gina
happens to be a very good friend of the whole family.
She has a weekend cottage not far from my father's
house so she's a frequent visitor there, too. But as for
her and Jake. The idea is absurd. Apart from which,
I would hardly have wanted you to meet her if she and
Jake had been lovers, would I now?'

'Brett ...' she began. This had gone on long enough.
'I think you ought to realize....'

'That we are running late,' he interrupted smoothly,
glancing at the mahogany school clock on her wall.
'I've booked a table for 8.45. So if you're ready, we'll
make a move.'

The Italian trattoria was small and the atmosphere
was both cosy and intimate. The waiter seemed to
know Brett well and they were immediately shown to
a table in one of the little alcoves tucked away behind
a screen of plants. But as Luigi fussed around her
solicitously, she couldn't help wondering about the
other girls he must have brought there in the past.
The idea disquieted her.

They ordered immediately. Samantha decided to
start with the antipasto – slivers of anchovies, baby
mushrooms, beetroot cut into tiny shapes, olives and
pimentos. She had hesitated caught in a delicious
dilemma as she tried to make up her mind between

the fettuccine all'Alfredo and the chicken cooked Roman style with tomato, wine and rosemary. But recalling suddenly how Tim had loved fettuccine, she chose the chicken.

Brett barely glanced at the menu that Luigi handed him, ordering the minestrone and a steak, together with a bottle of Frascati.

Despite her misgivings, Samantha found him a pleasant companion and was soon chatting easily about her work.

'In some respects, you could say that our jobs have certain elements in common.' Brett refilled her glass.

'Dusty documents for one!' she laughed. 'I seem to spend a lot of my time rooting around in the archives.' She glanced up. 'This chicken really is delicious, Brett.'

'Good. Although where you manage to put it is a mystery. Most women I know are on a diet of some kind.'

'When I was at school, I felt very left out of things because I was so thin! Nearly all of my friends seemed to be on some highly exotic and exciting diet. I used to wish desperately that I was fatter and could join in the fun!'

'I wouldn't have said that you were a girl who wanted to be one of the crowd,' he observed. 'You strike me as being something of an individualist.' There was a look of frank assessment in his eyes. 'In my opinion you and Jake are well suited in that respect. He has always seemed popular but basically my young cousin is a bit of a loner.'

All roads seem to lead to Jake, Samantha thought wryly. It was as if he was always present like some kind of a ghostly chaperone. Sensing dangerous territory, she attempted to change the drift of the conversation.

'Does your family live in London, Brett?'

'No. In Minchindon. My parents are in Australia at the moment but my uncle – he's the other trustee, remember? – is staying there and keeping an eye on things.'

'Minchindon. That's in Suffolk, isn't it?' Samantha nibbled at a grisini stick. 'I seem to remember a rather picturesque churchyard in the neighbourhood, with some very interesting tombstones.'

'That's right.' He shook his head with a smile. 'I tend to forget that you're the kind of girl who haunts places that other girls wouldn't be seen dead in!'

'All in a day's work,' she replied cheerfully.

She found herself humming the catchy little tune that was playing softly in the background. It was only after some little time that she became aware that he was watching her closely.

'Brett?' Her head tilted and she smiled at him enquiringly.

'I was just thinking,' he said and she heard the teasing note in his voice. 'Here am I, with a very charming young lady. The lights are soft, the music romantic and what do we talk about? Churchyards and tombstones!'

'Oh!' Her surprise showed in her voice. 'I'm sorry. It's just that...' she broke off in confusion, aware that she was blushing and hoping that it didn't show in the rosy glow of the table lamp.

'I suppose you and Jake usually talk shop over dinner. Don't worry about it! It's nice that you two have so much in common.' But that slight edge had again crept into his voice and she looked down at her plate unhappily.

The appearance of Luigi saved Samantha from answering.

'Would the signorina care for dessert?'

'Some ice-cream, I think. Cassata, please.'

'And a slice of your Genoese tart for me, Luigi. And two coffees. With cream?'

Samantha nodded. Luigi whisked away their plates and disappeared.

Once again, she attempted to change the subject. 'Did you ever think of becoming a barrister, Brett?'

'I've certainly thought about it, but I wouldn't have liked to spend so much time in court. Although the distinction between solicitors and barristers in this country could well be a thing of the past soon.'

'I remember hearing talk of that. So we could see you playing Perry Mason in court yet!' She smiled at him mischievously. He would look great in the outfit, she reflected.

He laughed. 'In reality, it's a lot less dramatic than is made out by television series and plays! As it happens, Samantha, I have an uncle in the theatre and he often plays the lawyer on stage. Naturally, his cases are much more dramatic than mine!'

'Really? Perhaps I've heard of him.'

'Quite possibly. He's Jake's other trustee. Harry Barrington.'

'No! I don't believe it. Are you really related to him?' Samantha stared at him, her spoon poised in mid air.

'You sound as if you're a fan of his. I'll have to

introduce you sometime. Or you must ask Jake to do it.

'That won't really be necessary!' she smiled at him impishly. 'I've already met him! But not with Jake!'

He sat back in his chair and looked at her searchingly. 'From the look on your face, I can guess that I'm about to hear an unbelievable story! Meeting up with Harry usually involves some larger than life incident!

'This certainly was!'

He listened attentively whilst she told him all that had happened before her accident, gleefully emphasizing the shock she had received when Harry and Paul had visited her in hospital. Seen now in retrospect, she could see the funny side of it all. So, apparently, did Brett and his laughter rang around the room.

'Oh Samantha!' he managed at last. 'What are we going to do with you? Is your life always as hectic as it sounds?'

'Not usually,' she replied quite truthfully. 'It does seem to be an incredible coincidence though. Coming straight out of your office and then seeing your uncle!'

'Not really. He'd been in my office just before you arrived. Half a minute earlier, and you would have met him then.'

Samantha thought back. Now that he mentioned it, she did recall someone passing her when she had arrived at the outer entrance but she had been studying the nameplates and hadn't noticed his face.

'I understand the camera team often uses that location around the cemetery. Very atmospheric, isn't it.'

'It is indeed,' said Samantha fervently. 'Particularly just after you've been told that you're virtually bankrupt!'

'Poor Samantha! My family do seem to be giving you a hard time, one way or another! So you met Paul, too. He often comes up to the Hall. That's the main reason we manage to keep our housekeeper. She is glued to the box on Tuesdays and Fridays. It seems the whole village is! But I was almost forgetting the reason – one of the reasons,' he amended hastily, 'that I wanted to see you.'

Here we go, she thought. I suppose I ought to have brought my bank statements with me. He's going to ask me how much I've been spending, and how I'm paying those confounded bills!

'I was talking to Harry only a few days ago about the difficulty you are in and he said he would very much like to meet you. If you are free, we could go up this weekend. He doesn't know that he's met you already, of course.' His face became boyishly conspiratorial. 'I think we'll surprise him with that.' Then he frowned. 'Like me, Harry feels less than happy about the way Jake is behaving.'

'Hold on, Brett!' Samantha retorted annoyed. 'I'm not a charity case, you know. Not yet, anyhow!' she added pointedly.

'Samantha. As I've said before, you don't want to look on the black side. I've a feeling that things will sort themselves out well enough in due course.'

'It's OK for you to say that, Brett! It's not your home and livelihood that are at stake.'

Samantha heard her attempt to appear jocular fail miserably and he reached across the table and covered her hand with his.

'I'm not a villain, Samantha. Neither is my uncle – nor my cousin, despite his disappearance.'

Then he smiled at her so disarmingly that Samantha caught her breath. She glanced down at the hand that so completely obscured her own, and a sensation of delicious excitement quivered its way through her body.

The long, strong fingers tightened around hers and she looked up. Although the smile still hovered around the corners of his mouth, his eyes had darkened and looked back at her with such intensity that Samantha sensed a powerful charge leap the gap between them. Without a word, he signalled Luigi to bring the bill.

Hand in hand they walked to where he had parked his car. Then without any warning, he pulled her into the shadow of a lime tree and wrapped his arms around her.

As Samantha felt the strength ebb from her limbs a sudden surge of pure joy, stronger than she had ever known before, swept through her and she relaxed completely against him. Immediately he brought his mouth down on hers, insistently seeking from her the response that she willingly gave.

Above them the breeze gently ruffled the branches, causing the shadows to move sensuously in harmony with the lovers concealed in its shade. Moths fluttered around the street lamp, irresistibly driven to dash themselves against the heat that would consume them. One fluttered frantically against Samantha's cheek as if searching out a kindred spirit.

A single night bird, alerted to some danger as yet unknown, shrieked a warning. 'Sami, sami, sami!' It seemed to Samantha, her senses heightened to a razor sharp perception, that it was calling her name. She stirred slightly in Brett's arms.

Abruptly, he released her and for a long moment stood staring down at her. Whatever expression had earlier been in his eyes, Samantha now saw only the narrowed pupils and the taut, unrelenting lines of his mouth as he once again brought his feelings under control.

'I'm sorry.' His voice, already perfectly composed, sounded to her like that of a stranger. 'I shouldn't have done that.'

He makes it sound exactly as if he'd just trodden on my foot, she thought, her sense of frustration and bewilderment tipping over into annoyance as he turned away and walked unconcernedly to the car.

They returned to her flat in silence.

'I'll pick you up on Saturday, then? At about ten?'

'I'll give it some thought and let you know,' she replied tersely. 'Goodnight, Brett.' She stepped back and saw him hesitate before turning away. Her heart gave a jolt as she saw the look in his eyes.

'Brett?'

She heard the invitation in her voice with a sense of dismay. But she knew that she couldn't let him leave like this. She saw his body tense and she knew that he was willing himself to resist. Then once more she was pinioned in his arms and her body joyously welcomed the searching touch of his hands.

'Damn!' he muttered harshly his lips against her tumbled hair. 'You know how much I want you!'

She heard the pent-up passion in his voice as from a great distance. Then, as her own thoughts began to

spin away giddily, she felt him shaking her roughly by
the shoulders. Her heavy lids drifted open lethargically
to face the silver fires blazing from his eyes.

'One day,' he gritted, and her heart plummeted to
hear the menace in his voice, 'you'll play games once
too often!'

Then, she found herself alone.

Samantha leant against the doorpost completely
bereft until she heard the car door slam. Then she
banged her front door shut, suddenly wishing that by
doing so she could shut him out of her life forever.

Seven

Despite her reluctance, Saturday found Samantha walking with him through the intricately wrought-iron gates towards the Hall. Already she was feeling sorry that she had let him persuade her into coming. Persuade, is hardly the word, she mused. Steam-rollered would be better!

'I'll call for you at ten, as arranged,' he'd told her brusquely when he'd telephoned her yesterday.

'We didn't arrange it Brett,' she protested. 'I just said I'd give it some thought.'

'And?' he challenged.

'I really am very busy at present. With Jake still away there seems to be double the paperwork to do.'

'Surely it can wait a day or two. Or, if you're really having so much difficulty, I'll loan you my secretary for a few days. She'll soon get you sorted out.'

Samantha remembered the rather officious lady who had ushered her into his office. She had no wish to be "sorted out" by her – or by anyone else for that matter!

'That's very kind of you,' she demurred politely, making a face at herself in the mirror across the room, 'but there are some things that need my personal attention.'

The line went silent for a moment. 'Your personal attention, Samantha?' His voice was soft and she instantly recalled the kiss he'd given her and the way his hands had moved possessively over her body. She subsided weakly into a chair.

'You still there?' This time there was a smile in his voice and Samantha couldn't help feeling that he could somehow see her confusion. 'Good. Ten o'clock it is then. Goodbye Samantha.'

Five minutes later she'd rung him intending to say that she definitely wasn't going. His secretary had answered.

'I'm sorry, but Mr Sinclair has already left for the weekend. You can leave a message but I'm afraid he won't get it now until Monday.'

Liar! she'd thought, putting the phone down with some vehemence.

When he'd arrived to pick her up, he'd announced that they were going by train.

'Car out of action, Brett?'

'I'm afraid I've already promised it to Gina. Her car is in dock. You don't mind, do you?'

'We could use mine,' she suggested, feeling more than a little put-out that Gina appeared to have prior claims on him.

'I've already bought the tickets.'

Throughout the journey he had been charmingly polite but Samantha was constantly reminded of how he had seemed to her on their first meeting. Remote – wary – distrustful. Despite anything she might say to him to the contrary, she knew that whenever he looked at her with that penetrating silver glance, it was Jake's girl that he saw.

Now as they crunched up the wide gravel path, she wished that Jake would somehow miraculously appear and relieve her of the burden of the past few weeks. She was tired of worrying about their bills and her flat. And she was tired of being in a state of almost constant warfare with the man at her side.

'Samantha dear,' a voice boomed, 'lovely to see you!'

Narrowing her eyes against the bright May sunshine, she recognized with pleasure the portly figure bouncing down the drive towards her.

'Harry!'

He kissed her smackingly on both cheeks and held her at arm's length whilst he scrutinized her, his bright blue eyes missing nothing.

'You're looking ravishing, I must say!'

'Hello, Harry.' Brett's face broke into an affectionate smile. 'Samantha tells me you've already met.'

'We have indeed.' He took her arm in a proprietary fashion. 'And in the most curious circumstances possible.' He looked shrewdly from one to the other. 'Did Samantha tell you how it happened?'

Brett laughed. 'She did indeed. But, knowing you both, I wasn't in the least surprised.'

'Is Paul with you, Harry?' Samantha's query had been purely automatic as she couldn't help thinking of Paul and Harry as a team. But she saw Brett's eyes grow cool. He still seems intent on casting me in the role of a Jezebel, she thought ruefully. Then she met his eyes defiantly. It wasn't her fault if he consistently misjudged her.

'He'll be down later this afternoon, dear. I'm sure he'll be delighted to see you again. But enough of my partner in crime for the moment. He'll probably have enough to say on his own account when he gets here. Did Brett tell you that we'll be filming in the village later this week? *The Case of the Scarlet Lady.* All very gruesome, my dear, but a way of earning an honest crust!'

Samantha smiled. She suspected that his "honest crusts" were very well buttered indeed!

Harry guided her across the lawn to examine a bed of roses that were shooting strongly.

'These are coming along well. I do believe that they have some greenfly already.' He squashed the offending creatures with his free hand. 'Would you believe, Samantha, that I once had a rose named after me. A beautiful blush pink, with white tips. A very vigorous grower too! I have a whole bed planted up with them at my home in Wiltshire.'

Samantha laughed aloud at the idea. 'What an honour! Was the grower one of your fans!'

'No. But I understand his wife was. So much more perceptive the ladies, I've always found!'

'I'll leave you two to get reacquainted, Harry,' grinned Brett when they rejoined him. They watched until he disappeared through the door of the front entrance.

'But enough of roses for the moment! Tell me about you and Brett,' he said archly. 'Are you what our American cousins insist on calling "an item"?'

'Good heavens, no!' Samantha's emphatic denial, which was accompanied by a sudden rush of colour to her cheeks, brought a smile from her questioner.

'Well then. What...?' he questioned delicately.

'Brett's acting as my solicitor. Jake asked him to draw up our business documents, you know.' She smiled impishly. 'I'm his partner, you see.' Then she laughed at his comically astounded expression.

'Really? So you are Jake's mysterious partner. I thought that Brett was being very secretive! Just fancy that!' He chuckled delightedly. 'Business is such fun these days!'

Samantha's face sobered a little. 'You may have heard that we're having a little hiccup. But Brett's kindly helping me to sort it out.'

A keen glance showed him that the so-called "little hiccup" was a lot more serious than she had let on.

'I knew, of course, that he was setting up some business venture with a friend of his but I had no idea that it was a girl – and a very charming one at that. But then I haven't actually seen him since – now when was it – the Christmas before last it must have been!'

They had reached the front entrance and he bustled around ushering her into the hall like a mother hen with a chick.

Brett put his hand under her elbow. 'I'll show you to your room, Samantha. Then we'll have some tea.'

'Thanks.' As she left the room she glanced across at Harry. He was looking out of the window with a curious little smile hovering around his lips.

From where she was standing, she couldn't see either the road or the dark blue estate that sped past the gates on its way to the village.

'I do believe we're in for a storm later,' he remarked brightly.

Samantha looked at him curiously and wondered what made her think that it wasn't the weather he was talking about.

After tea Brett offered to show Samantha the rest of the house.

'It's been in my mother's family since it was built in the late eighteenth century,' he explained. 'Although she had never actually lived here until we moved from London.'

'It's really lovely. Has it an interesting history.'

'It has indeed. It was built for one of my mother's ancestors – a very beautiful woman apparently – by her lover.'

'Sounds romantic,' she murmured, smiling.

'It was. He was one of the princes at Court and from all accounts idolized her.' He was very close now and she could feel his breath raising little tendrils of hair at the base of her neck.

'They never married?'

'No. They were both married already. Though, naturally, everybody knew of their affair.'

'Customs change,' she said, acutely aware of the warmth of him reaching out to her. 'Did she love him in return?'

He laughed and she saw his brows peak humorously.

'Who knows? Who can tell what a woman is feeling, Samantha?'

'Or a man!' Her eyes met his boldly.

The smile that curved his lips acknowledged her comment. Then he lightly picked up her hand.

'You might be interested to know that this ring,' he indicated the seal-ring Jake had given her, 'was a gift from her prince.' The tip of his fingernail traced the intaglio carved crest.

Oh God! thought Samantha in dismay. What on earth had possessed Jake to give it to her! She must return it when she saw him.

He drew her towards the window and a splendid

view of the landscaped gardens leading down to the river — its little boathouse almost hidden by trees. Samantha could just make out the shape of a rowing boat moored alongside it.

'You can't actually see it from here, but over there' — he indicated a clump of mature elms some little distance from the river — 'is a small cottage. It was built as a trysting place for the lovers. To afford them some privacy.'

Samantha stood on tiptoe. His arm tightened around her waist as he steadied her. But she could see nothing.

'Can you imagine it,' he murmured in her ear. 'The lovely lady of the house dallying away the long summer evenings in the arms of her prince.' His lips brushed against her cheek so softly that Samantha was not at all sure that she hadn't imagined it. 'Whilst all the time her husband would be playing backgammon in the house with his friends.'

His arm pulled her closer and Samantha momentarily closed her eyes as the magic of his voice and the warmth of his body so close to hers began to weave a languorous web around her. With an effort, she turned to face him.

'The games lovers play!' she commented lightly.

She felt his hands come up and entwine themselves in her hair as he looked down at her.

'And what sort of games do you like to play, Samantha' — the mouth was smiling faintly but his eyes glinted with a disturbing mixture of mischief and malice — 'whilst your lover is away?'

Her eyes held his challengingly. 'Maybe the same ones that you do, Brett!' Yet again an image of him and Gina danced before her.

His eyes narrowed.

'The game I would like to play' – his hands moved to cup her chin and to tilt it up – 'is one that I'll have to forgo, tempting though it may be!'

Samantha stared at him. She could see her own desire mirrored in his eyes. But she also saw a steeliness that sent a shiver of foreboding down her spine. The ghost of Jake stood between them as surely as if he were there in the room with them. Nothing she could say or do would change that.

'But don't tempt me too far, Samantha.' His voice was dangerously soft. 'Or there may be consequences that we will both regret.'

Abruptly, he released her and turned away.

'Brett ...' she began hesitantly.

'Come along!' He smiled at her distantly. 'You haven't yet seen the west wing.' Then his eyes gleamed with a touch of humour. 'It has been said that it's haunted!'

As Samantha dressed for dinner that evening, she was conscious of a mounting sense of excitement. She surveyed her reflection in the mirror critically. The simple, high-necked, fine wool dress, the colour of a stormy sea, clung to her slender body, flaring slightly towards the hem as she twirled around in her delicately strappy sandals. She had brushed her copper hair until it glinted with the lustre of a newly-minted penny and lightly shadowed her lids in a shade of amethyst-blue that made the eyes that stared back at her seem enormous.

As she ran lightly down the curved staircase, Harry advanced to meet her.

'My!' he said with apparent satisfaction, taking both her hands in his and holding her at a distance in order to see the effect better. 'You do look stunning! We're going to have to keep you well out of Paul's reach this evening. I'm afraid his reputation is quite scandalous where the ladies are concerned!'

Samantha smiled as he tucked her arm in his and ceremoniously escorted her to the dark oak-panelled dining-room.

'Hello, again.' The curiously husky voice came from the direction of the window. Looking across, Samantha was astonished to see Gina standing with Paul and Brett.

'Samantha, isn't it? I must say, I hardly recognized you!' Gina turned to Brett and touched his arm possessively. 'Why didn't you mention that Samantha was coming down, darling? We could all have come together! It would have been such fun!'

'I didn't know I was coming down myself until the last minute,' he said smoothly, moving towards the drinks table. 'What will you have, Samantha?'

Samantha, wholly disconcerted at the sight of the elegant Gina, looked at Brett coldly. If he had mentioned that Gina was to be here, she wouldn't have come herself.

'Vermouth, please. Dry.' She smiled politely in Gina's direction but moved closer to Harry. 'Nice to see you again,' she murmured, trying to inject an element of warmth into her voice.

Paul looked from one girl to the other curiously. Then he casually strolled over to stand beside Samantha. 'Did you get my message?' he asked, smiling down at her, blue eyes crinkling at the corners.

Samantha breathed a sigh of relief. Paul at least was reassuringly normal. 'Yes, I did, thanks.'

'And?' His brows twitched comically.

Samantha laughed. She'd almost forgotten the message he'd left about a charity fun-race he was involved in and suggesting that she be his partner.

'It sounds fun!' she smiled. 'Although I must warn you, Paul, I'm hopeless at anything sporty!'

'Great! I'll ring you again next week to let you know what time I'll be picking you up.'

'Such a small world, I always say,' remarked Gina gaily. 'Jake – Brett – Paul – Harry! We seem to move in the same circles, Samantha.' But there was an edge to her voice that belied the smile.

'I doubt that.' Samantha's answering smile was the sweetest she could summon up.

Gina turned to Brett. 'Who would have thought that your pretty little client would know so many interesting men!' She smiled up at him from beneath her lashes. 'Are you sure that your dealings with her are strictly business, Brett.'

He laughed and shook his head chidingly. But there was no mistaking the affection in his look. 'You can stop your teasing, Gina. Samantha is a friend of Jake, as you well know already!'

That's put me very firmly in my place, Samantha told herself wryly. My only valid identity these days is as Jake's girl! A quick glance at Gina showed her that she was pleased with this small triumph. But she also saw a gleam of malice in her eyes.

'It must be pretty serious between you and Jake if you've come to meet the family,' she observed, looking at Samantha speculatively. 'Funny that he hasn't mentioned you to me before. But then Jake has always been rather secretive about his women, hasn't he Brett?' Her glance at Brett was all wide-eyed innocence.

He merely shrugged. 'I don't see much of him these days,' he murmured noncommittally.

'Are you and Jake going to make it legal, Samantha?' she went on with a pretty show of interest. 'Or do you prefer just to go on living together? All the fun and none of the chores,' she added brightly.

Samantha could sense her cheeks flaming. She saw Harry frown suddenly. Paul shuffled uneasily. Brett's expression was unreadable. But she was saved from answering by the housekeeper's announcement that dinner was ready.

'You will stay for dinner, won't you Gina?' asked Brett. 'Matty always makes enough for a small army.'

So Gina hadn't been invited. The thought provided Samantha with a touch of consolation.

Despite the air of tension, Harry and Paul were both in good form at dinner, sometimes slipping into the familiar banter that characterized their performances in *Stepney Mansions*. It was easy to see why their programme regularly topped the charts.

Samantha realized that Paul was quite shamelessly setting out to monopolize her and she found herself responding easily to his light-hearted banter. She could readily understand why he and Harry made such a good team. His down-to-earth, bed-rumpled, roguish charm complemented perfectly Harry's genial and relaxed style.

She remembered reading somewhere that Paul had been in show business since early childhood. She knew, too, that he had made a series of disastrous marriages and his liaisons with a succession of beautiful women featured prominently in the gossip columns. He had several small children, all of whom he adored. Dinner that evening had been brought forward so that Paul could leave early as he intended driving back to London where he was picking up his son at Victoria for the weekend.

Having finished a hilarious anecdote about the eccentric behaviour of the producer when shooting a recent episode, he turned to Samantha. 'I bet you and Jake turn up some curious things in your line of work.'

'We certainly do. But we find that the main problem is getting the producer to realize that the romantic setting he's set his heart on isn't authentic.'

'And are you a romantic, Samantha?' asked Paul, gazing intently into her eyes.

Samantha laughed, 'About as much a romantic as you are, Paul!'

Paul, who was as well known for his hard-headed business acumen as for his success with women cast his eyes to the ceiling.

'My lady has a heart of stone!' he exclaimed dramatically.

'Shut up, Paul!' said Harry amiably.

As Paul refilled her glass, she glanced over at Brett. He met her eyes and she was conscious of a vibration passing between them of such intensity that she hastily took a gulp of her wine to cover her confusion.

Harry who had intercepted their unspoken communication looked amused. One eyebrow quivered roguishly. Then he glanced at his watch.

'Paul, you really must be going if you're to meet that

train at Victoria.'

'I'm on my way,' he said jumping to his feet. 'Samantha.' He took her hand. 'Will you walk with me to the car?'

'She'll do no such thing, Paul!' protested Harry, wagging his finger at his younger colleague reprovingly. 'Take no notice of him, Samantha. He always did have a weakness for beautiful redheads and is not to be trusted alone with one for a moment.'

Paul made a face of comic innocence.

'You must remember what happened last time,' added Harry with mock severity.

'I remember well enough,' grumbled Paul. 'I was taken advantage of!'

'From what I've seen, I'm sure that Samantha could cope quite adequately,' remarked Brett drily. But the look he gave her held a definite warning.

Cheek! thought Samantha. Anybody would think that he owned me! Even if it were only in trust for Jake! She smiled at him sweetly, then rose to her feet.

'I'll be very happy to walk with you to your car, Paul, if it means that you'll be off in good time to meet your train.'

Paul raised her hand to his lips and kissed it extravagantly. But from the corner of her eye she had seen Brett's eyebrow flick at her ironically and noted Gina's basilisk stare.

With just the slightest toss of her head, Samantha ignored them both pointedly and turned her attention to Paul. Taking his arm defiantly, they walked companionably to where his car waited in the drive.

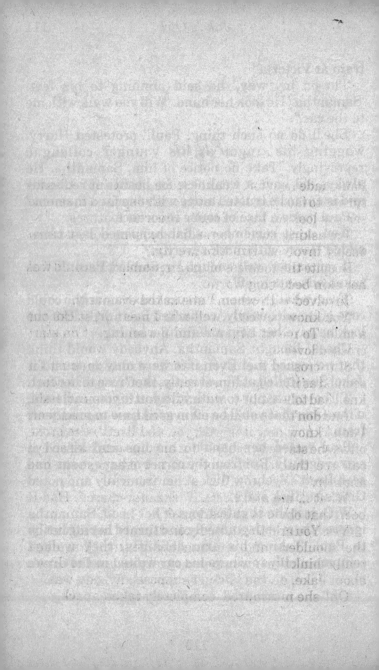

Eight

Paul made no effort to unlock the car door. But, as he turned to face her, Samantha was surprised to see the serious look on his normally cheerful features.

'I'm asking purely for selfish reasons but just how deeply involved with him are you?'

Despite the coolness of the air, Samantha could feel her skin becoming warm.

'Involved with whom?' she asked evasively.

'You know perfectly well who I mean. It sticks out a mile. To me at any rate and I'm an expert on star-crossed lovers.'

Star-crossed lovers! His words struck deep and it seemed as if in the deepest recesses of her soul a death knell had tolled. She could only look at him soundlessly.

'And don't look at me with eyes like a wounded deer! I don't know how it is with you and Brett' – he broke off as she started visibly – 'but anyone with half an eye can see that the two of you are crazy about one another.'

'What ... me and Brett...?' she stammered. Had it been that obvious to everyone?

'Yes. You and Brett,' he replied firmly, taking her by the shoulders and shaking her gently. 'You don't really think that I was fooled by all that spiel of Gina's about Jake, do you? I don't suppose anybody was.'

'Oh!' she murmured, completely taken aback.

'I've no idea what reason you've got for wanting us to believe it. I can only hazard a guess that you've been badly hurt in the past by someone.' Her eyes widened. 'Ah. I can see I'm right! But it's no good trying to deny your own feelings. Take it from me, sweetheart.'

He pulled her closer.

'Now I'm going to say this once and once only because I'm a selfish bastard and would be happy to help you pick up the pieces myself.'

Samantha gave a tremulous smile.

'Especially if you are going to make a habit of smiling at me like that. Now just listen! Brett is a great guy and a good pal and he's been like a brother to me. But he can be an arrogant wretch at times with women and if you hurt his pride he'll probably hold it against you for ever! I've seen it happen before. And no, I'm not going to tell you about it!' he added, as Samantha opened her mouth to speak.

'What I'm saying, Sammy, is this. Don't play games with him! It's not worth the candle! You'd be a great couple, if I'm any judge! Both in and out of the sheets. So don't chuck it all away for some silly fancy. End of lecture!'

He kissed her on both cheeks.

'And when you get back to town, I'll give you a ring. I promise faithfully I won't jump you!'

He's nice, she thought, watching him as he sauntered around and got into the car. He wound down the window and looked up at her cheerily as he started up the car.

'Oh and Sammy' – his grin was the one she remembered from her schooldays – 'there's one more thing you should know before you go.'

'What's that?' she called as the car started to move.

From halfway down the drive his voice drifted back.

'It's just that I should warn you! I never keep my promises!'

Samantha was still chuckling when she returned to the house. Paul really was impossible, she thought. But fun.

She passed Gina on her way out. She seemed in rather a huff and the look she gave Samantha was blatantly hostile.

'You off?' asked Samantha in surprise.

'I am. But don't think your little games have gone unnoticed!' Gone was even the slightest pretence at civility. 'You'll find that Brett Sinclair won't put up with that sort of thing! I'd advise you to confine your attentions to Jake. If he ever decides to come back, that is!' she added spitefully.

Samantha lifted her shoulders nonchalantly and stood aside to let her pass. Gina was the least of her worries! she reflected.

She found Brett alone in the library lounging in a high-backed leather chair.

'He's quite a character, isn't he?'

Samantha nodded her head, smiling as she did so.

'Gina's gone home,' he said. 'She has another engagement.

'I know. I passed her. She seemed in rather a hurry.'

'It seemed that she was rather upset at the way you allowed Paul to monopolize you at dinner,' he said casually.

Samantha stared at him. 'Gina was? Why on earth should that interest her?

'She is fond of Jake. She doesn't like to think of him

getting hurt. As it happens, I agree with her.'

Privately, Samantha thought that Gina's concern wasn't for Jake but the sudden cynicism in his voice caught her completely unawares.

'Meaning what, exactly?'

'I think you know well enough what I mean.'

'Brett. Why not say what you mean and be done with it!' Her voice was icy calm. 'You asked me here as a guest and now you're treating me like some – some – nineteenth century kitchen wench caught sneaking out to meet her lover!'

She turned smartly and met his eyes defiantly. 'It's the twentieth century we're living in. Not the feudal ages! So please don't ever try to tell me whom I can talk to!' Then head held high, she walked blindly past him.

Back in her room, Samantha threw herself down on her bed and closed her eyes. He could be an arrogant wretch with women, Paul had said. And he was obviously right! She buried her face in her pillow. It felt cool and fresh against her heated skin. He may be Jake's cousin but she didn't owe him either an explanation or a detailed blow by blow account of her movements!

Needing some air, she sprang from her bed and went over to the open window, leaning her elbows on the sill. Despite her anger, she felt a quickening of her senses at the beauty of the garden stretched out before her – its deepening shadows hinting at hidden and mysterious depths. Gradually, she felt the tension in her body leaving her as she began to succumb to the evening's heady magic.

The waving elms seemed to beckon an invitation. A

night for lovers, she thought. But her anger had now gone and she felt only a pang of nostalgia for those balmy long-gone days at college when being loved and in love seemed as natural a part of her life as breathing.

As they had dined early, the light was only just beginning to fade. She remembered the glimpse of the rowing boat that she had seen by the boathouse at the bottom of the garden. Some exercise would do her good and it wasn't yet too late.

Swiftly she changed into a pair of chestnut-brown cords and pulled a toning sweater over her head. Her sandals were substituted for a pair of walking shoes. Then, quietly, she went down the back stairs and out of the side door.

The sun was already setting behind the trees of the little wood that lay between the house and the village, making them look like black cut-outs against the rosy palette of the sky. An aura of peace lay over the scene and she breathed deeply, drinking in the mild early summer freshness.

Taking the path that led past the small water garden, she lingered for a few minutes at the pond to watch the antics of the multitude of toads that leaped in and out of the water and the rock garden nearby. A black and white cat sat as still as a stone statue on a flat rock, watching the scene through narrowed slit eyes. Seeing him about to spring on an unsuspecting victim she crouched down, gently plucked the small creature out of his path and put it down behind a sheltering rock, watching whilst it leaped joyously away.

Careful little fellow! she thought. I understand how it feels to know that someone is waiting to pounce on you the moment you least expect it!

'I thought I'd find you here, Samantha.'

The quiet voice broke into her thoughts. She looked up startled, her blue-grey eyes darkened to indigo in the gathering dusk.

'I came to apologize for what happened earlier.' His voice was distant. 'I'm sorry I upset you. I had no right to behave the way I did.'

She stared up at him silently. He doesn't really mean that, she thought. He still feels that he has every right to say whatever he pleases to me.

He stretched out his arm to help her to her feet. Samantha looked at the strong hand with its crooked little finger. Then, ignoring it pointedly, she rose to face him.

'I didn't mean to upset you, truly. Am I forgiven?' She noticed the remoteness in his voice. He is merely playing at being polite, she thought. After all, I am his guest.

Then he smiled so engagingly that Samantha almost felt herself weaken. But she caught herself up sharply.

'But you did upset me, Brett.' She could see the thick brows arch questioningly. 'It hurts to feel that someone who hardly knows me at all should consider himself qualified to pass judgement on everything I say or do.'

He was silent for a moment. When he spoke, Samantha detected a note of appeal that she hadn't heard before.

'Perhaps that's the trouble, Samantha. I know I haven't known you long, but it feels as if I have. From that first time when you sat in my office looking so forlorn but so full of fight, it has seemed as if I were meant to play a special part in your life.'

'As my guardian angel, Brett?' Samantha couldn't resist asking.

'It certainly seems as if that ought to be the case, in view of our professional relationship.' He moved a fraction closer. 'But I must admit that isn't the role uppermost in my mind when we find ourselves together.'

'Oh!' Samantha's voice was noncommittal, but her heart was beating rapidly. 'And just what role is it that you feel you have in my life, Brett?'

This time he reached out a hand and touched her shoulder tenderly. 'I'm not sure!' he murmured frankly. 'There are times when I feel that....' His voice trailed off and Samantha could feel his fingers tighten and the gap between them begin to close.

'There are times when you feel...?' she prompted, her eyes holding his steadily.

She saw him lower his gaze as he gently traced the line of her jaw, tilting her chin towards him.

'I think you know perfectly well what I feel.' The coolness in his voice had gone and had been replaced by a vibrancy that shattered any pretence she might have to calm. As he ran both hands through her silky hair, his eyes suddenly glowed with a silvery fire. He drew her close, his hands sliding down her body, moulding him to his own that curved towards her like a tightly strung bow.

'When I hold you like this I could forgive you almost anything,' he murmured.

Samantha, who had been on the verge of abandoning herself to the magically sensuous feeling of languor that was stealing over her, caught his words and alerted herself to listen.

'I can almost forget that what you are feeling now is just a natural response of a passionate woman towards a man.'

Instantly, the spell was broken and she stiffened. There he goes again, she fumed silently. Acting as if I fall into bed with any available man!

'And what do you mean by that precisely?' she demanded, giving him a little shove.

'I thought that would be obvious! You are a very attractive girl, Samantha, and it's quite natural that you should enjoy the power that a pretty woman has over a man.' He seemed oblivious to her scathing look.

'Go on.' Her voice was deceptively calm.

'I didn't choose the role that I have been given. The guardian angel, as you put it. But there have been times when I've been hard pressed to remember the relationship that exists between you and Jake. And to be truthful, Samantha, you haven't exactly made that easy at times have you now?'

'Meaning?' Her voice now was ominously chilly.

'I know that I had no right to behave the way I did earlier. But I don't think you had the right to behave as if my attentions would have been welcome.'

'Oh? Would you mind explaining that remark, please!'

'Do I really need to?' She saw his mouth harden to a single implacable line. 'You've certainly made it very hard for me to think of you as someone else's girlfriend. That night we had dinner, for instance. I had to be the one to draw the line. Or we'd be lovers now!'

'Damn you, Brett Sinclair!' she hissed furiously.

'How dare you speak to me about my morals! How about your own? How about Gina? Or is it one rule for the men and another for women?'

He made no reply but Samantha could see his eyes glittering dangerously.

'Well?' She folded her arms belligerently and stared back at him. 'Or am I too close to the truth for an answer?' With that she turned on her heel and started back down the path.

In her haste to be gone Samantha didn't notice that a small rock had become dislodged from the rockery and had fallen across her path. She tripped and nearly fell, stumbling back against Brett. Automatically, his arms came up to steady her. Samantha felt his hands on her waist as she hopped from foot to foot in an effort to regain her balance. Then, just when she thought that the arms encircling her were about to set her free, they tightened into steel bands, pulling her roughly up against him.

'Let me go, please!' Samantha was surprised to hear the frostiness in her voice. *He treats me like a child's toy that can be picked up and discarded at will,* she thought furiously. With a superhuman effort she fought against that insidious sense of lethargy which again was threatening to engulf her.

All at once, his arms released her. Samantha again lost her footing. Then, regaining her balance once more, she whirled around to face him and smacked him hard across his face.

In the moonlight, she could see his eyes glinting ominously as he stared down at her. Samantha lifted her chin defiantly but was devastated at the look she saw there. Suddenly his arms came up to hold her in a vice-like grip.

'Is that what you really want?' His voice was mocking. 'For me to leave you alone.'

Then his mouth came down on hers and Samantha felt her body melting into his as her resistance began to ebb away. His lips became more gentle as he sensed her response. Then, with a sigh, Samantha's arms came up and she clung to him. For a long moment they stood locked together, swaying rhythmically like aspens caught in a summer breeze.

Then totally without warning his arms dropped and he pushed her away.

'But even you can't make me completely forget' – a tired note had crept into his voice – 'that you are Jake's girl.' Abruptly, he turned on his heel and strode away.

Samantha stood watching him until he disappeared in the direction of the house, her senses still reeling from the onslaught. Then, tears of anger and frustration in her eyes, she turned on her heel and fled unseeingly down towards the river.

Why on earth do I let him do this to me! she thought despairingly. Every time we are together it ends like this. She remembered Paul's warning about playing games with him. If she had been more firm in her denial of any romantic involvement with Jake right from the beginning, would Brett have believed her? Then her eyes fell on Jake's ring. A family heirloom: not to be parted with lightly! What imp of mischief had prompted Jake to give it to her? No wonder Brett believed she was Jake's girl. She could almost believe it herself.

But deep down she knew that she was partly to

blame. Paul had been right. She had let her previous experience with Tim colour her actions and hadn't wanted to acknowledge the attraction that this man who had come so suddenly into her life had for her.

Sooner or later, Brett would be bound to learn the true state of affairs from Jake and would inevitably think that she had just been playing a game with him. But by then he would be out of her life for ever.

Thoughts tumbled through her mind in such rapid succession that in her headlong rush she almost missed the boathouse altogether. Collecting herself with an effort, Samantha pulled open the door with a jerk and went in.

The interior was pitch dark and she stood for a few moments whilst her eyes gradually became accustomed to the gloom. Making out the shape of oars standing in the corner, she took two and went up to the landing stage. In less than three minutes the boat was untied from its moorings and she was pulling away from the bank.

As the boat skimmed through the water, Samantha's tenseness began to slip away. The air felt cool against her face and soothed away her feverishness. The back gardens of the riverside houses slid by. As the dusk deepened, their lights began to come on, cutting the gloom with startling swathes of brightness.

Then she rounded the bend in the river, leaving the gardens in her wake and the scene became wilder as the stream widened and left the village. As it skirted the wood, the trees along the bank became denser and their boughs, some not yet fully in leaf, stood out starkly against the rapidly fading amethyst and rose-splashed sky.

Samantha became acutely conscious that she was now entering an alien territory as the inhabitants of the riverbank joined in protest at her intrusion. Owls hooted and birds screeched a warning at her approach. Unseen creatures slid into the water and glided smoothly away from her, their hostility filling the air with an oppressive sense of outrage.

Once, as she pulled too close to the bank a swan, maybe sensing danger to its brood, advanced menacingly towards her, spreading its wings and flapping at her in annoyance. She rested her oars and let the gentle current take her downstream. The white shape – ghostly in the dusk – kept her company until, feeling that the danger had passed, it gave a final admonitory flap at the boat before majestically taking off upstream.

Unexpectedly a clearing appeared and Samantha caught her breath in delight. A magical scene. Through the willows at the water's edge she glimpsed two primeval duelling oaks, their branches intertwined, set in the centre of a semicircular grassy knoll. Between them stretched an ancient log, trailing ivy. Other trees formed a waving, living backdrop.

Just like a stage setting, she mused. Any minute now the characters will appear and take up their places. Oberon and Titania, perhaps? She smiled at the thought. On impulse, she moored the boat to a convenient stump and lightly jumped out. Moving over to the ivy-draped log in the centre of the clearing, she sat down.

The rising moon illuminated the scene like a strategically placed spotlight, silvering all it touched with its cool, ethereal magic. Samantha sat quietly for a while letting the peace of the enchanting setting steal through her.

Lost in her reverie, she at first barely registered the faint sound of twigs snapping somewhere nearby. Then the noise increased and she became uneasily aware that someone – or something – other than herself had been attracted to the clearing. Her senses alerted, she listened intently, trying to discover the direction of the sound.

'Is anybody there?' she called softly and started to her feet. But nobody – or nothing – appeared.

'Hello?' she called again, her uneasiness increased by the silence that whispered back. She had heard something! She was sure of it. 'Who's there?'

'Well met by moonlight!' murmured a voice behind her.

Her heart in her mouth, Samantha whirled around. And came face to face with Jake.

Nine

With a little shriek, Samantha hurled herself into the arms of the slim figure who stood grinning down at her.

'Jake! You wretch! Where have you been hiding? When did you get back? What on earth are you doing here?'

He stood there, his eyes full of laughter, his arms wrapped about her. 'Hold on Sammy! Anyone would think I'd been away for years, instead of a few weeks! Let me get my breath back first!'

'Get your breath back?' She held him at arm's length, suddenly suspicious. 'Why? What have you been doing?'

'Shadowing you for the past mile or so. And a merry dance you've led me, I must say! I've been waiting for the opportunity of seeing you alone ever since you arrived!'

'How did you know I was up here?'

'The arrival of an unknown young lady at the Hall is bound to be a juicy titbit of gossip in these parts. Particularly when she's also a tasty redhead! I do have my spies, you know!' He tapped his nose signficantly. 'I was going to catch up with you in the boathouse but thought that cousin Brett might still be lurking around.'

'You were in the garden?'

'Afraid so! Watching your every move! And a fascinating scene, if I might pass an opinion!' There was unrepentant laughter in his voice. 'Saw you slap Brett down too. That's quite a wallop you pack, Sammy, love!'

He backed away, holding his hands up in a gesture of surrender as Samantha advanced theateningly.

'Come and sit over here, Sammy. I've a lot to tell you.' He indicated the fallen tree trunk. 'But first, what's been happening to you. Why are you up at the Hall?'

Samantha told him briefly about her meeting with Brett, touching only lightly on the subject of the car he'd purchased. Jake listened in silence until she had finished.

'Poor Sammy,' he said affectionately, putting his arm around her shoulders. 'I wouldn't have had you worried like this for the world! It didn't cross my mind for a minute that Brett wouldn't arrange an advance like he'd done before. After all, it wasn't as if I'd wanted to squander grandfather's money!'

Samantha nodded her head in agreement. But she had to admit that during the past few weeks she'd begun to see the trustees' point of view.

Then he smiled wryly. 'Even so, I really shouldn't have rushed off like that without clearing things up first. Although I did have a reason. I'm so sorry, Sammy!'

Samantha rested her head on his shoulder comfortably. At no point had she really doubted his intentions, but it was an enormous relief to know that he was back.

'About that car. I've already resold it for quite a nice

little profit. In the company's name, of course! The money should be in our account in a few days. So that's one worry off your mind.'

As he turned his head, the moonlight drained the chestnut hair and hazel eyes of their normal hue and emphasized the strong underlying bone structure and his resemblance to Brett became more pronounced.

'I'm sorry I didn't get a chance to tell you before,' he went on. 'But as you know, these cars are a hobby of mine. I can't afford to buy them for myself yet, of course. So the next best thing is acting as the highly knowledgeable middleman!'

Samantha gave a sigh of relief. 'Thank heavens for that! Brett said I might have to sell the flat.'

She saw his mouth harden. 'He had no right to say that to you,' he said quietly.

'He did have your interests at heart, you know. And you, partner dear, were nowhere to be found!' Samantha wondered why, in the light of Brett's behaviour earlier, she was trying to justify him to Jake.

'That advance was meant to purchase the car. I'm really sorry, Sammy. It does look as if I hadn't thought things through properly.' His voice sounded so repentant that Samantha gave him a hug.

'It doesn't matter now that you're back,' she said quickly. For a few moments they sat companionably together whilst around them the night sounds in the wood resumed their normal level.

'That business with Brett in the garden, Sammy. Anything going on there?'

Samantha giggled. 'That's the fourth time today that someone has asked about my love life! With different men too! Do I look like a temptress?'

Jake looked at her sitting beside him, her face lively
with laughter, the moonlight turning her pale skin to
alabaster.

'As a matter of fact, Sammy darling, you do! Had we
not known each other so well, I might have been
inclined to fancy you myself!' He leaned forward and
kissed her chastely on the cheek. 'We've been through
a lot together, haven't we, love?'

Samantha hugged him again. They had, indeed.

'But you haven't told me the reason for all this cloak
and dagger stuff. Why didn't you come up to the house
instead of skulking around in the garden?'

'I had my reasons,' he said cryptically. 'Actually,
although I think the world of him, I didn't much fancy
getting a lecture from Harry about my spendthrift
ways! Not until I'd had a chance to talk to you,
anyway. And Brett, too, can sometimes be a bit prickly.
As I'm sure you've already noticed,' he added slyly.

'You can say that again,' said Samantha feelingly.

'And dear old Carter has already given me a dressing-
down on the subject for not keeping him fully informed
about what was going on.'

Samantha thought of the elderly accountant they
had employed to keep their books in order, recalling
his repeated warnings about making sure they kept
him up to date with their financial outgoings.

'Apparently Brett tore him off a strip for not keeping
a more watchful eye on us.'

'Oh God! Poor man! It wasn't his fault! We really
must be more careful in future!'

'Agreed.' Now that his voice had taken on a more
serious tone, Samantha could hear the resemblance it

had to Brett's quite clearly. But when he continued, it was in a lighter vein. 'Now my news – or rather why I rushed off as I did. It was partly business, of course. I was sussing out locations for the follow-up on that Channel 5 thriller we were involved with last year. The one set in Florida.'

She nodded. She remembered it well. She also recalled it starred a very sparky American girl. She and Jake had hit it off immediately.

'See anything of Caroline, whilst you were there?' she asked mischievously.

He looked at her in astonishment. 'How on earth did you guess?'

'Not too difficult. Brett told me you were thinking of getting married.'

'He told you that!'

'He did indeed! Unfortunately, I couldn't convince him that it wasn't me you wanted to marry!'

'You're joking!'

She shook her head, laughing ruefully. 'I'm not, you know! He's been guarding me like a dragon. But I'm really happy for you both. Caroline certainly is a stunner and seemed a very nice girl altogether!'

Samantha heard the note of reassurance which had crept into her voice and smiled to herself. It was nice to think that Jake had at last got over Becky. She thought of Tim but his image was shadowy and produced no painful sense of emptiness as it had once done.

Jake was looking at her curiously and she knew that he too had been thinking along the same lines.

'It all seems a very long time ago, doesn't it love?' he murmured softly.

He took her hand and they sat quietly, watching the moonlight dancing on the water and Samantha knew that they were both exorcizing the ghosts that had held them bondage to the past.

When she at last spoke, she mentioned the break-in at the flat, briefly itemizing the things that were missing. So far as she could tell, little of Jake's had been taken, but he had to know about it.

He looked shocked. 'How awful for you Sammy! When did it happen!'

'It was when I was in hospital,' she said, forgetting for the moment that Jake knew nothing about her accident.

'Hospital! What hospital?'

Samantha recounted the incident, deliberately making it sound amusing and of no real importance.

'Harry! It's hard to believe! What a curious sequence of events. I know that cemetery quite well. Did you know that Brett has a fantastic pad near there?'

Samantha remained silent. There was really no need for Jake to think that her involvement with Brett was more than it actually was.

'Harry would know the area well too, so perhaps the coincidence isn't as great as it seems.'

A cool breeze began whispering through the trees and Samantha shivered slightly. Instantly, Jake turned to her in concern.

'You're getting cold. Isn't it about time you went back? Harry and Brett will think you've done a runner!'

'Why don't you come with me?'

'And face the music? I think I'll give that a miss for a bit, Sammy! I'd better get all my bills and documents together and go cap in hand to them with something positive to show. Although with what I made on the car, we're almost certainly in the clear.'

'You're probably right.' But it was too late, she thought, for Jake to be able to clear up the misunderstandings that had arisen between her and Brett. Anyway, she knew that she had been partly to blame.

They hugged goodbye, Samantha refusing Jake's offer of his jacket to keep out the chill. He helped her into the boat and pushed her off the bank. When she looked around, he had disappeared into the night. Only then did it occur to her that she hadn't asked him where he was going. She smiled ruefully. Dear Jake! She rather wished that she could have gone with him.

She made her way back to the boathouse deep in thought, her oars making scarcely a sound as they dipped through the water. She saw how the moon had silvered the water to mercury and smiled to see how its globules reformed in her wake. Just as if I had never been there at all, she thought. Just as Brett's life will be after I'm gone, an inner voice whispered.

This time she was conscious that the night crowding in all around seemed to accept her presence with perfect equanamity. She heard no screeching warnings; felt no hostile night creatures protesting against her intrusion. Just an almost perfect moonlight night.

With the reappearance of Jake, a great burden seemed to have lifted from her shoulders: yet she was still conscious of a weight lying like a stone in her heart.

Why? she asked the night. Jake was safely home; their business seemed sound once more. Even the break-in at the flat appeared just one of those unfortunate things that happen from time to time. Yet even as she reassured herself that everything was fine, she knew she was fooling herself.

She pulled into the landing stage with barely a ripple. Instantly, she was conscious of someone watching her. She looked around.

'Brett?' she murmured into the night.

Her senses told her the answer before her eyes had time to recognize the tall figure that detached itself from the shadows of the boathouse. Without a word, he came forward and tied up the boat. Then taking the oars with one hand, he grasped her hand firmly and helped her on to dry land.

Samantha felt a tingling sensation travel through her palm to every nerve fibre in her body. She had the powerful feeling that she had travelled safely home through some perilous sea. He pulled her close and they clung together wordlessly. A lone owl hooted and it sounded to Samantha like a lost soul that had finally found its way.

'I came to find you,' he said at last, his face troubled. 'My behaviour was unforgiveable!'

'You've been waiting all this time?' Samantha put up her hand and gently traced her finger along the furrows in his brow. He took her fingers and pressed them to his lips.

'I saw Jake go after you. I had to know if....' He broke off and drew her over to the bench outside the boathouse.

The silence between them built up until Samantha felt it was almost tangible. Then she took a deep breath and told him all that had passed between her and Jake that evening. He listened silently whilst she talked. All the while he held her hand, stroking it lightly.

'And there has never been anything between you? I'm sorry. I've no right to ask that.' He sounded apologetic but Samantha felt as if the course of her whole life depended on the answer.

She looked at the river and into the past. 'There has been a great deal between Jake and I,' she said quietly. 'We've been through a lot together. In a way I do love Jake. But we've never been lovers.'

He gave a sigh that melted into the breeze. 'You really should have told me, you know.' His voice was soft, the reproach gentle.

'And if he had been?' Samantha couldn't resist asking.

He put an arm around her shoulders and pulled her close. 'In that case' – his lips were against her hair – 'I should have had to challenge him to a duel! Pistols at dawn behind the cathedral!'

The answer was lightly given but she knew it was not the one that she would have got had her own reply been different.

'And Gina?' She sat up very straight. She had almost forgotten Gina.

'A good friend. A very good friend, Samantha.' She heard the inflection in his voice and felt an instant stab of jealousy. 'I know that she can at times seem rather abrasive. But she's been a family friend for years and we are all very fond of her.'

'Nothing more, Brett?' She heard the uncertain note in her voice and felt ashamed.

'Not now, no.' But she could tell from his tone that

at one time Gina had been very much in the picture. He pulled her head back to rest on his shoulder. 'Poor love, you must be tired! All that rushing around,' he murmured wickedly.

'I've certainly covered a lot of ground today,' she confessed.

'You're just like a will-o'-the-wisp, darling. One moment you're in my arms and the next....' He made an expressive gesture with his hands and shoulders. 'I'm going to have to watch you very carefully in case you are spirited away before my eyes.'

Samantha closed her eyes, revelling in the sensation of warmth that radiated from him. Then abruptly, he stood up.

'Come along! There's a place I want to show you.'

'Now?' she protested weakly. 'Brett! I'm really too tired to go on a guided tour. Can't we leave it until the morning?'

'It's not far.' He seized her hand and Samantha let him lead her unresistingly along a little paved path to their right that she had not noticed before.

It seemed to her that the evening had taken on a dream-like quality, as if she had passed through some magical barrier and entered another world. There was a sense of inevitability that, when Brett stopped, there should be an enhanted cottage in front of them.

Silvery vines shimmered eerily over the ancient door and clematis and honeysuckle trailed around the latticed windows, filling the air with a seductively heady perfume. Samantha gazed at it in delight. If I reach out and touch it, she thought, I'll find that its made of gingerbread!

'The trysting house,' murmured Brett, still clasping

her hand, and Samantha remembered the story he had told her that afternoon about the lady of the house and her prince.

They walked up the winding path, Samantha on tiptoe, unwilling to disturb the friendly spirits that seemed to surround this place. Brett stooped in front of a stone urn and took a large key from underneath it. As he inserted the key into the lock, Samantha's hand closed over his. Sealing a pact, she thought, just between the two of us. The door creaked slowly open.

Instantly, Samantha felt herself swept off her feet as he picked her up and effortlessly carried her over the threshold. The door creaked shut behind them. She closed her eyes and felt his breath warm against her cheek. Another door swung shut behind her then she felt herself cushioned by a soft mattress as he gently put her down.

Slowly she opened her eyes. For a moment she could see nothing, sensing Brett bending over her before she saw him. His expression was inexpressibly tender. His hands passed expertly over her body, charming away her clothes. Then unhurriedly and with a casual grace he shrugged himself out of his own.

At that moment, the moon went behind a cloud and the room was plunged into darkness. Samantha closed her eyes.

'Brett,' she whispered.

'I'm here, my love.' The words appeared to be whispered from an immense distance. In an instant Samantha felt his lips caressing her face. Then she was in his arms.

A swishing sound tugged at Samantha's consciousness

as she lay curled up beneath the covers. She stirred only slightly as the morning sun invaded the room, busily seeking out the shadowed corners and claiming them as its own.

Samantha was dreaming ... she could tell that even as she lay still cocooned in the warmth of sleep. The figure in her dream remained misty and though she tried her hardest to see his features, they faded before she could make them out.

In her dream the figure approached her and she could feel the heat of his body and it hung like a haze around him obscuring her view of him. She felt a gossamer soft touch on her cheek as his head hovered over hers and she felt a warm sensation at her throat that sent sensations of pleasure to the very centre of her being. 'Mmm ...' she murmured drowsily as she abandoned herself sensuously in the feelings that washed over her. Still in her dream, she saw the figure rise and stand looking down at her. As the features floated in and out of her consciousness, she reached out to him, still struggling to see his face.

'Tim?'

The syllable softly escaped her parted lips with a sigh. But instantly she realized that the face was Brett's and with a sense of delight raised her lips to meet his, waiting for the embrace that would.... But abruptly the figure disappeared. Samantha made a small sound of displeasure.

Then, as her eyes began to flicker open, a maliciously mocking voice cruelly invaded the territory of her dream and pulled her back to the edge of wakefulness.

'My word! We do seem to have a short memory this morning, don't we?'

Samantha's eyes jerked fully open. Staring in bewilderment, she tried to reconcile her dream world with reality. Quite unconsciously she repeated the gesture of her dream and raised her face to his, her parted lips inviting his kiss. He ignored her but she could see those silvery eyes lazar into hers with an intensity that shocked her.

'I'm so very sorry to disappoint you,' – each syllable seemed shaped to wound – 'but it seems that you've found yourself in the wrong bed. Or in the right bed, maybe, but with the wrong man.'

She made no move but stared back at him in total bewilderment.

'I'm afraid Tim – whoever he might be – couldn't manage to get here himself. But as I was closest to hand....' He shrugged with an awesomely telling eloquence.

'Tim?' The fateful syllable became stuck in her throat and emerged as a croak. 'Tim?' she repeated. What on earth had happened that he should ask her about Tim?

'Yes. Tim, Samantha. Surely you must remember him? Yes, obviously you do for you called his name whilst I ... whilst I....'

He turned away but not before she had glimpsed an expression of such cold fury that she could only continue to stare, for the moment completely mesmerized.

With an effort he regained control.

'But maybe you don't. Perhaps he means no more to you than I do myself – or, indeed, any of the men who might have loved you.'

He came closer, glowering at her with such malevolence that Samantha wanted to hide her head under the pillow. Instead, she struggled to sit up.

'What's the problem?' His voice was icy. 'Have you had so many lovers that you find it difficult to recall their names?'

Samantha felt a wave of heat creep through every millimetre of her body. Then anger took the place of confusion and she raised her head.

'It has never been like that, Brett,' she said sharply.

'No? I suppose you are going to tell me now that you and Tim were like you and Jake. Just very good friends.' The derision in his voice speared through the room like a deadly weapon. 'I should have known better than to believe that.'

'You can choose to believe whatever you like!' Her eyes blazed furiously.

He came closer. 'Purely from curiosity, Samantha, what was Jake really to you? A rather good-looking young man with more money than was good for him? Or was it just convenient to have a man handy whenever you were feeling ... amorous?'

But despite the mockery in his voice, Samantha was shocked by the desolation that was written in his eyes. For a brief instant she had an impulse to take him in her arms and to reassure him that the dreadful things he was implying had no substance. But immediately on its heels came a surge of anger at the way he was treating her. How dare he behave like this! She shook back her hair defiantly and it tumbled around her face like a windswept red-gold cloud.

'You would do well to realize, Brett Sinclair, that I'm not your property. Nor Jake's. Nor any one of the countless lovers that you seem intent on bestowing on me! What I do – in or out of bed – is nobody's business but mine.'

Then she pulled the covers up to her chin and glared at him challengingly. He glowered back and she saw anger, scorn and an indefinable look of sadness chase themselves across his face. Brett, she thought, suddenly despairing. Why are you doing this to me – to us?

For a long time he continued to glare at her flinty-eyed. Then she saw him turn and stride over to the window. As he looked out into the sunlit garden, Samantha saw the room darken in the way that it had at that first meeting in his office. But when he spoke his voice was calm, impersonal almost.

'If we get a move on, there'll just be time for you to catch the 9.30 train.'

Ten

Samantha closed the door to her apartment with a sense of relief. The last few weeks since her visit to the Hall had passed in a frenzied whirlwind of activity and she was grateful.

Jake was in Ireland, researching a documentary. With Jake's sale of the vintage car, the company's bank balance was once more in credit. Thinking of Jake and his new fiancée brought a smile to her face. She was pleased that he, at least, had managed to find happiness.

Then, as it had been doing with alarming frequency, her mind returned to that last morning at the Hall.

At first it had amazed her that she had actually called Tim's name in her sleep. No doubt a psychiatrist, trained in the labyrinthine workings of the human mind would have explained it as a simple transference of her feelings for Tim to Brett. But she knew that episode with Tim had been only a dress rehearsal for that with Brett. It had just been unfortunate, she thought wryly, that the ghost of Tim – who had been wandering around in her subconscious for so long – had chosen that particular moment to surface.

Samantha had asked herself just how she would have felt if the positions had been reversed and it had been Brett who had called a woman's name in his sleep. Would she, too, have had such an overwhelmingly hostile reaction?

She thought not. Even in our modern world, she reflected, women are still judged by different standards to those used for men. But she was bitterly disappointed – and angry – that Brett had behaved the way he had.

After making a cup of tea, she sank back in her comfiest chair to listen to her answerphone messages. The voices of her callers filled the room. Then Jake's voice, a little fuzzy from atmospherics, crackled from the machine.

'Hi, Sammy. Jake here. Just to tell you that everything is going well over here and I'll be back on Monday. Bye, love. Have a nice day!' Samantha smiled. Over the years he had grown very dear to her.

Then an achingly familiar voice cut through the air. 'Samantha?' There was a pause, as if the caller were waiting for an answer. 'Brett. I need to speak to you. Could you ring me, please. At home or the office. Before Thursday if possible.' The call ended with the sound of the phone being put down decisively. No personal – or even polite – greeting.

Samantha just sat there, letting the emptiness that swept over her gradually be replaced by cold fury. How dare he expect her to act as if nothing had happened between them? How could he be so insensitive? If he wanted to discuss business, he would have to wait until Jake got back. To talk about anything else was now completely out of the question.

After a long, cooling shower, she slipped into a silky shirt and floating palazzo pants in a shade of jade green.

A quiet evening at home won't hurt me, she thought.

Watch a film or maybe catch up on some of the paperwork. She made herself a snack meal, curled up with it on the sofa and switched on the television.

As if on cue the doorbell rang once, paused then rang more insistently as if someone had decided to keep a finger on it. As she opened the door, Brett strode inside.

'Good. You're home at last.' His voice was pleasant but completely impersonal. 'I've been trying to reach you all week.'

'Oh?'

Samantha was pleased that she had managed to put into that one cool syllable all the pent-up annoyance that had been plaguing her since their last meeting.

'You didn't get my message?' One brow arched enquiringly.

'I've only just arrived home. I've been in Devon all week.' She was disappointed to hear the defensive note in her voice. Then she lifted her chin and stared back coolly.

'Never mind. You're here now. Get your jacket. We're going out.'

He could have been talking to a child, she thought, irritated. But she stared back at him balefully.

'*You* certainly are, Brett. You are going to leave this very minute! But, equally certainly, I'm not! I've had a long drive, an exhausting week and I'm dead beat. All I want to do now is to have a quiet evening and an early night.'

How odd, she reflected. I've thought of little else but him all week. But now I really do want to be left alone. She had played this scene with him in her imagination many times. But it was not running according to the script.

The grey eyes looked at her quizzically.

'Waiting for your friend, perhaps? Tim, isn't it?' he enquired pleasantly. 'He's not here is he?' He strode through to Samantha's bedroom and returned a few moments later holding a jacket.

Samantha walked over to the door and purposefully held it open.

'For the last time, Brett, I'm staying in and I'd like you to leave. I really don't think we've anything left to say to one another.'

But he ignored her protest and instead held out the jacket with a smile – its sleeves ready for her to slip her arms into, like a parent with an obstreperous child. 'Please, Samantha.'

Despite her annoyance, Samantha felt herself being drawn into the scenario he was creating.

'Just where is it you want me to go?'

'You'll find out soon enough,' he said calmly. 'I don't think you'll consider it unpleasant. Honestly.' Then the smile became so disarming that Samantha hesitated.

She couldn't think of a single reason, apart from curiosity, why she should go with him. Not after the way he had behaved at their last meeting.

To her intense surprise, curiosity won.

'No more trouble since the break-in,' he asked as she locked up.

'You could say that I've had the odd unwelcome visitor,' she replied pointedly. She was already regretting her decision.

They drove in silence. After ten minutes she turned

to him.

'You may as well tell me where we're going, Brett. I'm not a child on a mystery tour.'

He shot her his quicksilver glance.

'I have never at any time thought of you as a child, Samantha. A rather dangerous young woman, perhaps.'

'Don't let's start all that again, for heaven's sake! I'm hardly cast in the mould of a *femme fatale*!'

She was rewarded with a sideways glance.

'I wouldn't say that,' he said quietly.

Samantha looked at him suspiciously. Was he laughing at her?

'It's been a long time since anyone has had me acting like a moody, totally smitten teenager!'

'You must be coming down with something nasty!' she said waspishly.

'I only wish it were as simple as that!'

Yes, she thought, he definitely was laughing at her. But despite herself, she felt drawn into his game. Though it's a game I can't win, she told herself sadly. Gina was right about that, at least. He did play by different rules!

'What are the symptoms?' she enquired offhandedly, looking out of her window.

'Sleepless nights? No concentration to speak of! Loss of appetite! Irritability at all times!'

'Sounds hopeless, I must say.'

'I think I know the cure.'

'There's no problem in that case.' Samantha yawned loudly.

'You're tired?'

'I've had a very busy week!'

He negotiated a bend with skill. Samantha's eyes were drawn to the strong hands on the wheel and for a moment a feeling of longing swept through her. She stifled it quickly.

'Samantha.' His tone was level.

'Mmm?' Hers was offhand.

'Will you stay with me tonight?'

She looked up startled. 'Certainly not!'

'Why? I thought we got on rather well together.'

Samantha blushed furiously. 'I thought the reason would have been perfectly obvious.'

'Not to me, it isn't. Tell me, please.'

'I talk in my sleep, remember, and I wouldn't want to shock you again by reeling off a list of my past lovers!'

She risked a glance and saw that he had raised an arm in a mock gesture of warding off her sarcasm.

'Anyway,' she continued, driving her point home, 'you should have realized that I make it a rule never to sleep with the same lover more than once!'

'Ouch! I think I deserved that. Couldn't you make an exception in my case?'

'Especially not in your case!'

'I stand rebuked!' He put out a hand and rested it lightly on her knee. 'You're sure you won't change your mind?'

'Perfectly sure!' She made a gesture towards his hand. 'And I'd rather you didn't do that.'

'Sorry.' But she heard a hint of laughter in his voice.

Hateful man! she thought and looked with unseeing eyes at the scenery that appeared to be flashing past at an alarming rate. "Will you stay with me tonight," he'd said, as casually as if he were asking her for a dance. How little value he must have put on the experience. And how foolish she had been to let it mean so much to her.

She stole a quick look at the profile of the man beside her and found herself fighting back an urge to smooth away the heavy fall of hair lying across his forehead. Oh Brett! she thought sadly. If only things had been different between us.

She came to a decision.

'Brett. I'm sorry. I shouldn't have agreed to come with you. But I'd like to go home now, please.'

'We're almost there now.' His glance was brief. 'I promise to bring you back later, if you're sure that's what you want.'

'I'm perfectly sure now.'

'Later, Samantha.'

'Brett, I said now! What do I have to do to get you to turn this car around? Scream rape?'

The slow look he gave her burned into her.

'I think it's a bit too late for that now, don't you?' He turned his eyes back to the road. For a moment there was silence.

'Do you still see him?'

'See whom?'

'Tim. That was his name wasn't it?'

'I don't think that's any of your business. You have no right to question what I do or whom I see. I've never asked you about your love-life. Don't tell me that you and Gina were never more than just good friends!'

'That's a completely different matter.'

'Why?' she challenged.

'If you don't know already, I see no point in discussing it.'

'And that's your answer, is it? Nothing more?' She frowned. 'You've got no more sensitivity in you, Brett Sinclair, than ... than' – she looked around furiously for inspiration and found it in the fields racing by – 'than those rabbits over there!'

'Rabbits!' His eyebrows shot up in alarm. 'Rabbits!' he repeated and this time she heard the amusement in his voice. The car began to slow down perceptibly. 'Samantha, my love. Just what am I to think? You shared my bed. Yet never once have you said you love me!'

Despite her anger, Samantha's eyes widened in astonishment. Those should have been my lines, she thought, not his!

'Love you?'

'Yes, Samantha. Love. Or has all the love you possess been used up on your precious Tim?'

Samantha was lost for words. "My love," he had called her. The only other time he had used that term was that night in the little cottage in the garden – the trysting house, as he'd called it. Her face grew warm just thinking of it.

'Love you?' she repeated at last, conscious that she was beginning to sound like a cracked record.

'Don't play games, Samantha.'

Paul had warned her against that, she remembered. Had he really thought that she was playing games? Surely not, she reassured herself uncertainly.

'Brett,' she began tentatively, 'I think we should talk.'

'Talk? Do you really think that talking will solve our problems?'

'What would you suggest, then?'

'I made an alternative suggestion earlier, but I understood you to turn it down flat.'

Samantha stared ahead. He'd asked her to stay with him that night. But despite the signals that her body was sending her to the contrary, she knew that wouldn't be the answer either.

'You're very quiet. Perhaps you've changed your mind?' he murmured.

Samantha shot him a sharp glance. 'No!'

One hand left the wheel and came to rest lightly on her shoulder. 'Sure?'

'Absolutely,' she said firmly. He withdrew his hand without comment. 'But if you won't turn around, could we at least stop for a coffee, please?'

He glanced at his watch.

'Might as well. We are probably too late for what I had in mind.'

'Too late for what?' Her voice sounded flat. All curiosity about where they were headed had long since disappeared.

'It doesn't matter now.' His voice softened. 'You really do sound tired. Do you desperately need that coffee now? Or would you prefer to go straight home.'

'Straight home, please Brett,' she said in a very small voice. He nodded without a word.

She remembered little of the journey home. The emotionally charged atmosphere of the outward journey had all but disappeared and she felt an aching lethargy creep through her. At some stage she must have dozed off, for when she became conscious that the motion of the car had ceased, it was already dark. She found her head resting on Brett's shoulder and yawned as she sat up, rubbing the back of her neck.

'Have we been sitting here long?' she asked, as Brett withdrew the arm that had been around her shoulders.

'I didn't like to wake you.' Then she heard the smile in his voice. 'To be honest, Samantha, I've never had a girl fall asleep on me before.'

As she glanced out of the window and saw his apartment building, she suddenly registered where she was.

'Brett! You said you would take me home!'

'I have. My home,' he said simply. 'You were right. We do need to talk and I thought you would prefer to do it at my flat rather than yours.'

'I had been thinking of neutral territory,' she demurred, but she got out with a sense of relief. In the car, she had seemed to be in a hostile world, one which was directly under his control. Now, stepping out into the quiet of a summer evening, she felt once again in charge of herself.

'It's been raining!' she said in surprise, breathing in the freshened air.

'We needed it,' he said, taking her arm. 'It will help to clear the air.'

A lot has happened since I was here last, she thought, as he once again ushered her into his living-room. The plants, as if awaiting their arrival, seemed to wave a welcome.

She sank into one of his comfortable sofas, kicking off her shoes and curling her legs beneath her whilst he bustled around in the kitchen area making coffee. Then he subsided into the seat opposite.

'I'm sorry about tonight. I had wanted to spirit you away somewhere romantic. But things just didn't seem to work out the way I'd planned,' he said ruefully. He reached into his pocket and took out something which he placed on the little table between them with an apologetic smile.

Samantha glanced at it. Her passport. She looked at him questioningly.

'I took it when I went into your bedroom to get your jacket,' he explained. He sounded somewhat abashed. 'I remembered seeing it there when we were tidying up after the break-in. I thought it would have been nice for us to have a quiet dinner in Paris in a little place I know near the Madeleine.'

Samantha continued to watch him steadily. She felt no surprise at what he had just revealed. I've had so many surprises in the past few weeks that I think I'm immune to them, she thought. The idea saddened her.

He went to sit beside her, his weight causing Samantha to slide a fraction towards him.

'Instead, I found myself acting like a jailer to a lovely but extremely unwilling captive.'

She sat completely motionless. It's as if I'm in the audience, watching something being acted out without any need for intervention on my part, she thought.

Almost imperceptibly he began to edge towards her. Samantha could feel the warmth of him reaching out to envelop her.

'I've been behaving like a lout and I'm sorry, Samantha.' He smiled disarmingly at her. 'Am I forgiven?'

The scene seemed to be set for her to murmur "yes" before melting into his arms with a sigh. But I'm not a character in a romantic novel, she told herself firmly. There are things that we have to get straight first. Life isn't all romance.

'Samantha?'

He was prompting her. One little word and she would be in his arms. For tonight, at least, she thought ruefully. But tomorrow their doubts would return with the inevitability that day follows night. Maybe ours was meant to be just a passing affair. Something as fleeting as a shaft of moonshine, she mused, the idea lending a softness to her eyes and mouth.

'Samantha, love?' This time an edge of doubt mellowed the tone of the deep voice. 'Am I forgiven?' But he drew back a little.

She was acutely conscious of his withdrawal. It felt as if part of her was being drawn with him.

The silence deepened. Then Samantha lifted her eyes to meet his.

'No,' she said quietly. The word hung over them like a sword. 'No, Brett. I think we should both be more truthful with one another. Until we do, neither of us will have any real peace of mind.'

'You're right. To be honest, Samantha, I've tried very hard these past few weeks to get you out of my mind. When I thought you and Jake were lovers, it was easier to do and I steeled myself to resist you. For Jake's sake. But, as I think I've said before, you didn't make it easy.'

Samantha half opened her mouth to reply, but he leaned forward and gently laid a finger on her lips.

'Not now, love. Not when I'm in the middle of my confession!'

His brows lifted comically and she smiled. His

finger traced the curve of her mouth gently.

'As I was saying, despite temptation, I resisted you! Then I learn that you and Jake are not romantically involved and things begin to look quite promising!'

His eyes glinted wickedly at the memory.

'Then, no sooner had I staked my claim to you,' – he smiled as he caught hold of Samantha's arm which had taken a none too gentle swing at him – 'than you began calling for this man Tim! I'm afraid I thought the worst. That you just wanted a little flirtation with me – like you did with Paul – and that there was someone else you really cared for. I must admit I tried to prise the information out of Jake,' he went on. 'But he completely clammed up.'

'Tim worries you, doesn't he, Brett?' She knew that this was something she had to get out of the way before there could be any chance of happiness between them. 'There's really no need, you know! I've thought and thought about this but I still can't imagine why I spoke his name when I did. Nobody could have been further from my thoughts at the time! I suppose it was just my subconscious playing tricks!'

She looked at him candidly and he gave her such a penetrating look that Samantha felt he was trying to read her soul.

'I'll accept that,' he said at length. 'And I promise most faithfully that I'll never mention him again.'

'Thank you,' she said gravely. She was glad that Tim would no longer be a point of contention between them.

'I must say that I had already decided to do that before I saw you again this evening,' he said, taking her hand. 'But you looked so annoyed to see me that

I felt very piqued. It was ridiculously childish, I must admit.'

He looked so penitent that Samantha had to fight down the urge to smile. But first I have to tell him why I behaved as I did, she thought. She bit her lower lip. Brett gave her hand a little squeeze.

'Your turn now,' he prompted gently.

'You were right, I suppose,' she said at length. 'I was playing games. I told myself I needed to.'

He looked puzzled. She avoided the question in his eyes and fastened her gaze on their interlocked hands.

'Firstly, Brett, I thought you were already involved. You certainly seemed to have a pretty heavy scene going with Gina.'

He shook his head decisively.

'Gina and I have been friends for a long time. But neither of us have ever wanted a more permanent commitment.'

Maybe you didn't, thought Samantha. But I'm not so sure about Gina! She had a moment of genuine sympathy for her. She'd seen the way that Gina had looked at him and guessed that she'd found him as impossibly attractive as she did herself.

'Then I tried to convince myself that you only wanted to keep an eye on me because you thought I was Jake's girl and you didn't want to see him hurt. Then there was the financial bit – your knowing that Jake and I were partners and responsible for each other's debts. That didn't help matters. I felt you might be trying to safeguard Jake's money. Family money.'

'Only partly right there, darling!' His arm came around her shoulders. 'I certainly thought that you were Jake's girl. And, as I've said before, I tried desperately hard not to fall in love with you. But I did.'

Samantha's heart began to beat very fast as she heard the determination in his voice.

'I must admit that I despised myself for it.' His face suddenly looked sombre. 'But I wouldn't have given you up, even for Jake! I was only waiting for him to come back before I did the dishonourable thing and claimed you for myself.'

Samantha gave a little shiver as his fingers twined themselves in the hair at the nape of her hair.

'I wish I'd known that,' she said simply. 'I found my real problem was that I found you very attractive but' – she paused, choosing her words with care – 'I had been given reason in the past to mistrust my feelings and didn't want to commit myself.'

He gave her hand a reassuring squeeze. 'That happens to us all from time to time.'

He turned her face towards him and gently bent his lips to hers. His kiss was tender but she could feel the tension in his body and knew the effort he was making not to rush her.

Instinctively she knew that they now had all the time in the world. She recalled Paul's comment about star-crossed lovers and smiled. Not this time, Paul, she thought thankfully.

'Why Paris?' she asked suddenly.

'It seemed a good idea at the time,' he said, shaking his head in self-mockery. 'It's indisputably romantic and I felt I needed all the help I could get.'

He took both her hands in his and raised them to his lips.

'After all, it's not every day that a man gets around

to proposing.'

She sat there looking at him whilst the seconds ticked away.

'Well? Do I get an answer?' His voice held a note of uncertainty. 'Perhaps you need time to think about it?'

Samantha's eyes widened as she stared at him wordlessly. Then suddenly she jumped to her feet and walked slowly to the door. He watched her, motionless.

'Brett?'

'Yes, Samantha.'

'Do you still have those tickets?'

'I do indeed!'

'Then I think we'd better get a move on! A quiet romantic dinner sounds really great and I'm absolutely starving!'

In a few strides he was at her side.

'Oh no you don't! he said firmly. 'You're not getting away with that sort of an answer.' He put his arms around her and looked into her eyes. 'After all the trouble you've put me to these past few months, I'm not having you keep me at a distance now.'

'I really don't know what you mean, Brett,' she murmured lowering her eyes demurely.

'And that is one game, you are definitely going to have to stop!' he said severely, raising her chin so that he could see the mischievous look in her eyes. 'At least, with other men. You really are the most outrageous flirt, you know.'

She smiled. And the smile licked at the corners of her mouth like a cat at the cream.

'So you keep telling me, Brett! It must be that passionate nature of mine!'

'Hm! I can see that I'm going to have to take you firmly in hand once we're married,' he murmured some moments later, still holding her close. 'You will marry me, won't you?'

'I'll have to give it some very careful thought,' she said looking up at him provocatively from beneath her lashes. 'After all, it's not every day that a girl gets proposed to!'

Swiftly, he swept her into her arms and whisked her through the door to a flurry of helpless laughter.

Behind them the moonlight filtered through the leaves creating a tapestry of fantastical shapes and leaping shadows on the walls. Then from somewhere came the sound of a muffled sigh and the room settled down to wait for their return.

A Touch of
Spring Fever

One

Julie decided to walk to work that morning. It was a beautiful day; the pale early spring sunshine suddenly made everything around her look fresh and clean. The air still held a touch of cool crispness, but Julie loved it. Tall daffodils stood proud in the tubs and flower beds in front of the imposing Town Hall, the crenellated buildings of the Colleges. The heart of the busy centre of Cardiff gleamed white in the sun.

Oblivious of admiring glances from passers-by, Julie's long slim legs covered the distance in no time at all. Her thick brown hair, bronzed chestnut in the sunlight, swung like a curtain across her smooth cheeks. Shoulders straight, there was a spring in her step, a surge of pulsing life in her heart, and a feeling, too, of ... what...?

She humped her briefcase over to her other arm, a slight frown marring her otherwise firm brow. Lately, she had been conscious of a feeling of emptiness – a slight dissatisfaction with her work, her home-life, everything. A feeling that somehow she was missing out on something. She sighed softly; perhaps it was all to do with the burgeon of spring she thought wryly as she turned the corner to reach her office.

As always, a warm glow of pride flooded through her as she glanced at the lettered inscription on the glass panel of the outer door. JP Agency – Julie Prescott's own thriving business – the result of a lot of hard work and many anxious moments. She was early, the building quiet and as she lingered in the tiny cloakroom, her thoughts went back to

5

how it all started....

After the trauma of her divorce and with much soul-searching, she had asked to be transferred from the Birmingham head office down here to the big growing branch in Cardiff – to make a new start, pick up the pieces away from everything that reminded her of her broken marriage; to leave her parents in Sutton Coldfield; not to see her married sister, Helen, and her two little nephews so often. She had talked it over with her father for a long while.

'Try it, Julie love,' he'd urged. 'And remember, we'll always be here if you want to come back.'

'I'll miss you....' She had always been close to her father. Although in looks she took after her mother, deep down, she was her father's girl, always had been.

'There's a good train service from Cardiff to Birmingham. And,' he smiled gently at her, 'there's always the phone.'

Knowing the long time her mother spent chatting on the telephone, Julie grinned back at him lovingly, and decided to take his advice. It had not been easy at first. It took ages to get used to the lilting Welsh accent, and a slower, more laid-back pace of life. She wasn't used to strangers who wanted to know every last detail of your life. But Julie soon grew to realize that it was warm friendliness that prompted their questions, not nosy-parkerness.

She smiled reminiscently remembering her first day and how the girl in the next desk had introduced herself.

'I'm Megan Williams, see.' The girl's dark eyes had been friendly, her round face beaming. 'What shall I tell them I called you then, cariad?'

'Julie – Julie Prescott,' and she smiled at the quaint way Megan had asked her name. That had started a deep friendship that still endured. She soon learned to slow down a little, not to fume with impatience when everyone stopped first to chat before doing a job; soon learned the warmth and true worth of these softly-voiced Celtic folks.

She had been there a month when, one day, she had to go to the chief accountant's office. Alun Jones had soon made her feel at ease – his dark eyes showing instant admiration.

'Settling down, are you then, Mrs Prescott?' His quiet voice was as attractive as his open smile and Julie liked him on sight. Of medium height, slightly thick-set, with the round features and dark hair of so many Welshmen, he treated her as a friend. She remembered clearly the day she had found him waiting near the lift; the way his face had lightened at the sight of her.

'Everything going well, Julie?'

She nodded, guessing there was more to follow. The lift reached the ground floor and as the occupants spilled out, Alun had gently taken Julie's elbow and walked her to the car-park.

'I wondered, Julie...? I have two tickets for a concert at St David's Hall for tomorrow night.' He paused and then rushed on nervously, 'It's a very good concert and it would be a shame to waste a ticket, see.'

She turned and smiled at him, putting him at ease.

'I'd love to go, Alun, thank you.' Patent relief crossed his face.

'Good. Shall we go for a bite to eat – straight from the office?'

He swallowed nervously. 'I'd like us to get to know each other, Julie.'

She nodded once more and said quietly, 'I'd like that, too, Alun. I need a few friends down here.'

Julie remembered that following night so well. She'd tidied herself in the cloakroom. Megan of course wanted to know 'why she was wearing a new dress and putting on a new face, like?' Realizing by then that she could keep nothing secret, Julie told her, 'I'm going to a concert with Alun Jones from Accounts.'

Dark eyes wide, Megan made a face in the mirror.

'Oh him ... ' she shrugged, 'he's a nice enough bloke, but he's old – about forty-three, I'd say.' To young Megan that was over the hill, Julie though wryly.

'Well, I'm coming up to thirty-five myself, Megan.'

'No? Well, there's a thing! You don't look it, pet, and that's for sure.' Julie gave her a quick grin and renewed her lipstick, thinking that perhaps the other girl was right. Just then she didn't look her age.

Alun took her to a little Italian trattoria where they had pizzas and a bottle of red wine. As they ate, she was conscious all the time of the admiration in his eyes and knew she had to put him in the picture right away if they were to be friends. With a soft sigh, she put down her fork and took a sip of wine, hardly knowing where to begin.

'Are you...? She paused and then plunged on, 'Are you married, divorced or what, Alun?' Pleasure at her interest lit his eyes and he leaned forward.

'I'm still single, Julie.'

'Oh.' She didn't know how to go on. Single, at his age?

'I'd like to tell you,' he began and she nodded, watching his face closely.

'It's almost twenty years ago now. I was to be married to a girl I'd known since childhood.' His voice grew husky as he went on, 'I loved her very much and we were very happy, so good together. We'd got a little house; the banns had been read, everything was getting under way for a nice wedding.' He stopped as if he couldn't go on, and Julie reached out to cover his hand as it lay clenched on the table.

'Go on, Alun,' she encouraged softly. He took a deep

breath.

'One day, Gwennie took her little car on a shopping spree, full of excitement, over the moon. She never came back; her car was hit by an articulated lorry out of control.'

'Oh Alun …' Julie breathed, dismay and sympathy tightening her throat.

'She lay in a coma for three weeks – she never knew us.' Alun's voice was bleak with remembrance. 'She died two days before our wedding day.'

'How awful for you; what a terrible thing to happen.' Julie's voice was softly sympathetic. Alun nodded, then his face lightened a little.

'Of course, I got over it – eventually. There's been quite a few affairs, one or two relationships, since then. But no, I'm not married, Julie.' Looking at her, he asked, 'And you? I know you're divorced. Like to tell me what happened?' He saw a shadow cross her face. 'Not if it bothers you, mind.'

Slowly she began, remembering as she did, how she'd met Jeff; how it was in the beginning....

' "Julie and Jeff – even our names go together, darling," he once said. But you seen, Alun, the trouble was that so many other girls' names went with Jeff's! I tried hard to tell myself I was wrong – was only imagining things; that Jeff was telling the truth, not just making excuses for his late nights, his absences....'

Julie bit her lip, her fingers clasping and unclasping on the little table between them.

'I forgave him, tried to patch things up, to forget his lapse. After all, lots of husbands strayed once and came back, I told myself. But Jeff didn't stop at the once, Alun.' Her eyes clouded with memories as she went on, 'Soon he was bedding and shedding one new girl, one new face after another.' Alun shifted in his seat, concern for her showing in his eyes. 'I tried hard to forgive him, to understand, but at last, sheer self-preservation made me sue for a divorce. For ages I was so low, so lonely; blaming myself that there was something in me that couldn't keep a man faithful to me. I felt so unloved, unlovable. Then I decided to leave Birmingham and come down here to the Cardiff branch, to start afresh. So I collected the remnants of my pride and moved on. Pride makes a poor bedmate, Alun, but it was all I had left from my marriage with Jeff, who collected girls like a small boy collects stamps!' Bitterness had tinged her voice then as she tightened her lips.

'So, Alun, it's no deep relationships for me. It's too soon; the hurt's too deep yet. I'm off men.' She gave him a twisted smile. 'But I do need a friend.'

He was thoughtful for a moment and then said, 'Let me be that friend then, Julie. Let me show you my city, my Wales. Who knows, perhaps...?' His words held a wistful note of hope.

Julie shook her head, her chestnut hair catching the light from the guttering candles on the table between them.

'Just friends, Alun – please.' And so the rules had been laid down from the start.

Alun had tried hard to keep to those rules, but Julie would have been blind not to notice that he was beginning to care deeply for her. It showed in a hundred little ways....

As she stood before the mirror in the small cloakroom, her mind went back in time – that time over two years ago now – remembering how Alun had helped her get over her broken marriage, helped her to settle down into such a different way of life. Through contacts, he had helped her to find the pleasant little flat on the outskirts – not too far from town. He had taken her to concerts to listen to the glorious sound of male voice choirs; introduced her to the game – an almost sacred pastime to the Welsh – of rugby. Scoffing at her protests, her pleas of ignorance, he had taken her to Cardiff Arms Park and she'd enjoyed it immensely. The singing of hymns as well as the ribald parodies; the sight of lusty young thighs, of a heaving, steaming scrum, had seemed a different world to Julie, but with Alun as her mentor, she had enjoyed it all.

They had been friends for a while when Julie gradually began to want something more in her life, some greater challenge than her present job gave her. One evening when she and Alun were eating at their favourite Italian restaurant, she had been telling him of the difficulty of getting the right secretaries, even temps, for her department. As always he had been listening sympathetically, and as she paused, he suggested quietly, 'Well, Julie my girl, why don't you start your own business? Cardiff could do with another decent employment agency for good secretaries and temps. You know, with really top qualifications and so on....' As he spoke, Julie had felt the excitement growing. To be her own boss! Yes, of course, it was just what she wanted; something to aim for, that she could do, without anyone else's help.

No, she held the thought, she would need Alun's help and advice. Did he mean it? Her eyes had widened; was Alun joking? But he had been deadly serious, and Julie found that she couldn't dismiss the idea from her mind during the following weeks.

They had been climbing one of the steep hills before going for lunch at a favourite pub. Half of her attention had been on the story Alun had been telling her of a local legend about the mountain; the other half still mulling over the ideas buzzing around her brain.

'Could I do it, Alun?' she'd burst out as they paused to look at the view of the Severn Estuary. Puzzled, his dark eyebrows rose as he turned to look at Julie's face.

'Do what, love?'

'Could I really run my own business? An agency, as you suggested the other week?'

'Why not? You know your job. You get on with people, especially other girls.' He paused and then smiled confidently. 'Yes, I'm sure you could do it, Julie.'

'But the money, Alun? I've got some put by, but I'd need an office....' Doubt crept in her voice.

'And enough to keep you going until you got established,' Alun added firmly. 'But the bank would help, also the WDA....' And he went on to explain the scheme whereby the Welsh Development Agency helped ambitious beginners to set up in their own small business.

They had reached the summit and turned back once more downhill and Julie stopped again looking across at him.

'Will you help me, Alun, please?'

'You know I will, love,' his voice husked. 'I'd do anything for you, you know that, Julie.' He reached over and took her slim hand in his warm one. 'If only....'

Quickly, she reached over and placed her finger gently on his mouth. 'Don't, Alun....' she begged. Kissing her fingertips, he sighed.

'All right, all right. But I meant it, Julie: I'll help you all I can.'

And that help had proved to be endless. As before, he helped her to find the right office.

'It must be central,' he'd advised. 'A small office in the right prestigious block will be more suitable than a larger, cheaper one out of the way. And I think I've found just the thing.'

It was, too. By careful partitioning, it was divided into a

small reception area, an office for Julie and a comfortable room for interviewing job applicants and clients.

'I can't borrow all that amount from you, Alun,' Julie's smooth brow furrowed anxiously. He had insisted on ordering expensive office furniture and fittings and she had begun to worry. Would she make it with no monthly pay-cheque to fall back on? The outgoings were high ... she had nibbled her bottom lip, eyes worried as she looked across at Alun.

'No cold feet now, cariad.' He pulled out a sheaf of papers, a smile round his mouth. 'Here it is – the help from the WDA. I had a job getting it, Julie. They like their projectees to be on a new industrial estate, but I did it.'

'Oh Alun, what should I do without you?'

'You won't have to try,' he told her softly, and she felt a pang of regret that she couldn't return his affection.

Finally it had been decided to make Alun a partner – 'a sleeping partner,' he'd suggested wryly.

Her colleagues had given her a farewell party. They had all seen the advert announcing the opening of the JP Agency and wished her luck. Megan had been rather quiet and thoughtful ever since Julie had confided her plans. Then, glass in hand, she'd asked seriously, 'Can I come and work for you, Julie?'

'Oh Megan, would you? Thanks, pet.' Julie's face lit up and then clouded. 'The pay...? It won't be as good as you're getting now, not at first.'

'That's OK. You'll soon be on your feet and I'll expect a rise then.' And so it had started.

At first, both Julie and Megan had had to go out as temps until they gradually got a few good secretaries on their books. Alun was a great help, constantly passing good business her way, and Megan quickly became her Girl Friday, handling both the temperamental skilled secretaries and fussing, fuming bosses alike.

The future looked good, and now into their second year she was gradually getting a name for top quality, reliable staff and her list was growing all the time.

Alun was still her faithful escort; taking her everywhere, to see and be seen; making the right business contacts, helping her to keep up with the latest requirements in office staff. He still had hopes of making her care for him, she knew, and while she didn't mind his good-night kisses, his fond embraces, she still wouldn't let their relationship grow any deeper.

With a faint sigh, she now looked into the mirror. Long-lashed, large brown eyes looked back at her wryly, her generous mouth curved in a faint smile. The make-up on her smooth cheeks didn't need renewing and she passed a slender hand over her already tidy hair. It was beautiful; thick and shiny with bronze glints; expensively cut and layered so that a daily shampoo and blow-dry kept it immaculate. She squared her shoulders, and then dismissing the effects of the blossoming spring, she went through to her office.

Megan was just sorting the post, leaving separate piles on her desk.

'Hi Julie. You're early.' Megan's face looked a little flushed as she hurried on. 'There's a young chap in Reception waiting to see you. I told him to wait, that I'd ask you....' she floundered to a halt.

Surprised, Julie looked up at her usually calm assistant.

'Who is he? Does he have an appointment, Megan?'

'Yes – er no. Not with you, with me. But he says he'll only see you, so I didn't know what to do. He insists on only seeing the "boss lady".' Megan paused and then added, 'He's – er, rather dishy, Julie.'

At that Julie's smile deepened. Recently engaged herself, young Megan had suddenly redoubled her matchmaking efforts all round.

'All right, I'll see him. Leave his notes and give me a couple of minutes.'

'Oh thanks.' Still smiling, Julie opened the file and glanced through the details it contained before buzzing through to Megan to send in the waiting client. A moment later, after a sharp rap on the door, a young man came in. Surprised, Julie only had a second to ponder – he was young to be a boss needing a secretary, wasn't he?

'Hello, Miss – er – Mrs Prescott. I'm Mike Stephens.' His voice was warm and pleasant and Julie felt her heart skip a beat as she took his outstretched hand. Megan was right – he *was* dishy! Tall, broad-shouldered, with a good-looking face – a young, sure-of-himself sort of face, with laughter lines crinkling the corners of his dark grey eyes as they sparkled across into hers. His tall litheness made him seem only just out of his youth, scarcely a man. And yet there was nothing uncertain in his stance – head high, shoulders squared.

Yes, very sure of himself, Julie mused inwardly. His suit was not new, but it fitted him well, and his toning shirt and tie were immaculate.

'You do take males, don't you, Mrs Prescott?'

'Some male secretaries, yes,' she answered slowly. 'Please sit down, Mr Stephens.' She indicated the chair opposite. 'This agency deals mainly in supplying highly-skilled girls, secretaries and temps.'

To her ears, her voice sounded a little breathless, and suddenly she wished she'd insisted on Megan interviewing this applicant. Her fingers still tingled from the touch of his, and those dark laughing eyes were wreaking havoc with her heartbeat.

'Actually, I've been thinking lately of expanding the agency to take more men – executives and so on, on to the books,' she paused, surprised at herself. She hadn't mentioned the idea to anyone else, so why to this man, a stranger?

She swallowed to steady her voice.

'Tell me, Mr Stephens, what have you done up to now?' Another quick glance at the details before he gave his age as twenty-five. A decade younger than me, she though inconsequentially.

Quietly, efficiently, he gave her a quick résumé of his past experience. For his age, his qualifications were very good.

'So why do you want to leave London and come here to Cardiff to work?' Her hands ruffled the papers unseeingly before her, avoiding the look of open admiration in the dark eyes. He leaned back in the chair and crossed his long legs.

'Suddenly …' he shrugged his shoulders and then went on, almost as if explaining to himself too, 'I got sick to the back teeth of London – of high rents, costly commuting, the never ending rat race, of dog-eat-dog, of working all hours just to make a living, never having anything over – money or time.'

He paused, pushing his hand through his thick black hair. 'And then something happened. My grandmother died and left me a cottage here in south Wales. But it's occupied by an old couple who used to work for Gran, and I can't very well turn them out. So I'll have to get a room or something until....' Again he paused uncomfortably. 'They're pretty old – no need to buy another place until....'

There was an endearing awkwardness in his words – a look in his eyes that touched her heart. He seemed very young, and he was trying to cover up his soft-heartedness, she could tell.

'I can come for interviews, but I need someone to look out for my interests meanwhile. I'll move down as soon as I can; I don't suppose I'll starve. Well, not quite.' He grinned and suddenly she found the idea of his going hungry strangely disturbing. She made a few more notes, deciding to do her very best for him. She had plenty of good contacts. Over the last years, she had built the JP Agency up into one of the best, and this young man's application had reminded her that it was time to expand....

She buzzed Megan and asked for two cups of coffee, and as they waited, she found herself chatting easily to this Mike Stephens. He was relaxed and quite happy to sit there, a look in his eyes telling her he found her attractive. And that look made her heart beat faster, as it hadn't done for such a long time. A pulse of excitement, an awareness of how masculine he was, made her feel almost shy and rather nervous. There was a slight breathlessness in her voice, and she told herself to stop being a fool!

She gripped her coffee cup tightly, reminding herself that she was thirty-six in a few weeks' time, with a disastrous marriage behind her, not some silly schoolgirl with her first admirer!

After a while, Mike Stephens looked across at her, and without disguising his curiosity or excusing his presumption, asked her frankly, 'Is there a Mr Prescott on the scene?'

She shook her head. Then trying to put him in his place, to regain her usual cool and business-like manner, she replied abruptly, 'No, I'm divorced. Now about this post you're seeking, Mr Stephens, suppose you leave it with us. We'll put out a few feelers and then let you know if anything comes up, mm?'

At that he rose, towering tall above her and he smiled that little-boy, heart-stopping smile of his again.

'Thanks, Mrs Prescott, I'll do that.' He moved towards the door and then turned to smile at her. 'That face doesn't suit you – that boss-lady face, I mean. Bye for now and thanks.'

Well! The pulse beating madly in her throat made her breathe deeply, struggling to regain her composure before

Megan's sharp eyes saw her!

It was ages since she'd felt like this – this tingling, alive, excited feeling of heady delight at knowing someone found her good to look at. She went across to peer into the little mirror over the filing cabinet and saw that right then she could have passed for ten years younger. Or was that just wishful thinking? But no, her brown eyes shone darkly and the slight flush made her creamy skin look clearer, younger!

Then: You fool! she told herself through the mirror. She'd avoided brief, passing affairs, shallow relationships with other men since she and Jeff had been divorced. She had taken good care to see that she hadn't been hurt again; taken care not to lose her heart or her head after the trauma of losing her husband.

And yet here she was, peering into the mirror, examining her face for flaws, telling herself not to be a fool just because the expression in a young man's eyes had told her he found her attractive. Yet it wasn't a bad face. She had her mother's fine bone structure, the sort that didn't blur with age. Her skin was clear, but *she* knew only too well how sallow it could look on her 'off' days, when she was extra tired or worried. But the fine lines around her mouth disappeared when she smiled, didn't they?

She grimaced at her reflection and went back to her desk to scan again the form in the file. *Mike Stephens, aged 25* she read again; she was ten years older and a damned silly fool as well!

'I'm going shopping in my lunch-hour, Megan. I'll try not to be too late back.'

Megan looked up with an inquisitive grin.

'Buying something nice then, are you, love?'

'I might. I don't really need anything though,' Julie mused avoiding the knowing look in her assistant's eyes.

'Just the time to treat yourself, Julie. Don't hurry back.'

So Julie found herself dawdling in the pale sunshine, glad to be outdoors. She ate a quick sandwich and then, in her favourite store, she bought a new lace-frilled blouse, old-fashionedly Edwardian-looking enough to be really trendy, and some slender-heeled shoes in black patent leather.

Taking a chance, she was lucky to get in at her hairdressers without an appointment and settled down to an hour's pampering, her thoughts on her date with Alun later.

But that night, some of her restless bubbling unease made her dissatisfied with their usual place, their usual meal. She wanted … God, what did she want? She saw the puzzled look in Alun's brown eyes and felt ashamed. He wasn't a bore; it was just that … she almost shrugged in the effort of trying to get rid of her silly fancies, her undefinable longings.

'What is it, Julie?' Alun leaned across to touch her hand as her fingers played restlessly with a spoon. She sighed softly.

'It – it's nothing, Alun. Touch of spring fever, I guess.'

'Marry me, Julie,' he burst out quickly, watching her face as he did so. 'You must know how much I love you.'

Her eyes bright with unshed tears, she shook her head.

'I'm sorry but I don't love you. Oh darling, I'm so sorry. I'm very fond of you, but it's not enough. It wouldn't be fair to you.' Swallowing the tight lump in her throat, she whispered gently, 'You ought to find someone else, dearest, not waste your time on me....'

But even as she said the words, she knew what a gap in her life his going would leave. Who else would be there always for her; to listen to her problems, to help her solve most of them? Who else would know just when she needed to talk or keep quiet? They went out a lot together. She was his partner at business dinners and he at hers. It was such a comfort to have him there – always ready to take her out – to take away that awful odd-woman-out feeling she'd known before she had met him.

Yet now there was a strange wistful ache inside her as she wondered just what she did want.

'You need a break, Julie. How about coming to the Mumbles with me next weekend?' Startled, Julie's eyes widened. He touched her hand again, smiling ruefully, anticipating her protests. 'It's all right, pet. All kosher, separate rooms and all that.'

At that her throat tightened again. If only she could love him as he deserved to be loved.

'I'd like that, Alun.' And they went on to discuss arrangements – quietly as loving friends, but not lovers....

Two

Several days later, Julie asked Megan to phone Mike Stephens and tell him she had arranged an interview for him with a large firm of aero-engineers. Something in her voice must have given her away, for she saw Megan's eyes watching her face closely, a pleased smile around her lips.

'You'll see him yourself?'

Julie nodded, shuffling the pile of letters in front of her.

'Well, seeing that we are fairly new at placing men, I think I'd better, don't you?'

'With the gorgeous Mr Stephens – oh yes, I do,' Megan laughed and dodged out of the office quickly.

Two days later, Julie found herself almost holding her breath waiting for Megan to show Mike Stephens in. Found herself waiting with a thudding heart to see if he was as she remembered him; if she had imagined the admiration in his eyes, or if he had just been trying to charm her into helping him find a job? His face had been there before her ever since his first visit in spite of telling herself she was being a fool. All she knew was that she wanted to see him again. And no matter how many times she told herself to stop being a fool, reminded herself that he was only a boy – well, almost only a boy – she could not dismiss her eager anticipation as Megan showed him in.

'Mr Stephens for you, Mrs Prescott,' and Julie caught the sparkle of mischief in Megan's eyes.

'Thank you, Megan.'

She hadn't been wrong! He was as handsome as she'd remembered. He smiled as if he was sure of his welcome, his eyes alight with pleasure at seeing her. He had the most fantastic dark grey eyes; a person could drown in those eyes, she thought dreamily.

In his hand he carried a long-stemmed rose – a ridiculously out-of-season, beautiful red rose.

'For you, boss lady, with my thanks.' He looked at her blatantly up and down, taking in every detail. And she wondered if he guessed how carefully she'd dressed and made-up her face that morning? Or the effect that look in his grey eyes was having on her foolish heart?

'Thanks for seeing me, Mrs Prescott,' he repeated as he took a seat,' and for getting me this interview so quickly.'

Quietly she explained that the firm had the post coming vacant shortly, and as she knew he was anxious to get back to London, she had fixed up an early interview.

Together they scanned the details of just what the job involved – the responsibility of the whole purchasing department and stock control of thousands of pounds worth of components to be purchased and the stock lists to be computerised. It was an exacting job with the whole department in one man's hands.

Would he be too young, she wondered? As if reading her thoughts, Mike Stephens said firmly,

'I won't let you down, Mrs Prescott. It's just the sort of position I've been trained for.'

'I'm sure you won't.' Their eyes met in a glance that spoke volumes; both attracted by what they saw in the other. The tension in the air between them had nothing to do with business or jobs or contracts. In that long pause, each was reaching out to the other in mutual attraction.

Julie was first to break the silence.

'You'll have plenty of time before the interview,' she began.

He rose, still watching her face.

'Will you – er, would you have lunch with me, Mrs Prescott?' And then, somewhat impatiently, he asked, 'What does the J stand for, by the way?'

'Julie,' she told him breathlessly.

'Julie,' he repeated, 'nice name for a nice girl.'

'*Girl*!' Again her heart lurched, but the thought made her voice cool. 'I'm sorry, Mr Stephens, I've another appointment I must keep, but please, give me a ring and let me know how you get on this afternoon, will you?'

'Will do.' He reached out and took her hand and the warmth of his touch seemed to spread a lick of fire along her arm. 'If and when I do come down to Cardiff to live, may I give you a call? I'd like us to meet again – outside the office, that is.'

She nodded. 'I'd like that too,' she heard herself reply. When he'd gone, she again berated herself for her stupidity. He was far too young. Besides he was probably only being grateful for her help, feeling himself a stranger in a new town.

But for the rest of the day, a pair of attractive dark eyes came between her and her work, and when Megan put through his call just before closing time, she had to swallow past the beating pulse in her throat before answering.

'I got it, Julie. I got it!' How young his voice sounded.

'Oh good, Mr Stephens, I'm so pleased.' She kept her voice calm and impersonal, wondering if Megan was evesdropping next door. 'We'll be sending our account. May I wish you all the best...?'

'Why don't we celebrate tonight?' he put in. 'Please....' And the plea in his tone almost made her weaken. Then again she remembered those years – the years that she was older than him and she said quietly, 'I'm sorry, Mr Stephens, I can't.' The pips interrupted and she repeated, 'I can't, I'm sorry.'

'Well, I shall be in touch soon and I won't take no for an answer.' His voice was firm and deep now. 'I mean to get to know you, boss lady.'

'Bye,' and with that she hung up before she gave way to the longing inside her. She had never felt like this before; how silly could you get? He would forget her the moment he got on the London train.

But she couldn't forget him. Throughout the pleasant weekend on the lovely Mumbles peninsular, she kept remembering how he looked, telling herself she was an idiot. She ought to have accepted his invitation to dine. What harm would one date have done?

She and Alun took long walks in the pale sunshine, contented and happy in each other's company. Only occasionally did he show how much he wanted their relationship to deepen, and Julie's heart ached, hating the thought of hurting him.

They had a wonderful long leisurely dinner in the old oak-beamed dining-room, followed by drinks and a peacefully pleasant time round the log fire. At last Julie stifled a yawn.

'It's no use, Alun, I'm whacked. It's me for bed. How about you?'

He rose, his brown eyes twinkling as he murmured, 'Is that an invitation, Julie?' Despite his grin, his voice held a wistful plea. She shook her head, not quite sure if he was teasing or serious.

'Sorry, Alun, besides you did promise....'

'I know, I know. But you can't blame a chap for trying or hoping you'll change your mind.'

As they climbed the creaking stairs, ducking to avoid the

low beams, he held her arm close to his side, his voice thickening with emotion.

'We'd be so good together, darling, and I do love you, you know.' Outside her door, Julie paused and looked into his face, her lovely eyes troubled.

'I'm sorry,' she repeated softly. 'I'm very fond of you. You're my best and dearest friend, but....'

She heard him sigh deeply, and put her arms round his waist and dropped a gentle kiss on his cheek. His arms tightened around her and she felt his body grow taut with desire. Before she could pull away, his mouth covered hers in a fierce and hungry kiss. Dismayed she struggled in his arms, her mouth trembling, tears stinging her eyes.

'Oh, Alun....' Misery and remorse almost choked her then. Perhaps this weekend had been a mistake? Was she to lose his friendship; ought she to stop seeing him?

Seeing the concern on her face, he endeavoured to regain his composure.

'I'm sorry, Julie love. Don't worry I've no intention of coming on strong again, so sleep tight.' He dropped a gentle kiss on her forehead. 'Goodnight. See you in the morning, eh?'

She nodded, a lump in her throat.

'Goodnight, Alun.'

Deeply troubled, she tossed and turned on her pillow for a long time before sleep claimed her. Why couldn't she love Alun as he deserved to be loved?

On Sunday they spent a long, lazy day in the pale sunshine, both careful not to mention what had happened the night before. Remorse and regret tinged her thoughts on and off all through the day, but Alun went to a lot of trouble to let her see that nothing had changed between them. That, as ever, he was her friend, her confidant. All the same when he kissed her good-night outside her flat that evening, she felt as if the break had done her little good, solved nothing....

'I agree, Julie, it *is* time you expanded. So, tell me, just what do you have in mind?'

They had just finished the light meal she had knocked together in her little kitchen. It was a quiet, cosy scene; the gas flames flickered giving out enough warmth to take away the evening chill; the shaded lamp cast a soft glow over the room as they sat together comfortably on the soft leather settee, coffee and drinks on the small table beside them.

It was time to discuss things with Alun and get his opinion about her new ideas.

'I'd like to start a special register of highly-skilled executive males, and females too, of course, but something more up-market than just secretaries and temps. You know the sort of thing, Alun, doing the 'head-hunting' for the specialists in top management brackets, chief executive types; exclusive posts that are not always advertised. I'd like to be able to go into it deeply, be able to sort out and short-list the special applicants....' She paused, wondering if Alun would think she was going a bit over the top?

'You'd need to do quite a bit of training and research yourself, Julie, wouldn't you? Possibly take in a partner, a second-in-command who knows all about that sort of thing.'

She nodded, adding quickly, 'But do you think I could do it?' For a moment self-doubt tinged her words. 'And is there a need for another such agency in town?'

'Yes.' Alun leaned back, sipping the fragrant black coffee. 'Yes, to both questions, Julie. You'd need more space,' he said thoughtfully. She leaned forward, the firelight reflected in the amber of her eyes, her vivid face alight with eagerness.

'That's just it! The people next door are moving to bigger

premises. I've just heard. Oh, Alun, their place would do fine. Two medium-sized offices and a large one that I'd sub-divide for individual interviewing rooms.'

He laughed softly, pleased to see her so excited by the whole scheme.

'Got it all thought out, haven't you, cariad? So – you want me to make an offer for that next-door suite of offices then, I take it?'

'Yes, please. Oh Alun....' Impulsively Julie clutched his arm and hugged him tight. 'What should I do without you?' She paused then, seeing to her dismay, the sudden gleam of hope in his kind eyes. 'You – you're the best friend a person could ever have, I reckon.'

He groaned wryly. 'Best friend? Ah well, half a loaf and all that.....'

'I wish, Alun....' For a moment Julie's voice was thick with emotion. He patted her arm fondly.

'I know, love – don't fret.' He drew in a deep breath. 'Now let's get down to some details, shall we? And what are we calling this new agency?' Looking at her face, he laughed. 'Come on, out with it!'

'I thought – how does 'Exclusive Executives' sound?' She waited anxiously as he considered the title in his mind and on his tongue.

'I think that's great.' He raised the brandy glass. 'Here's to you, Julie my darling, and to the launching of Exclusive Executives.'

She reached across and placed a gentle kiss on his cheek.

'Bless you, Alun. Here's to our new venture....' And solemnly they drank a toast to each other.

Julie took time off to see her folks, mainly to discuss her new venture with her father. He had a good head for business; had always encouraged and advised her and she valued his opinions.

'Sounds promising, Julie, but don't go in too deeply over your head, pet. Keep the JP Agency going. And don't forget, I've got some money put by if you get strapped for cash.'

'Bless you, Dad.' And she reached over to kiss his bald spot. 'But you're retiring soon; you'll need all you've got then.' As he made to demur, she added, 'How about that round-the-world cruise Mum's always on about?'

The next few weeks were the busiest, most worrying weeks of her business career. A new bank loan was negotiated, the lease of the extra offices signed, her new firm's title registered. Decorators were busy dividing the larger office, fitting a new communicating door between the two suites. Workmen were arranging shelves, fitting new carpets, desks and filing cabinets.

Julie and Alun had spent several evenings pouring over drafts of advertising lay-outs; scanning trade papers, house magazines, for suitable outlets. They had put forward Julie's name for one or two business management seminars and courses.

'I'll need a new girl for the office next door.'

'I think you'll need another computer, Julie, also a special girl to work at it. One also used to helping others to programme and set-up computers – all sorts of jobs like that. And I think I know just the girl. She came to my office recently to help us with our programming.'

'Oh....' Her interest caught, she watched Alun closely as he went on, 'She works for a large firm selling and installing computers as their glamourous dolly-bird – following the salesmen, demonstrating and helping customers with their new equipment.'

'But would she leave them?' Julie asked.

'For the right salary, yes, I think she would. I'll contact her for you and fix up a meeting, shall I?'

For some reason, Julie wasn't quite sure, but she nodded slowly. After all, it wouldn't hurt to see the girl Alun sounded so keen on, would it?

'A personal call for you, Julie – the gorgeous Mike Stephens – remember him?' Megan's voice sounded pert on the intercom. Remember him? Julie was surprised just how well she did recall every moment of their meetings; just how often she'd wondered how he was getting on in his new job.

'Thanks, Megan, put him through.'

'Hi, boss lady. How are you?' Even his voice over the phone made her heart beat faster, so that she made her reply sound cool.

'I'm fine, Mr Stephens, thanks. And you...?'

'It's Mike – remember? Can I see you, Julie – soon? Like tonight, maybe?'

And Julie knew she wanted to see him again, but that would be foolish. He affected her far too much, and what was the use? She was too old for him and she didn't think she could trust herself to treat it as a casual date with a client.

'I'm sorry Mike, but I have something on for tonight.' And she had – with Megan and her fiancé and the man who was to be best man at their wedding. They were all having a meal together and then going on to dance at a night-club. Quickly she explained to Mike.

'That's OK. I'll ring you again, Julie, soon.'

When Megan came through with the post, she asked, 'What did the hunky Mr Stephens have to say for himself then?'

To her dismay, Julie felt her cheeks grow warm.

'A date tonight, but I told him we're going out.'

'He'll ring again, I bet. I could see he fancied you,' Megan laughed and Julie's lips tightened.

'And if he does, please tell him I'm out!'

Megan shrugged her shoulders. 'Suit yourself, but I'd give him a whirl if I were you,' she said as she left the office.

Julie told herself she wasn't looking for trouble; that somehow she could get hurt if ever she saw too much of Mike Stephens.

The evening was great fun; the young chap who was to be best man kept her laughing all night. She recognized his type almost at once. Keen to get on, determined to stay free and unfettered; the way ahead of young James didn't include a walk down the aisle for himself, or the encumbrance of a real commitment. He was fun to go out with for an odd date, to dine and dance the night away and then say good-night with a brief kiss.

Oh yes, Julie knew the drill; knew she was what he was looking for too – a self-supporting, smartly-dressed, unattached female who knew all the rules and kept to them. She had enjoyed the evening.

Then why, she asked herself as she removed her make-up before getting into bed, did she feel this feeling of dissatisfaction – seeing the evening's date and herself as two of a kind. Yet wanting something … she bit her lip, the hazel eyes reflected in the dressing-table mirror puzzled and rather unhappy looking. Just what did she want? Damn this touch of spring fever!

A few days later, Megan told her that Mike had rung again.

'He won't take no for an answer, I reckon, Julie.' She saw her boss's face tighten as she shrugged her shoulders.

'By the way, Alun's set up and interview for this afternoon, Megan – a Miss Debra Deane. I'll see her in here.'

'The new computer whizz-kid? Right, I'll show her through

then when she comes.'

'And, Megan, keep her chatting for a few minutes; let me know what you think of her, mmm?'

'Will do.' Megan knew all about the new expansion plans. She intended staying on after the honeymoon, for which Julie was grateful; they worked well together and she trusted her completely.

Tall, as slender as a reed, Debra Deane was a stunningly beautiful girl; more like a model than a computer expert, Julie thought as she watched her take a seat. Her dark business suit was well-cut, her blonde hair smooth and shiny. But there was something about her blue eyes – some hardness that Julie didn't quite like. Her CV was most impressive; her qualifications impeccable; her manner pleasant and friendly, and yet...?

'Why are you leaving your present post, Miss Deane?' she asked.

'I just think I could better myself. When I talked about it to Alun Jones I felt that this job would suit me very well – something I'm keen to do; a chance to get in at the beginning of a new expansion. You see, Mrs Prescott, I'm in a bit of a rut just now and I'd like to be able to move on – and up, if possible.'

'Fair enough. I understand.' They chatted a while longer, and in spite of herself, Julie was impressed and said so.

'I'll need to give a month's notice, of course,' the blonde girl told her.

'That will suit us fine; we'll be ready for you by then. I'll send your contract on then, Miss Deane, and look forward to having you on our team.'

After she'd gone, Julie rang for Megan.

'Well, what did you think of her?'

'Gorgeous looking. She'll be an asset, Julie, in that respect.

Bit of a cool customer, I'd say, but perhaps she was nervous and that was only a cover, but....'

She paused and Julie put in pensively, 'Yes, me, too. I found her very competent and so on, but....'

At that Megan grinned across at her boss.

'Couldn't stand the competition, could we, Julie?'

Was that it, Julie mused, or was it the fact that Alun had spoken so warmly of Debra Deane? Was she jealous, in a dog-in-the-manger-kind of way?

She was busy at her desk later that afternoon when the door burst open and a young girl flung herself across the office and slumped into the chair opposite.

'It's no good, Mrs Prescott, I've quit.....' Anger was almost choking the young temp, and her eyes filled with tears of exasperation.

'What on earth....? Quietly now, Carol. Tell me what's happened.' Gently Julie soothed the angry girl and waited until she had calmed down a bit.

'It's that rotten ... that Mr Boscombe! He's got more hands that an octopus and I'm not standing any more of his groping and touching.' She gulped, gradually getting her breath back. 'You know how it is, Mrs Prescott, it's almost an occupational hazard for secretaries and temps. They often just try it on. You can't blame a bloke for trying, and usually the one slap-down does it. But not Mr Boscombe – his hands always linger longer than necessary. He never misses a chance to pat and paw you – the old lecher! His beady eyes never get above your cleavage; always brushing up against you. That sort of thing....'

'I'm sorry, Carol,' Julie put in.

'Yes, well....' The indignant girl was determined to have her say. 'No wonder he can't keep a secretary, always wanting another temp. Well, *I'm* not going there again! This time, as I waited for him to sign some letters, the dirty old slob was creeping his other hand up my leg to my crotch.' She looked across at her boss, her eyes angry and resentful. 'This time I struck out – nearly knocked his head off. Then I came straight here to see you.'

'Quite right, I'm sorry, Carol, that you've had to put up with this harassment, but leave it to me. And I'll be taking his firm off our books, don't worry. See Megan about another assignment before you go, will you?'

Fuming, she tried to get through to Mr Boscombe on the phone at once, but he'd already gone home. It was getting late, but damn it, she wasn't going to leave it until morning!

'Give me his home address, please. It's urgent,' she requested, and a few minutes later she was put through to the dreadful man, via his wife.

Losing no time, she told him in no uncertain manner just what she thought of an old lecher with wandering hands who tried to take advantage of the young girls sent as temps to his office. Pulling no punches, her voice cold and angry, she told him she would be sending no more staff ever! Flushed and breathless, she slammed down the phone and leaned back in her chair.

'Well, I'm glad I wasn't on the receiving end of that little tirade, boss lady.....' She looked up, her face pink, brown eyes dark with anger still to see the tall young man behind a huge bouquet of flowers. It was Mike Stephens standing there, a wide smile on his good-looking face. And at the sight of him, Julie felt her heart leap, her pulse race even faster.

He was every bit as attractive as she remembered she thought once more. Just in time she stopped her hand from reaching up to her ruffled hair.

'Er – hello, Mike. I didn't hear you come in.....'

He grinned showing white teeth and creased laughter

lines.

'No, you were far too busy tearing a strip off some poor bloke!' He laid the flowers on the desk and sat down, casually crossing long legs and watching her flushed face. She looked lovely right then, sparkling with annoyance, with no sign of the usually cool business-like Mrs Prescott.

Taking a deep breath, she told him briefly about the lecherous customer.

'I feel so responsible for the young girls I send out,' she finished. 'Anyway, Mike, thanks for the flowers, they're lovely. How's the new job coming along; have you settled in down here?'

Holding up a hand, Mike laughed.

'I'm going to tell you all about it – over a meal. Get your coat, Julie, I've booked a table.'

'But – I'm sorry. I hadn't planned to go out tonight. It's not really necessary, you know, Mike, we did send the account.'

He leaned across and placed a long cool finger on her protesting lips.

'I'm not taking no for an answer. Now go and powder your nose; put these in water; lock up and we'll go.' Masterfully he took her by the shoulders, raising her out of her seat, his dark eyes sending messages she couldn't help but understand. He really wanted to take her out. Her pulses tingled at his touch; she ought not to let him treat her like this. Where was her usual calm and competent self? It seemed that she lost her cool every time this attractive young man came into her life!

She couldn't help noticing how vibrantly alive her face looked in the mirror, and she knew that, although it was unwise to go out with him, she would forget her qualms for tonight.

He had booked a table at Cardiff's best hotel and as they had a drink in the bar waiting to be called he smiled down at her.

'Cooled down now, Julie? You were breathing fire and brimstone, you know.'

'I know, but it's sickening that young girls should be harassed like that. I'm no prude, but I do feel kind of responsible....'

'It works the other way, too, you know,' he said.

'What do you mean, Mike?'

'We chaps get the same in reverse. Young, luscious females brushing against us in quiet corners; giving us the come-on.' His eyes were full of mischievous laughter, and though she knew he was teasing, she felt a tinge of jealousy tighten her throat, thinking of all the lovely *young* girls Mike saw every day.

'Tell me about your new job,' she asked later, spreading scrummy pâté on crisp thin slices of Melba toast.

'Well,' he began, 'I'm responsible for the purchasing and stock control of thousands of small parts – for components for the aerospace programmes. All very hush-hush, Julie – all secret stuff.' And he went on to tell her that his firm was at the moment competing with the French for a huge Middle East order.

'Sounds very high-powered stuff,' she mused aloud.

'It is. I'm having a tough time getting used to it all, but I'll manage. In a few more weeks, I'll have it all at my fingertips.'

How confident he was, she thought. Young, eager and keen, he would go far if nothing cropped up to spoil things for him. Through the long leisurely meal, they chatted quietly, each deeply interested in the other's views.

She felt both comfortable and excited with him. Her senses were aware of him to a degree she'd never know before; her nerve ends still tingling at the memory of his hands upon her arms.

'Did you get a place or is your cottage empty now?'

He grimaced as he explained, 'I've got a flat of sorts – cheap and not too good, but it's all I can afford.' Surprise must have shown then on her face; this meal alone was costing an arm and a leg, she reckoned. Reading her thoughts, he grinned.

'I know, I know. This is a one-off, Julie. My thank you. From now on, it's a burger bar or we go Dutch.'

So he had plans for seeing her again, had he?

'I need every penny I can scrape together from now on.' And he went on to tell her about the old cottage his grandmother had left him.

'It's near St Fagins and it's terribly run down. But, Julie, I've such plans for it; a double garage with extra rooms over. It wants rewiring, replumbing, central heating, new floors, walls pushed out....' He stopped for breath. 'I aim to do as much as I can myself.'

Somehow she couldn't quite see this London whizz-kid into DIY, and again he read her thoughts.

'I know. But I'm going to give it a good try, Julie. The thing is – the old folks who have lived there for years are in a bad way. A couple of weeks ago, the wife was taken into hospital with a stroke and is not expected to live.' His brow creased and she knew he was genuinely worried. 'The Social Services are rehousing the old man in a warden-controlled apartment near to the town and the hospital. The cottage is too cut off for him all alone. I wasn't going to do anything about the cottage until....' He paused and then went on, 'Now it'll be empty and I must start doing something with it a bit at a time and as I can afford it.'

He reached across and covered her hand with his.

'I'm telling you all this because – well, I'll be strapped for cash, Julie, so it'll be a pub meal next time, I'm afraid.'

'You think there's going to be a next time then, do you, Mike?'

'Definitely. I told you, boss lady, I want to get to know you. Now – how about a dance?'

The group was good, the tiny polished floor crowded, and as he took her in his arms, she felt her knees tremble. As if he knew how his nearness affected her, he drew her closer, his warm hand firm in the middle of her spine. And she felt as if her whole body was being remodelled to fit against his. As she felt his breath on her cheek, she longed to run her fingers through the dark hair at the nape of his neck. She couldn't believe the way the nearness of his body made her feel.

Did he know what he did to her with that gorgeous grin of his? She was a fool, behaving like a romantic schoolgirl, but she couldn't help it. And she didn't like what was happening to her, being out of control.

Since Jeff, she believed that falling in love never just happened. To drown in the sea, or in love, you must first have made the decision to go into the water. She was not, definitely not, going to get even one toe wet, if she could help it!

But as the night went on, Julie found it harder and harder to keep to this resolution. There was something about Mike that made her pulses race, made her want to stay in his arms all night. Must be the old sex urge, she told herself wryly. Blame that or the sap rising with the onset of spring. Whatever it was, she would have to watch herself. She could so easily be swept away by the sheer magnetism of his charm, his muscular charisma, his youthful zest.

At last as it grew late, Mike sounded as regretful as she felt when they finally walked to the car-park, his arm holding her close to his side. She had left her car at the office; she would enjoy the walk to work in the morning. Mike's car wasn't new, but it was a prestige model and must have set him back a tidy sum even second-hand.

It was amazing that after an evening together, they still found things to chat about on the short drive to Julie's flat. Although it was late, she asked him up for coffee, knowing deep down inside her that she shouldn't.

As she switched on the lights, Mike looked around with interest and open envy.

'Lord, I'd hate you to see my dump, Julie, after this....' But his description of the awful place and the dragon of a landlady, made the laughter bubble between them as they sipped the hot coffee.

'I'm getting hooked on you, Julie Prescott.' Calmly, he reached over, took the mug from her nerveless fingers and turned her face to his. She blinked at the look in his grey eyes, a look of desire and a hungry need that matched her own.

She swallowed hard, struggling to remain cool.

'Don't be silly, Mike. I'm too old for you. I'm almost....' Before she could go on, his mouth came down on her parted lips, closing them with his own in a kiss that sent her senses reeling. Gentle at first, it coaxed and persuaded hers to respond. Desperately she tried her hardest to resist; tried not to lose herself in the ecstasy of the touch of his lips.

As the flame flared up between them, the pressure grew and his kiss became fierce with passion and desire. She felt swamped, drowning. She couldn't stop herself as her hands crept up to the back of his neck as he held her tight – so tightly that she could feel the hard thud of his heart against her own.

'Oh Mike, it's – this is wrong! You and me – I'm so much older than you.'

His hand gripped her shoulders firmly and he held her away at arm's length, looking down into her eyes.

'Try telling that to my heart, Julie, my love. Older?' His eyes gleamed with laughter and reproof. 'Lord, you look like a young girl right now, boss lady. What does age, or money, or any of those things matter between you and me when we feel like this? When you can send me over the moon just by being near me?' He punctuated his words with kisses – on her eyes, her neck, her lips, filling her with heady delight, so that she forgot all else but being in his arms.

'So, Julie my girl, that's the last time I ever want to hear about age – understand?'

She struggled away from him, trying to calm the thud of her heart, to regain her composure.

'Mike, you're rushing me. You hardly know me! Besides, I'm not looking to get involved again – I learned my lesson the hard way. I don't intend to get caught again.' She saw the shadow cross his eyes and looked away, her hand pleating the hem of her skirt. He lifted her hand and turning it over, placed a gentle kiss in her soft palm.

'Well, Julie, I intend to make you change your mind. Meanwhile, will you let me see you, take you out? We'll explore the town and countryside together, eh? Have fun. Who knows, I might even get you to help with my DIY efforts!'

Again she watched that devastating smile of his; saw it crinkling his eyes, his mouth, and she shook her head before she weakened once more.

'I'm pretty busy, Mike. And you certainly are....' She paused seeing the denial on his face. 'Well, we'll see.'

She rose, indicating that it was time he left, hoping he wouldn't kiss her good-night. Her poise was delicately balanced and she could weaken so easily. But when he dropped a light, casual kiss on her forehead she didn't know whether she was glad or disappointed.

'Goodnight, Julie. Be seeing you....' And he was gone.

Three

It was fast getting near to the time of the launch of the new Exclusive Executives Agency, and Julie's nerves were often on edge. There was little peace at work these days; the hammering and drilling from the adjoining offices was deafening at times. She could barely hear Alun when he rang to give her more details of the business seminar they were both attending that weekend.

'It'll be good for business, Julie. Take plenty of advertising stuff with you – cards and so on. It's a great chance to get reactions; test the water, so to speak. I'll pick you up about two o'clock tomorrow, shall I? Oh, and Julie, it's glad rags for Saturday dinner and dance, don't forget. Bye.'

She replaced the phone and began making notes of what she needed, and what questions she wanted answering. She saw from the programme that there was to be a session on "head hunting – its problems and pitfalls." She had lots to learn and was glad Alun would be there too.

Later the phone rang again. It was Mike and her heart leapt.

'Hello, Julie, how are you?' The very sound of his voice made her breath catch in her throat.

'Oh, hello Mike. I'm fine thanks, busy as usual. What can I do for you?' She was pleased with the even tenor of her voice. She heard a faint chuckle from the other end.

'It's the boss lady speaking this morning, is it? Well, I just rang to fix up something for this weekend. What shall we do?'

Julie wasn't quite sure if she was pleased or disappointed that she had to tell him. 'I'm sorry, Mike, but I'll be busy all weekend.'

'Oh!' He sounded rather deflated and she could feel his disappointment over the wires. 'Not all the time, surely? What're you doing that'll take the whole weekend?' He sounded a bit put out and she bit her lip. Did a few kisses give him the right to expect her to be hanging around just waiting for his call?

'I'm going to a business seminar – an important one for me, as it happens, Mike. I'm sorry, but I shall be away....'

'Can I drive you there?' he put in quickly. 'See you just for that little while then?'

'No. No, I'm sorry. Alun's taking me. He's attending the seminar as well.'

'I see.' The words fell flat. 'One of those weekends, is it?'

How dare he? Julie's feelings were all mixed up. The dismay at the suggestion he'd made, disappointment at not being able to see him at the weekend and a touch of anger at him and herself, almost choked her.

'Alun is a good friend, a business partner, and what we do together is none of your affair, Mike. Now I'm busy, so I'll hang up.'

'Julie, wait....' But she cut him off, her hand shaking as she slammed down the receiver. Taking a deep breath, she resolved to put Mike out of her mind and concentrate on her work. But in spite of her resolution, she found his face coming between her and the papers before her for the rest of the day.

She kept remembering their evening out and how it had ended; felt again the warmth of his kisses and how they had stirred her blood.

She longed with all her heart to ring and tell him she would abandon the seminar and spend the weekend with him instead, but she knew how ridiculous that would be! She was a fool to let the thought of him and his kisses make her forget the importance of all else. He was just another young man – probably on the make, looking for a short fling until he found something better – a young girl more his own age and style probably. But did she have to be so week and so have to deny herself his friendship at least? Surely she was strong enough to overcome this crazy longing?

As she sorted through her wardrobe that evening she felt dissatisfied with her clothes. Weren't they all a little too *staid*? She dismissed the thought at birth, knowing that her choice of garments had always been right, suitable for her life-style, her job. Classic, expensive suits that complimented her colouring. But were they too...? She shrugged, annoyed with herself. What *was* the matter with her? Did she want to look like "mutton dressed as lamb" as her mother would have phrased it?

Finally she chose a mid-calf length black crêpe dress. Touched with silver, it fitted her beautifully, made her look slim and elegant and was eminently suitable for the high-powered business-lady image she wished to project that weekend. Nevertheless, she picked out a softly frilled blouse to go with her expensive formal suit. Slim, high-heeled court shoes, fine tights to tone, her most costly yet discreet perfume and make-up and she was ready. The briefcase matched her calf leather handbag and held all she thought she would need in the way of paperwork.

Spending an hour pampering herself, taking a long, leisurely soak in the bath, she knew she was ready for whatever the weekend brought her.

She was almost ready for bed when her mother rang.

'Sorry to ring so late, Julie dear, but I've been so busy.'

'Yes, Mum, I know.'

Her mother sat on numerous committees, had her finger in a good many pies, yet always found time for more.

'How's Dad?'

'Feeling tired these days. I'll be glad when his retirement comes round. Did I tell you, Julie, his firm's giving him a reception. And I thought we'd have a family party here, too. I'll let you know all about it later. You will come, won't you?'

Dear Mum, it was hard to get a word in sometimes.

'I will, I promise,' she said. 'How's Helen and the little horrors?'

'They're lovely,' the doting grandmother affirmed stoutly. 'It's time you settled down and had some children, Julie. You're not getting any younger.'

Julie grimaced and spent a few minutes diverting her mother away from her oft-recurring theme. At last, promising to keep in touch, she managed to hang up and put her mind to the coming weekend again.

However, she found it hard to get to sleep that night.

Alun was on time as usual, his eyes lighting up with pleasure when she let him in.

'Ready, Julie? You look very smart, I must say. This the lot?' With a warm smile he picked up her overnight bag and briefcase.

'Thanks, Alun.' Julie looked cool and calmly collected, successfully hiding the slight tremor inside her. This weekend could probably turn out to be an important one for her and her future plans, and again she was glad to have Alun along with her.

'New suit?' she queried later, looking him over fondly.

'Mmm, thought I'd do you proud,' he grinned; his round face seemed quite youthful and carefree at that moment.

'Seriously though, Julie, we stand to make a few good contacts if we seize our chances. The session on the legal technicalities of head hunting is the one we need to listen in to carefully. These days large firms tie up their top young men tightly, trying to avoid others poaching, industrial espionage and so on.'

'Yes,' she agreed thoughtfully, 'I'd marked that session down as a must. I've a lot to learn, I know.' She sighed softly, watching as Alun manoeuvred his sleek BMW into a parking space. Switching off the ignition, he turned to her for a moment.

'You'll need to know how to advise your young men on what to sign and what not to; there are lots of snags and pitfalls, you know.'

'I've got a small tape-recorder in my briefcase, Alun. Thought I'd tape that session.'

'Good girl.' As he helped her out of the car, he gave her arm a tight squeeze. 'Well, here we go....'

The seminar was being held in the conference suite of Cardiff's plushiest hotel, and already Reception was swarming with well-dressed business men of all ages, along with quite a few very smart females.

'Their secretaries?' Julie's eyes twinkled at Alun.

'Perhaps. A few top PA's and female bosses here, too, though, I reckon.'

Smooth-talking stewards gently eased them into an impressive lounge; soft-footed waiters passed amongst them handing out drinks. Round the edge of the large room, tables were loaded with leaflets and brochures and advertising material of all kinds. There were many firms there, too, to advertise office furniture, computers and all types of business equipment of the latest design and technology.

'Look, Alun.' Julie could hardly conceal her pride when

they came to the tiny display announcing the forthcoming opening of Exclusive Executives. It looked very discreet, impressive and up-market and her eyes shone with delight.

'Oh Alun, it's great! Bless you.' Blindly she reached out to squeeze the grey pin-striped arm nearest to her.

'Thank you, my dear, but what did I do to deserve that hug?'

'Oh!' Her mouth fell open in dismay; it wasn't Alun's arm she was clutching warmly! *He* had moved on a little to the next stand. Instead she looked up into the laughing florid face of a stout man she'd never seen before. 'I'm so sorry. I thought ... ' she stammered.

'I know, my dear, you thought I was Alun Jones; no such luck.'

'I'm sorry, I got carried away at the sight of my own little display.'

'Such enthusiasm is refreshing, Miss ... er?'

'Julie. Julie Prescott. I'm opening Exclusive Executives soon. And yes,' she beamed at him happily, 'I am thrilled and excited about my new project.'

'Tell me about it, young lady,' he commanded. And so she did, pleased to see that he really was interested.

'Here,' he gave her his business card. 'Send me some details, we might be able to use you.'

Quickly she gave him her own card and thanked him quietly.

'Good luck, Julie Prescott,' he said as he moved on.

She took in a deep breath and looked round for Alun. Her very first contact! With shining eyes, she told him about it, and he was pleased for her. If only her eyes would light up for him like that!

The proceedings began with a welcome address, brief introductory talks from the WDA, the chamber of Commerce and other dignitaries. After a short break for tea and biscuits, everyone went to find their rooms to change for dinner.

Julie had a quick shower and sat before the dressing-table, brushing her hair, trying to remember just a few of the many people Alun had introduced her to. One or two had glanced knowingly across at her and then back at Alun, while she tried to stifle her growing anger as she read their thoughts. Still, she mused, as she gently brushed her hair into gleaming highlights, it was no use fighting it; women still had to try harder to overcome this masculine prejudice. In business, it was still mostly a man's world. But by heavens, she was going to try hard and do her damnedest to alter her little bit of that world, wasn't she?

Her make-up was perfect; discreet and carefully applied. The black dress fitted her slim figure in all the right places with the hints of silver glinting as she moved. A pair of ornate silver ear-rings was her only jewellery, and as she took a close look in the long mirror, Julie was quite pleased with what she saw there. A final spray of perfume in the deep cleavage of her firm breasts and she was ready.

'You'll knock 'em cold, cariad.' Alun's soft Welsh lilt brought a faint flush to her cheeks as he led her into the opulent dining-room filled with large round tables. Each table sat twelve diners and there was only one other girl besides Julie at theirs.

As the meal progressed, she wondered if Alun had some-how managed to wangle their seating arrangement, for the other men there were very important and influential business men. As the wine flowed, and one sumptuous course fol-lowed another, talk became general and Julie was delighted to notice how skilfully Alun steered it around to the opening of her new project! Several of the men seemed interested, but the other female, as if resenting the attention Julie was attracting, suddenly put in clearly, her voice cool, 'Surely most firms would rather go to a well-established, experienced agency, with plenty of the right people on their books?'

Julie put down her glass carefully, and smiled round the table before answering quietly, 'That's true, of course, but the best *employees* seek a firm with shorter lists – that way they can be sure of creaming off the top jobs, and not be just one of a long queue waiting to be placed.'

There was a moment's pause, and then the grey-haired man on Julie's left put in, 'Quite, quite. As with all agencies, the best posts will only spread so far. A good bloke's got a better chance on a shorter list. I agree with you, Mrs Prescott. Good luck I say to your new venture. Old Alun here will put you right.'

'He does – he's my greatest help,' she acknowledged sincerely and then changed the subject. She knew she must push only so much and she'd had her turn and was well pleased by what had been said.

After dinner, they all split into different rooms; some just to talk, drink and smoke; others to "play" with the computers and other sophisticated equipment in a large room filled with long tables. There were several smaller rooms given over to various discussion groups, mini-lectures on all types of business problems. Advice for all was there for the asking and Alun skilfully conducted her to first one group and then another, making contacts, leaving cards, promising follow-ups and generally helping her to get known.

Julie reckoned that only about half of the promises were genuine; most of the older men were just interested in a pretty face, an attractive figure. Still by bedtime, she was feeling satisfied and pleased with all she and Alun had achieved.

'Thank you, Alun.' At the door to her room they paused, and she raised her face to his. 'Though thank you sounds a bit tame, but....' She shrugged her slim shoulders, lost for words.

'There's one way you could really say thank you, Julie. Say you'll marry me!' Alun's quiet voice had thickened with emotion. All night he had been longing to get her alone all to himself.

Julie's eyes clouded.

'Oh Alun, you know I've no intention of making that mistake again.'

'Marriage isn't such a bad thing,' he put in gently. 'Some people even manage to enjoy it.'

'That's as maybe, Alun, but I guess I'm just not much of an advert for it, that's all.' There was regret as well as a note of finality in her voice. She hated to see the longing in his brown eyes as she reached up to kiss him gently. But there was no passion, no commitment in her kiss and Alun knew it.

For a second he held her close and then said softly, 'Goodnight, cariad, sleep tight.'

'Night, Alun.'

Later, as she lay between cool sheets, Julie wished – not for the first time – that Alun wasn't in love with her. And immediately on the wish came the thought of a young, dark face and laughing dark eyes, and before she fell asleep, she wondered what Mike Stephens was doing with his weekend. One part of her – the restless, spring-fevered side of her – wished she could have accepted his offer to spend it with him.

The lecture on litigation was as important and well-attended as Alun said it would be. Julie managed to prop the tiny tape-recorder on a small table beside her. As the talk went on, she soon realized how careful the new agency would have to be when handing out advice about contracts.

Later over a drink in the bar, Alun suggested, 'I think it

would be a good idea to put my tame lawyer on hold over this one, Julie love. Get him to vet any contracts that look a bit tight.'

Sipping her gin and tonic and looking around the crowded bar, she agreed. The buzz of conversation was almost deafening.

'Such a lot of business is done under cover, isn't it, Alun? And the old boy network is still alive and well.'

'Mmm. So for a while, until you've learned all the pitfalls, you'll have to go warily. Check and check again, every step of the way.'

By the time the final meeting broke up, Julie's head was aching, her eyes tired from the cigar smoke and her brain felt it would burst with all it had tried to assimilate.

'I won't come in, my dear; you look all in.' Alun cut short her thanks and with a brief peck on the cheek, left her at the door. Julie slumped into an easy chair with a huge sigh of relief, kicking off her high-heeled shoes with a grimace. Why did the smartest shoes always give your toes hell?

For a moment, she smoothed out the pain in her forehead with a pensive finger, wondering whether to go through her notebook at once, or leave it till tomorrow. No, a cup of tea first. But as she rose to go and make it, her doorbell rang. Not Alun back for something, she cursed softly under her breath and went to the door.

With a quick indrawn breath, she looked up to see Mike Stephen's tall frame silhouetted in the doorway.

'So you're back?' he began and without waiting to be asked, passed into the hall, dropping his jacket on the small table as he did so.

'I've only just walked in.' Julie's voice was cool. What gave him the right to barge in uninvited and question her movements? 'What do you want, Mike?'

'To see you, of course. I've been ringing since lunch-time. Thought we might spend the evening....'

'Well you thought wrong!' Even as she stormed at him, Julie's heart was beating overtime, as angry with herself as with him. What on earth was it about this young man that knocked her off balance, made her whole being tingle with awareness at the very sight of him?

As she walked stiff-backed into the lounge, he reached out and gripping her by the shoulders, turned her to face him. In her stockinged feet, she had to look up, her eyes wide, her lips tremulous.

'Mike! I'm pooped. It's been quite an eventful week-end....'

Gently he passed a long finger down her cheek, his eyes tender. 'I can see it has, sweetheart. So ...' he paused and looked round, 'why don't I make us a cup of coffee or tea? And you can curl up and tell me all about it.'

Julie felt her anger drain away and submissively she flopped back into her chair.

'You win, Mike, but you can't stay for long. I've a busy day tomorrow.'

He grinned down at her and agreed. 'Me, too. And I hate Mondays, don't you?' He went through to the small kitchen to make the coffee, leaving her wondering if she'd have the strength of mind to send Mike away.

When he came back, he placed the mugs on the small round table in front of the settee and then reached over to pull her up out of her chair.

'Sit here with me,' he coaxed, but before she could lower herself on to the settee, he held her close and found her lips with his. Gently at first he moved them over her mouth; slowly, deliberately enticing her response. Julie felt herself weakening, wanting more. Of their own accord it seemed, her arms reached up behind his neck, pressing his head closer with a faint murmur, hungry to be nearer.

Again she was astonished by the strength of her feelings for this man, knowing they were not based on rhyme or reason.

'I've been wanting to do this all weekend, darling,' he told her and the coffee was almost cold by the time they finally began to drink it.

Mike watched her all the time as if he couldn't get enough of the sight of her. With an effort, she resisted the urge to tidy her hair – she knew she never looked at her best when she was tired and wished she hadn't switched on all the lights. There it was again! The ugly knowledge of the years between them. He reached over and turned her face to his.

'Not still thinking of Alun Jones, are you, Julie?' A tinge of jealousy shadowed his grey eyes.

Angrily she pushed herself upright, away from him.

'Did you share a room you two?'

'No, we didn't! Not that it would have been any of your business,' she retorted heatedly.

'I'm sorry love, but I *am* jealous; I hate the thought of you being with any other man but me. I want you all to myself, Julie.' As he spoke his lips travelled over her cheek, her neck, her ear lobes – gently nuzzling, making her heart lurch, wanting him to go on.

'Well then Mike, you're going to spend a lot of time being jealous in the near future ... ' she began and then went on to tell him all about the new Exclusive Executives project and of what she had learned that weekend.

His interest held now, he listened intently, nodding his head approvingly.

'That's great, boss lady, great! I know you'll do it and I

wish you all the luck in the world. But I wish *I* was the one helping you and not Alun Jones.' His face darkened again at the thought and she hurried to reassure him.

'Alun's an old and valued friend. I need his help and advice and probably more financial help too. I'm fond of him, but that's all.'

'But he's in love with you; wants you to marry him,' he stated forcibly. She felt the colour stain her cheeks and shook her head.

'That again is not your business, Mike. I'm sorry, but I can't help it if you're – well, jealous of Alun. I need him,' she finished flatly.

'And you don't need me? And I've no money to help you out with, have I, Julie?'

She couldn't bear the bitterness in his voice, the regret and chagrin in his eyes.

'I didn't ask you to come into my life, did I? I've worked damned hard to get where I am. I need to work even harder to get Exclusive Executives off the ground and not lose the lot. I'll have no time to pander to your hurt feelings!' She rose sharply to her feet and moved over to the window, to stand staring out into the dark night.

'I'm sorry, Julie love.' He came across and stood behind her and she saw their double reflection in the dark glass – he so tall and young and she...? She shrugged off the incipient though and turned to face him. 'I know you're ambitious and I promise I won't interfere; just let me see you, take you out when you're free, to want you all the time," he murmured into her neck.

Once more his kisses sent fire through her veins and her body responded with a surge of wanton desire which made her tremble with the effort to control it. She was frightened by the intensity of her feelings for him. She simply *had* to get things firmly in check before they swamped her completely.

'I – I like you a lot, Mike. You *know* you turn me on. But I won't let anything come between me and my new venture. With a failed marriage behind me, I'm definitely not looking for a husband, or a lover who'll be jealous and want all my time....'

He placed a finger gently on her lips.

'I know, Julie, and I promise – no more jealous tantrums. Just spare me what time you can. There's no way *I* can think of getting married. I'm going to be busy, too, in my new job and doing up the cottage. So … just loving friends it is then?'

Not quite sure whether that was what she really wanted after all, Julie nodded and taking his arm, pulled him over towards the settee again.

'That's it,' she agreed. 'The ground rules are laid now – no strings attached, no commitment, no pressures, no heel taps.'

There was a long pregnant pause, and then she began to ask him about his plans for the cottage, watching his face light up as he sketched out all he hoped to achieve in time.

'Every penny I can spare will have to go into it, darling. I'm hoping to do a lot of the labouring work myself. I wish you'd come and see it, Julie, you know – a sort of before and after look. Will you?'

She agreed with a smile and once more he took her into his arms. This time she called a halt while she still had the strength of mind to do so.

'Time to go, Mike.' She rose and held out her hand. He stood up and placed a warm kiss in her soft palm.

''Night, boss lady, be seeing you soon.'

The following week was a busy one for Julie and her assistant, Megan Williams; they both worked through their lunch hour and twice stayed late at night.

The alterations on the new office block were completed and Julie was grateful for the wholehearted co-operation she had received from her friend. Megan was also beginning to get her wedding arrangments under way, and chatting about them sometimes made a welcome break from discussing fittings, fixtures and office supplies! By lunch-time Friday they had got through most of the work and Julie called an early halt.

'You get off now, Megan, and thanks, you've been a real pal. Have a nice weekend and I'll see you Monday. Bless you.'

Deciding to leave early herself and cook a decent meal for once, she did some shopping for the weekend and let herself into the flat with a weary sigh. It had been quite a week! She was putting away her groceries when the doorbell rang, and she went to see Mike standing there, a rather limp bunch of flowers in his hand. He had an unsure-of-his-welcome look on his face.

'Hi, Julie,' he greeted her with a quick kiss. 'Fancy going out for a pizza or something equally expensive?'

'Come in. And thanks for these.' She gave the poor flowers a wry glance. 'If these are the best you can do, I'll feed you here – be cheaper for you. Come on.'

He followed her through to the kitchen to perch on the corner of a bench, his long legs taking up far too much room.

'Glad you're an up and coming tycoon lady,' he grinned. 'I'm even more skint than ever, pet. Car's in dock till Monday – MOT and sundry repairs.' He shrugged and reaching out pulled Julie up close until she rested between his outstretched thighs. 'So, Julie my pet, as well as feeding me tonight, how about us using your car to go to see my cottage tomorrow? You taking the picnic, of course.'

Between words, he gave her face soft little kisses, his grey eyes sparkling with a cheeky twinkle and the corners of his well-shaped mouth lifted mischievously.

'Can I afford all this, I ask myself?' Julie laughed. 'Now let me go or we'll never eat. And I'm hungry …' she was about to add, "and tired" and then once more she remembered that he probably rarely felt fatigue at his age. So she bit her lip and turned to the stove.

'Mmm, smells good,' he sniffed.

'Steak and all the trimmings. You can do the salad, Mike. And lay the table. Now – scoot and let me get on.'

It was a pleasant evening. They talked as they ate; sat on the settee and listened to tapes from her music centre, and kissed; drank wine and kissed again.

But Mike didn't rush her, didn't press her for more than she was prepared to give, and they finally said goodnight on the doorstep.

The quiet evening had soothed Julie's tired brain, left her pleasantly relaxed. And she fell asleep the moment her head touched the pillow, her lips still softly tremulous from his kisses.

It was a glorious spring morning, and when they set off just after eleven, the sun was already warm, the sky blue, with only a few puffs of cotton-wool clouds floating high above them.

'You'll have to tell me how to get to this country hideout of yours, Mike. I'm still quite new around here.'

'I often get lost myself,' he told her. 'But the nearest village is called St Fagins – from there I know the way.'

'Isn't that where the Welsh Folk Centre or something is?' she asked, her eyes fixed firmly on the antics of a shoppers' bus in front of them.

'That's right. Perhaps we could go there one day. I've

heard it's quite something worth seeing.' His plans for future dates lifted her heart and the sun seemed to shine even more brightly.

St Fagins was a lovely old village; quiet in spite of the famous Folk Centre.

'It's near enough to commute to your job, isn't it? When you move out here, I mean.'

'Yes, but lord knows how long that'll be,' he told her mournfully. And when they finally wound their way down yet another narrow lane and she saw Mike's cottage for the first time, she could see what he meant.

It was a squat, stone-built little place, sturdily tucked away in the fold of the hills. Snug, but lonely and oh so badly in need of repair. The roof sagged, guttering hung brokenly, fences and walls had all fallen away, window frames were rotted and the garden a wilderness. All so neglected. And yet it had an appealing air about it as if it was begging to be loved and cared for once more.

'It could be made really beautiful again, Mike. But there's an awful lot to do.' With the best will in the world, Julie couldn't keep the doubt out of her voice.

He swept away some dead leaves from the wooden bench seat in the rickety old porch and sat Julie down forcibly.

'Now darling, close your eyes and think how it could be – all repaired and renovated. Add a double garage – stone-clad of course, with rooms above. All the stone whitewashed, with black wrought-iron fittings on the door. Shutters to leaded-glass windows, a lovely garden, and round the back – a patio and conservatory for sitting out and admiring the view. Oh Julie, I can see it all, can't you?'

With her eyes closed, she could picture it all. Above all, she heard the excitement and longing in Mike's voice. And suddenly she wished and hoped with all her heart that his dream would come true! But inside, her consternation rose once more. Rotted floorboards creaked upstairs; plaster had fallen away leaving gaping holes in the walls; The low ceilings had flaked away with slats showing through in several places.

However, the electricians had already begun putting in new wiring, and one bedroom had fresh new floorboards and a new door. It was here that Julie spread out a travel rug and they ate their picnic.

'If your clients could only see you now,' Mike laughed as he reached over to brush away a few strands of cobweb caught in her smooth hair. 'Seriously though, Julie, what do you think? Can it be made into a decent place?' He flung out a wide arm. 'Can you see it as I do?'

'Yes, I can,' she agreed. 'And I can see it with chintz curtains and covers; a lovely old dark settee beside that fireplace downstairs; copper pans in the kitchen. Oh yes, Mike, it could be made into a beautiful little place. But it'll all take time and lots of money, and meanwhile you're stuck, half-starving, in that miserable room of yours.'

'Then I'll have to live on your picnics, sweetheart. This is scrumptious,' and he reached into the picnic basket for another little game pie.

As they finished the last of the white wine, Julie rose and stretched her legs, saying, 'Come on, this floorboard's hard.'

'Far too hard for what I had in mind.' Her smooth eyebrows rose in query, a smile playing round the corners of her mouth. 'Such as...?'

'Making mad passionate love to you.' Mike grinned and once again she felt her heart miss a beat at the sight of his smile.

She shook her head and brushed sawdust from her skirt, determined not to let him see how his words affected her. *She* would have enough sense for both of them; he was only a young man after all. A sexy, very masculine young man whom, for her own peace of mind, she'd do well to keep a little more at arm's length.

Downstairs, they decided to sit in the car, it being the only place with two comfortable seats. As he went on making plans, she interrupted, 'Exclusive Executives opens next week, Mike, and I'll be very busy, so I'm afraid....'

She paused and he put in, 'But you need to have some time off – at weekends, say? So let me see you then, Julie, please,' he begged. And in spite of her resolution, she nodded and agreed. 'I know how busy you'll be; how important your new project is to you, darling. So I promise I won't plague you, but I must see you – sometimes and often – for a little while.'

'All right, Mike, but no pressure though.'

'That doesn't mean no loving though, does it?' he murmured softly, lifting her curtain of hair and kissing her neck. Unable to stop herself, she turned her face and her lips close.

'No, I didn't say no loving, but ...'

He covered her mouth with his as his dark head blotted out the sun, and all else fell away. And Julie knew, whatever else happened, she couldn't say no to Mike's lovemaking....

Four

It came all too soon – the official opening to Exclusive Executives. With a soft buzz of conversation and drinks in hand, the guests were milling around in the new office block.

'Ladies and gentlemen....' With a wide smile and a sharp rap on a desk, Alun strove to get their attention. 'You all know why we're here – apart from drinking Julie's excellent wine – so without more ado, please raise your glasses. I give you – Exclusive Executives and all the very best of good luck to Julie Prescott and her colleagues.'

'Good luck, Julie!'

'Here's to Exclusive Executives! All the best.'

Her hazel eyes shining, Julie gazed round. It was all going so well.

'So folks ...' again Alun raised his voice, 'I now formally declare this new enterprise well and truly opened!'

There were loud cheers, some jovial, some ribald, and everyone drank the toast. She was delighted to see so many local dignitaries there, friends of Alun's she guessed, with some of her own too. Quite a few of the girls from her register had managed to turn up to see their boss launch her new firm. Best of all, Mike had managed to put in an appearance.

She looked round eagerly, peering above the crowd trying to see him. He was over the far side of the crowded room, his dark head bent, absorbed in talking to ... Julie's heart lurched as she saw who had caught his attention – Debra Deane, the computer consultant who was starting to work for Exclusive

Executives next week. Julie had almost forgotten her and now she was angry with herself, amazed at the pang of jealousy that half-blinded her for a moment. Her original antipathy came back then in full force. Debra was tall, slim blonde and beautiful. And as if they weren't tributes enough – she was young! At twenty-five, she's a decade younger than me, Julie told herself bitterly.

Just then someone caught her arm and began asking questions. Blinking rapidly, she struggled to dispel the hurt of the heart-burning jealousy and concentrate on answering him. Today was an important step forward, and she couldn't afford to falter. But even as she tried to collect her thoughts, she was conscious of the longing to turn and watch the tall, good-looking couple across the room – one so fair, the other so dark.

Later, she heard Mike's voice and saw him this time with another young man and he was trying to catch her attention.

'Hi, Julie. Congratulations and all the very best, darling.' Swiftly as he dropped a light kiss on her cheek, she turned her head, their eyes met, and she knew he really meant it. 'This is a friend of mine – Peter Rogers. Pete, meet the boss lady of Exclusive Executives.'

She held out her hand, liking the open, clean-cut look of the other man.

'Nice to meet you, Mrs Prescott. May I ...' he paused and cast a swift glance around and then went on, 'may I come and see you soon?'

She could see he didn't want to elaborate.

'Certainly, when?' Consulting her notepad, they agreed on a time, and she wondered if this Peter Rogers was to be her very first client?

'See you soon then. I must circulate,' she told them.

'I'll ring you, Julie. Don't overdo things. Bye.' Mike

glanced across at her with a warm intimate smile and she forgot the pangs of jealousy she'd experienced a short while ago.

'See you, Mike. Bye, Mr Rogers.'

As she moved away, she saw that Alun had been watching them closely. He dropped his eyes to the glass in his hand, but not before Julie had seen the look on his face. But for a while she had to concentrate on saying goodbye to her departing guests, making notes furiously as first one and then another asked for details and brochures to be sent on to them.

It was late the following Friday evening after a frantically busy week that Mike rang.

'Got your breath back yet, Julie?' Suddenly all her tiredness dropped away and her heart lifted joyously at the sound of his voice.

'Just about – and you?'

'Longing to see you. How about tomorrow? Could we have the day out? How about that Welsh Folk Centre thing, darling?'

'The whole day...?' She paused and then remembering, added, 'I've got an appointment early in the morning, but after then....'

He must know how much I want to see him, she thought ruefully trying to keep the eagerness out of her voice. They finally arranged that Julie would take the picnic and call at Mike's digs to pick him up and they'd spend the rest of the day together.

And if that isn't running after a bloke, then I don't know what is, Julie my girl, she told herself with a grimace.

The next morning, she wasn't long at the JP Agency's office, and changing into some flat shoes, she picked up her car and drove towards Mike's flat. As she turned down first one dismal street and then another, her spirits sank. Surely he could afford a better area than this? If the outside was depressing, the inside was much worse and even Mike's welcoming kiss couldn't erase her dismay. Seeing the look on her face, he shrugged.

'Yes, I know, love. It's pretty awful, isn't it?'

The one large bed-sitting room was gloomy and grubby with dirty, faded wallpaper and a cracked ceiling. The divan bed sagged in the middle and everything looked cheap and nasty and dark.

'Surely you can do better than this dump, Mike? After all, you're on a good salary.'

'I know, but it's costing a bomb to do up the cottage; more than I thought it would. And this won't be for ever. Come on, let's get out, it's a lovely day.' With all the optimism of youth, he dismissed his surroundings with a shrug, but Julie longed to see him out of there.

The Folk Centre was more interesting than she had expected. Set in acres and acres of open land, it took you back in the history and development of Wales. Tiny miners' cottages had been dismantled and then set up piecemeal in a row, all furnished with genuine items of furniture. An old zinc bath hung outside one back door; another had the original little bike shed and outdoor privvy.

They watched bread and scones being baked in an old-fashioned baker's oven; a tanner making a leather saddle – everything done by hand, using the ancient tools and crafts of bygone days.

Mike could hardly get her away from the little old village school, complete with well-worn double desks, slates and chalks. Even the teacher's cane was there!

With the warm sun on their faces, they sat beside the river and ate their picnic. Julie felt that her cares had faded, her nerves rested, her body beautifully relaxed. Leaning back on her hands, with the smell of the crushed grass, the gentle breeze ruffling her hair, she knew she'd never been happier. Being with Mike was all that she wanted right then.

'You're good for me, Mike. I never would have thought to come here myself, and I've enjoyed it all so much.'

There was a smug, almost complacent grin on his face.

'I'm right then, darling. You need to get away from your business whenever you can. And I need to see you, touch you....'

The husky timbre of his voice sent Julie's pulses racing and she turned to look at him, reaching out. Their fingers met, and the whole of her body felt alive and tingling. She'd never felt so aware of a man for ages and it almost alarmed her, because lately she had always been the one in charge of her being.

Mike was becoming far too important to her and she would need to think about it.

She heard him give a deep sigh of contentment as he leaned back, his dark head in her lap. Of their own accord, her fingers threaded their way through his crisp hair as she looked at his face, loving the thick long lashes that black-edged his brilliant eyes, loving the sensuous curve of his mouth, the firm chin.

Then she thought again of those awful digs of his; he couldn't stay there, she couldn't bear the thought of his staying there!

They spent an hour going through the glass cases in the final section until Mike said, 'Come on, Julie, my feet are killing me; we must have walked miles.'

Passing out through the turnstiles, she suggested, 'Come to my place and I'll rustle us up a meal. OK?' And his face lit up.

'I'd thought you'd never ask.' And there was something in his tone that made her wonder if she'd been wise to ask him back to her place.

She switched on the gas fire as Mike slumped on to the settee.

'This is great after my dump, love. Fancy taking in a lodger?'

Shaking her head, she laughed. 'I'll feed you and then chuck you out.'

'You're cruel, do you know that?' he mocked. Half an hour later, they ate and then relaxed with their mugs of coffee on the settee in front of the fire. Suddenly he reached over and deliberately took the mug from her hand, turning her face to his. She blinked at the look of desire and hungry need she saw there.

'Mike, don't....' But before she could say more, his mouth came down on her parted lips, closing them with his own in a kiss that sent her senses reeling. Gentle at first, and then, as the flame flared up between them, his kiss became fierce with fervent desire.

Her hands crept up to the back of his neck as he held her tighter. So tightly that she could feel the beat of his heart against her own. Then, his hands gripping her shoulders firmly, he held her away at the arm's length and looked down into her eyes.

'I want you, Julie. Now – all of you; just having you in my arms sends me over the moon.' He punctuated his words with kisses, on her eyes, her neck, her lips; filling her with heady delight.

She struggled to hold on to her spinning senses but she was dazed with happiness; deliriously, wonderfully happy. And all the pulsating desires she'd ever known flooded back, making her body quiver with longing. Feeling as if she was drowning, the crazy thoughts skittered through her brain like fire.

Why not love Mike? She was free and at her age she ought to grab happiness with both hands. As his caresses set her whole being tingling, she knew it was too late to draw back. She wanted him as much as he wanted her right then.

'Let me love you, Julie,' he begged and the pressure of his hard, muscular body against her softly yielding one awakened in her an answering hunger. She clung to him, forgetting all she'd planned for herself, forgetting everything but the feel of his mouth on hers, his hands caressing her body into eager response.

Sliding his fingers under her skirt, loosening her bra fastening, he cupped her firm breasts. She gave a soft moan as her nipples hardened at his touch, her whole body burning with its urgent need. Blindly, hurriedly, she fumbled with the buttons on his shirt, pulling it open, desperately wanting to feel him, to run trembling fingers through the mat of soft dark hair on his hard chest.

Like a love-starved teenager, her breath came in hard little gasps and as he rose and lifted her in his arms, she knew she had lost the battle to deny him anything. Swinging her close, Mike moved across to her bedroom and kicked open the door. As his hand felt for the light switch, Julie murmured,

'No, not the light....' Bemused as she was, she was still scared of letting him see her naked. She wasn't a young girl. Would her body please him – or repel him?

'Yes, my love. I want to *see* you. I want to look into those big brown eyes of yours when I take you.'

As he whispered the words, his hands were quickly divesting her of the rest of her clothes until she stood before him – a deep flush on her cheeks, her bronze hair a dark curtain concealing her eyes. Placing a fervent kiss in the dusky hollow between her breasts, he laid her tenderly on top of the bed while he removed his own clothes with shaking hands, to join her there.

Gently rousing her, he stroked her high round breasts as her fingers caressed the smooth compact muscles of his shoulders, his long straight back. Breathing hard, he nuzzled the soft hollows of her throat, then languorously, lovingly, his lips travelled down, ever downwards, to where there was a hard, burning core of hungry desire erotically inside her.

Julie moaned softly in her throat, moving, rubbing against him, wanting more.

'Oh please, Mike....' she begged and her head tossed from side to side on the pillow. 'Now....'

There was a soft triumphant note in his voice as he whispered, 'Gently, gently, my love.' And by the time he covered her burning body with the length of his, she was nearly out of her mind with yearning. With a deep, almost animal-like groan, she felt his entry; rode with him on the wonderful ride of love as he brought her again and again almost to the peak of fulfilment, only to pause, to look down into her face, and then begin again.

Then suddenly, the world spun out of control; stars blazed behind her closed eyelids and with a loud cry she gasped and then fell down and down earthwards again. Panting, her brow dewed with sweat, she felt his whole body shudder, his hoarse grunt of utter relief as he filled her with his warmth.

For a while he lay there gasping and then rolled away.

'Oh God, Julie, that was wonderful.' His chest heaving, he fought to regain his breath, the jubilant smile on his face so radiant it dazzled her eyes, and she reached up to place a kiss on the base of his throat, feeling the heavy thud of his heart beneath her lips as she did.

'For me, too, Mike. Wonderful....'

They kissed gently and quietly, with her head on his shoulder until finally, dreamily sated with love, they slept to wake a couple of hours later.

'I'll have to go, Julie.' For a moment, she wanted to keep him there, and then she reluctantly agreed.

'Yes. Shall you ring for a taxi?'

'No, I'll walk.' Tenderly he reached over and kissed her, tucking his shirt into his waistband. 'Right now I could float on air, my darling.' He kissed her again. 'Go back to sleep. Night....'

And Julie was asleep even before he let himself out of the front door.

She woke early the next morning, wondering why she felt so blissfully contented, and then stretched to get rid of the unusual little aches and pains the lovemaking seemed to have left her. As she groped sleepily for the bathroom she was glad that Mike hadn't stayed the night – to see her in the stark morning light like this. At her age, her face needed all the care and attention she gave it! Peering into the mirror, she searched for signs, some change, but the eyes looking back were clear and bright. She looked like a woman fulfilled!

Her first interviewee was Peter Rogers, Mike's friend.

'Hello, sit down Peter,' she indicated a smart new chair and rang for coffee. 'What can we do for you?'

For a long moment he looked at her across the desk and then leaned back to cross his long legs.

'Firstly, Mrs Prescott, every word said here this morning has to be in confidence, strictly between you and me. Understood?'

'Of course, that goes without saying,' she put in firmly.

'Well, I want a move. There's a post going soon that I think I'd like to get. But until I have full details, I can't openly apply. You see, my present firm mustn't know I'm doing it. They've got me pretty well tied up and I need a go-between – a really discreet, careful person to take care of my best interests and sort it all out for me first.'

'I understand. You don't want to burn your bridges too soon, Peter?'

'Quite!'

Coffee came and as soon as they were alone again, Julie began taking down the details. It appeared that Peter Rogers was a top flight salesman. In fact, he represented his firm in the whole of northern England. His CV was excellent; he also showed her a recent testimonial from his employers awarding him "top salesman of the year."

'The new firm wants an executive sales manager for the whole of the British Isles. It's quite a promotion. The salary's almost double, and I know I stand a good chance of getting the position.'

'Then why not apply direct?' Julie had to ask.

'Because of this damned agreement.' He passed over a copy of a legal-looking document and then sipped his coffee while Julie read it through. It was indeed full of tightly binding conditions. He couldn't take another sales position within three months of leaving, or in a similar area, or sell the same type of product. And confidences he duly disclosed about customers or products to a new firm made him liable for prosecution and so on.

As she read it, Julie's brow creased. And then remembering Alun's advice, she told Peter, 'I'd have to get our legal department on to this once we get the ball rolling. First, I think I need to see the new firm and, giving away as few details as possible, try and find out what you need to know.'

The serious-faced man opposite nodded, and a few minutes later rose to go, satisfied with all her suggestions.

'I'll leave it with you then, Mrs Prescott, and remember not a word to anyone else – not even Mike Stephens.'

Curious, Julie asked, 'You're a close friend of his?'

'Well, not really close. We play squash together, that's all.'

'I see. Well, we'll be in touch, Mr Rogers.'

After he'd gone she rang Alun to arrange to go and see his lawyer friend that afternoon. And then, putting down the phone, she leaned back and sighed. Exclusive Executives had received its first assignment!

Alun rang back in a few minutes, and before he hung up again asked her to have dinner with him that evening.

'We haven't had a proper date for ages, Julie,' he grumbled. She felt guilty because she really wanted to stay home in case Mike rang or came round. After last night ... for a moment her eyes grew dreamy and then Alun's voice brought her back down to earth.

'Well, Julie, shall I pick you up?'

'Er, yes please, Alun. About seven-thirty. But I don't want to stay out too late; I'm really busy.'

And indeed she hardly had a moment to spare, with the phone ringing constantly.

'Julie,' Megan's soft lilt sounded rather anxious as she put through another call. 'This firm have a rather serious complaint to make about one of our temps. Will you take it?'

'Put me through, Megan.'

Almost at once a deep voice, full of barely concealed anger, came over the wire.

'And we have reason to believe your girl has been leaking confidential information to one of our competitors, Mrs Prescott,' he finished.

With a sinking heart, Julie listened to the irate voice and then put in quietly, 'May I come and see you – in the morning, say about eleven?'

'Make it ten-thirty!' And with that the receiver was slammed down, leaving her nibbling her fingertip pensively.

'Megan, get me Sarah Carter's file, will you, please?'

'Anything wrong, Julie? That was one angry man just now.'

'I'm afraid so, Megan.' A frown creasing her smooth brow, she asked, 'What do you know about Sarah Carter?'

'Not much. She's a good secretary. Clever; on the ball. Must have well-off parents, or a rich boyfriend. She dresses really top label.'

Julie sighed, but refrained from any further comment. She'd need to sort this out herself.

After lunch, she kept the appointment with the lawyer Alun had recommended. Without wasting any time, she explained what she needed; told him about Peter Rogers' contract of employment.

His long fingers made a pyramid as he looked at her from beneath bushy brows.

'Mmm, I see. The usual sort of thing. It's pretty binding legally, and it'll take some litigation to break it. It can be done, by careful negotiation on both sides. We'll handle the legal bits; you do your best in the diplomacy stakes, Mrs Prescott.'

For a few minutes, he told her how to handle any forthcoming interview with Peter's present firm and then rose, and shaking hands, wished her well. So far, so good – she was learning fast!

Alun seemed in a funny sort of mood when they finally sat at their table that night. He had taken her to an expensive new place and it was crowded with obviously well-heeled clients, all anxious to see if the famous French chef lived up to his reputation. Soft music, shaded lights, attentive waiters gliding swiftly over richly carpeted floors, all augered well for its successful opening.

'Had a job to get a table,' Alun told her as they scanned the menu.

'You shouldn't have, Alun, it's so expensive.' It wasn't that that was worrying her, but she had a feeling Alun was only trying to offset Mike's attraction for her. *He* certainly couldn't afford a place like this.

'Please, Julie – let me make the running my way. Your young man's strong competition!' The words were lightly said, but his soft lilt failed to cover the pleading hurt in his eyes.

'You know you have a special place in my life, Alun, don't you?'

'And Mike Stephens?' A spoon halfway to his mouth, he waited for her reaction. And she inwardly cursed the faint flush she felt staining her cheeks. 'You've really gone overboard for him, haven't you, my dear?'

Just for a split second, she was tempted to refute his suggestion emphatically, and then the remembrance of the night before spent in Mike's arms made her bite her lip. She avoided Alun's brown eyes watching her and pushed the food around the plate in front of her.

'Yes, darling, I like him – very much. But,' she put in quickly, her voice gentle, 'you know he's years younger than me. Neither of us is looking for a serious commitment just now.' She reached across to touch his hand. 'So, Alun, stay my dear friend, please.' Her large hazel eyes begged for his understanding. 'I need you,' she said softly.

Alun swallowed visibly, his voice husky.

'All right, love. It's your own business and I'll always be here for you.'

'Thanks, darling.' Her grateful smile was beautiful to see and the man opposite knew he would still settle for that half a loaf!

As the waiter served their next course – wild duck à l'orange with tiny new vegetables – she gazed around with interest. The place was full, every table taken.

Suddenly she saw a face she knew. What a coincidence. Sarah Carter was sitting at a table across the big dining-room! She was beautifully dressed and as Megan had hinted, her dress was definitely not one of the off-the-peg variety! With her at the small table for two was a smartly-dressed man. Grey-haired and with a rather lined face, he could have been her father, Julie told herself.

And then Alun, following the direction of her gaze, said with a chuckle, 'Old Stan Evans got himself a young dolly-bird, I see. Hope his wife doesn't find out?'

Carefully Julie suggested, 'Perhaps his daughter?'

Alun shook his head, his grin still wide.

'No. He's just got the two sons. One still at college, I believe.'

'What's he do?' At the look of query on his face, she added, 'The girl's one of our temps. I just wondered...?'

'Oh, he's Caratech Caravans – the other side of Cardiff. Strange though,' he paused watching the other table with a frown, 'looks more like a business chat than a naughty night out, wouldn't you say, Julie?' Indeed the other two were talking seriously; no sign of intimacy between them.

Amazed by the second coincidence, she began to eat again, almost tempted to tell Alun about the irate call she'd had that afternoon, then refrained. It was something she must look into herself.

And so for the rest of the evening, she devoted her attention to Alun. They danced once or twice on the tiny floor, and then took their coffee and liqueurs in the opulent lounge. The soft hum of conversation, the smell of perfume, cigars and good food all lulled her into a sense of restful well-being.

As she thanked Alun later, she told him warmly, 'I have enjoyed tonight, darling. You're such a pet,' and she kissed him lovingly.

'I know, cariad, if only....' Alun sighed and then with a soft goodnight left her standing there gazing after him regretfully.

At ten-thirty sharp the next morning Julie sat, outwardly calm, facing the red-faced man on the other side of the wide table-top desk. She had taken extra care with her appearance; her lightweight suit and toning silk blouse were immaculate, and her chestnut tinted hair curved smoothly round her soft cheeks.

On arriving at the large industrial complex, she had been directed to the manager's office and now faced him, her heart full of misgiving, for this firm was also a manufacturer of high-class caravans! Once more the coincidence was all to obvious; she had seen Sarah Carter with this firm's greatest rival last night!

'Briefly, Mrs Prescott, the plans for an entirely new model caravan have been leaked to a rival firm. We now have word that they intend to use them. Your temp could have had access to them – the others were old and trusted members of the firm,' Mr Lloyd went on to explain that, like cars, new caravan models were exhibited every early spring ready for the summer season.

This year they had decided to bring out a revolutionary new model, incorporating many special features never tried out before. Production costs would be high and everything depended upon its surprise impact and exploitation early next year.

Now with this other firm about to do the same, the whole concept had been spoiled.

'I can't begin to tell you, Mrs Prescott, what this means to us. We've been holding on, saving up all the new features and ideas, to create this one beautiful and entirely new image of a caravan.'

His face grew sterner still and he had all her sympathy. 'We have almost positive proof that Miss Carter has been in touch with Caratech Caravans, but prosecuting her won't help us now.'

Just then a girl came in with a tray and poured out two cups of coffee. When she had gone, Julie said, 'I'm so sorry, sir. I'd no idea; Sarah Carter was just another good temp to us. I – I just don't know what to say – what I can do...?' She gave a soft sigh.

'We're not really blaming your Agency. Of course, you'll sack the wretched girl?'

'Of course, but I do blame myself a little. She was always dressed in very expensive clothes, but I never suspected anything like this. I'm so sorry.'

They sipped the hot coffee, both lost in thought. Julie knew that if ever this got out, her JP Agency, and possibly the new Exclusive Executives, would be ruined. Who would trust a firm who had supplied another with an industrial spy? she mourned inwardly. Dismayed, she looked around the cluttered office, seeing the pictures on the walls of caravans of the last twenty years. And then, like a flash, she had an idea!

She put down her cup, looking steadily at the man opposite. Dare she make a suggestion – or would he just tell her to mind her own business?

'Mr Lloyd,' she began nervously, 'I've just had an idea. Er

– may I tell you?'

He nodded brusquely. 'Go on.'

'You say you *all* bring out the new models each spring?'

'Yes, at the annual Caravan Show at the Earl's Court Exhibition Centre. Why?'

'Then why not put out *your* new model before then – say this autumn? Jump the gun; then Caratech would only be following you. You'd still be the first, instead of just one of two next year.'

The words tumbled out, watching as he digested what she had said, and she saw a flash of interest, of relief, cross his face. Slowly he rubbed his jaw, murmuring, 'Yes, I think you've cracked it, young lady! Yes, we could do it. Get out an early prototype, plenty of advance publicity to titivate interest beforehand....' In his mind's eye, he could see it all. 'No one has ever brought out a new model in the autumn. But then it's an entirely new concept all round. Not just one with a few odd changed features as is the usual. Yes, we could do it! Not a word to anyone mind; this'll have to be really under the wraps stuff.'

By the time she left Mr Lloyd's office, he was quite friendly, and she blessed her moment of inspiration, vowing to insert a new clause in the JP Agency's directive – no secret work for temporary secretaries!

Mr Lloyd's secretary smiled as she saw Julie pass her desk.

'All through, Mrs Prescott?'

'Yes, thanks.' Julie glanced at her watch. 'Just trying to decide whether I've time to have lunch and get back to base before my two o'clock appointment.'

'Why not join me here in our canteen.' The middle-aged woman's face was pleasantly friendly. 'Then you can use our locker room to tidy up and go on from here. Nice day for a walk.'

'I've got my car, but thanks, I'd like to take you up on the use of your canteen.'

It was noisy with the hum of chattering voices, the sound of cutlery, but Julie's guide found a fairly peaceful corner.

'Reserved for the MD's secretary,' she grinned. It was a nice meal. She chose a prawn salad, followed by lemon mousse and a pot of really good coffee. She found she had a lot in common with the secretary and time passed quickly.

'I'll leave you here to freshen up, Mrs Prescott. Nice to have met you.'

'Thanks, I've enjoyed it.'

She found that she'd got to drive through the town centre and out the other side. Lunch-time traffic was still dense, but for once she didn't fume. She had plenty of time and at each red traffic light, found time to admire the large beds of golden daffodils, the pink almond blossom on the trees lining some of the wide streets. Spring in Wales was beautiful, she thought, and wondered what Mike was doing right then.

And the longing to see him again rose like a real pain inside her. Just in time she stopped herself looking in the mirror. Lately she had been inspecting her face closely, looking for tell-tale signs of age; imagining any new wrinkle, the odd grey hair.

Today in her new suit and blouse, and with the sun highlighting the bronze glints in her hair, she knew she looked good. And the sense of well-being gave her the confidence she needed for her next appointment.

He was younger than she expected and within a few moments, she realised that this was a youth orientated concern. Quietly and concisely she explained who she was and what she wanted.

'My client wishes me to act as a go-between – for the time being.'

'So – how do we know he's any good?' The words were crisp, slightly harsh. But Julie smiled positively.

'He's the best! I know, I've seen his awards. His firm will fight to keep him. It'll possibly mean litigation. He – we want to know, will you go that far?'

'To get the best – yes, Mrs Prescott.'

At that, she was able to expand a little, and by the time she left the huge block of offices, she was certain Peter Rogers could go ahead with his application for the post.

Back at her office about three o'clock, she slumped behind her desk, suddenly feeling drained, but pleased with all she had achieved so far. A few minutes later the blonde head of Debra Deane poked round the door.

'Just finished with my first computer client, Julie. By the way, your Mike Stephens called.' She paused and Julie thought she looked like a cat who'd found the cream jug. 'He's a dish; we had quite a chat....'

Swallowing hard on a fierce surge of blind jealously, Julie asked thickly, 'Did you now. What did he want?'

Five

Debra was examining her highly polished nails. 'He wondered if you could meet him for lunch. Seems he'd had to go into town about a planning permission or something.'

'What time did he ring?'

'About noon.' The blonde girl paused, her slanted green eyes gloating. 'I told him I didn't know when you'd be back and ... well, I offered to meet him. We had a quick snack in St David's Centre. Hope you don't mind, Julie?'

Feeling like she'd like to strangle the other girl, Julie said huskily, 'Mind? Why should I? Mike's a free agent.'

'Heaven knows why – he's gorgeous,' Debra breathed as she closed the door behind her, leaving her boss fuming.

I'm right, Julie told herself fiercely, Mike is a free man – I just can't let him clutter up my life. She bit her soft bottom lip, the ache inside her getting worse as she pictured he and Debra together. Was he another like Jeff, her ex-husband? She couldn't bear that.

That night, she waited anxiously for his phone call, but it never came. She went to bed early to lie there chiding herself for wanting him so. After their lovemaking, she had expected to hear from him the following day, to see him the next night again.

She was almost asleep when the phone rang. Reaching over to switch on the bedside lamp, she saw that it was past eleven o'clock.

'Julie? Hi darling, it's me. Sorry to ring you so late, but I've just put in a hard slog over at the cottage. How are you?' The deep timbre of his voice sent shivers of longing through her.

'Sleepy!' she answered with an affected little yawn. 'I've had a busy day too. Sorry I wasn't able to meet you at lunchtime, Mike, but I hear that Debra consoled you nicely.'

She heard his chuckle and was annoyed with herself for letting him know that it had bothered her.

'She's a bit too pushy for my taste, Julie. Won't take no for an answer. Had to pay for her lunch, too,' he grumbled. And at that she laughed aloud.

'Are you in bed?' he asked.

'Mmm,' she murmured, quite unaware of how seductively enticing her voice sounded.

'Wish I was there with you, don't you?'

'Don't I what...?' she teased, her lips close to the receiver.

'Wish I was there in bed with you,' he repeated.

'And not with the glamourous Debra?' There was a pause, and then she heard him say, 'What about the affluent Alun?'

'Oh, he's still around. Took me to the ... ' she mentioned the new eating place, wanting to make him jealous too.

'As long as you only talk business, I don't mind. Don't forget, boss lady, I'm going to be the man in your life from now on.' The possessive masculinity of his words made the pulse in her throat tighten as she murmured, 'I'll have something to say about that, Mike.' Again there was the sound of his soft laughter.

'I'll be over tomorrow night. Is that OK?'

Weakly, still longing to see him, she gave her assent.

'Oh and Julie, I'll bring my toothbrush this time. Night darling, sleep tight. I shall.'

And with a click, the phone went dead.

Damn, he thinks he can walk into my life just as he likes. She thumped the pillow, angry with herself and her weakness where Mike was concerned. Ever since he'd first walked into her office, he'd turned her life upside down. It has got to stop, she thought. But somehow the resolution was cold comfort and before she finally slept, she found herself planning what to give him to eat the next evening!

She had to work hard the next day so that she could leave earlier. She skipped lunch and shopped for food instead. She planned to give Mike lamb chops and all the trimmings, a bottle of good red wine and liqueur with their coffee. And then remembering his appetite, she bought an expensive cheesecake from the delicatessen.

Like a young girl on her first date, she showered and changed into a low cut sweater and full skirt, liberally dabbing her pulses with perfume. The chops were cooking nicely and the table looked inviting as she switched on the wall lights and gas fire. And all the time her heart thudded like a drum inside her ribcage, her whole body aching with longing.

At the sound of the doorbell, she drew in a deep breath, trying to still the pounding inside her. He stood there, a bunch of wild flowers in his hand.

'Hello, Mike.' God, he looked young. Or was it just the sparkle in his dark eyes? She raised her face to his like a child – and kissed him like a woman!

'Mmm, you smell nice,' he nuzzled her neck. 'And you taste good enough to eat. I've missed you, boss lady....' And his fervent kisses on her mouth showed how much.

Julie felt the room spin, dazed by the effect he had on her. After all, she'd been kissed many times before. But she knew the difference was that she'd never enjoyed it so much before; never felt the complete devastation of having her feelings laid bare, leaving her nothing of herself that wasn't affected by him.

'You missed me too?' he murmured and a faint smile of satisfaction touched the corners of his mouth. Without answering his question, she asked, 'I suppose you're hungry?'

'Starving! And sick of baked beans. I'm a lousy cook.' As he spoke, he was peering into a saucepan on the stove. 'I don't know which I'm hungriest for – the dinner or the cook!'

It was a great meal, with Mike wise-cracking as he ate, telling her every other bite what a fantastic cook she was. Telling her of the progress he'd made at the cottage, discussing the problems lightly.

'It's going to be a hellish long job though, Julie. I'm worried you'll be gone off me long before it's finished. I get sick to my stomach thinking of Alun Jones and all the other prosperous blokes you meet. They can afford to take you out and dine you. Instead, here you are at home – feeding me.'

'Poor Mike,' she teased, 'when I'm broke and you're an up and coming property owner, you can wine and dine me. Talking of wine....' She held out her empty glass and he refilled it. 'Does it matter these days who pays what? I like being with you, so stop griping. Here's to chops and down with beans on toast.'

As they ate the cheesecake they began to talk shop. Mike was settling down well in his new job and listened intently as Julie discussed hers, putting in a suggestion now and then.

'Trouble is, things are not too good all round; lots of firms are laying off key men, not taking them on,' he told her. 'Only today I heard that one of our chaps is being made redundant. Good bloke, too....'

'What does he do?' she asked.

'He's in the engineering section – a designer in aerodynamics – streamlining stuff. Top class chap.'

As she cleared away the plates and started the coffee, she

suddenly remembered something.

'Mike, when I was at that caravan builders, I heard that they needed a chap to help design a new model – a specially streamlined thing. I'm not too sure if I've got it right, but....'

'Say, that's great! I'll tell him to give you a call; go on your list, and you can see if you can place him.'

They had finished their coffee, sipped their brandies, half listening to a throbbing country and western tape she'd left running. Putting down his glass, Mike reached out a long arm, and with a contented sigh, pulled her close to his side.

'Now, my darling, the eating's done, the drinking's over, and no more business talk.'

'So,' she grinned up at him. 'What had you in mind to follow?' As if she didn't know!

'This.' He kissed her cheek. 'And this.' And he kissed her mouth. 'Lots and lots of this....'

At his touch, her body was traitorously aware of every masculine inch of the man who held her. She wanted him so badly; couldn't wait for him to take her to bed. And her cheeks burned at the thought of her own wantonness, disgusted by her weakness.

'Did you bring your toothbrush?' she asked, hoping he'd stay the night.

'And my razor and a clean shirt. Can I stay?'

'Right now, you help with the dishes.'

As he dried the pans, she couldn't help thinking of the morning and how she'd look. Usually she cleaned and creamed her face every night and wore a comfy old nightie. And her lips twitched as she pictured Mike's face if he saw her looking like that!

As she rinsed round the sink and wrung out the dishcloth, he slid his arms round her waist with his lips nibbling at the nape of her neck. The tingle from his touch ran right down to her toes.

'Hey, let me dry my hands....' she protested.

'Can't wait any longer.' And he turned her into his arms, holding her close to the lithe length of him. As she knew the strength of his arousal, she felt a tiny answering flame curl in the pit of her stomach. Beneath her hands, his heart was beating a rapid tattoo, and his breathing seemed to be giving him some trouble.

'I'm mad about you, you know that.' He punctuated his words with kisses on her eyes, her neck and her lips, filling her with heady delight.

'Oh Mike, this is stupid. You and me ... I'm older than you....' He stopped the words with a hard kiss that cut off her breath too.

'Look, darling, what does age, or money, or any of those things matter between you and me when we feel like this? This is all that matters – that this is good between us, my love.'

And it was *so* good to feel his hands caressing her spine under her sweater and then the roughened feel of his thumbs coaxing her nipples into taut erection, turning her breathing into little gasps of desire.

'Can I stay, Julie. You're not going to turn me out later?' Dazed, besotted by her need for him, she nodded her head.

'Stay,' she whispered. And even as she did, a warning voice in her brain made her wonder if she'd regret it later.

After Mike had used the bathroom, she brushed her teeth and grimaced at her image in the mirror; tonight she would leave her face. As she went into the bedroom, she saw that he had switched on bedside lamp and turned down the duvet. Her fingers shook as she began to undress.

'Here let me. I have this fantasy all the time – of undressing you like this....'

Sensually, slowly, he kissed each part of her body as he laid it bare, until at last she stood there before him – naked. His eyes darkened with ardour, and his hands on her breasts tormented them to a heavy fullness, her nipples rigid with longing.

'Oh Mike,' she breathed, 'I don't think I've ever felt like this before.'

'Or me, darling. God, I want you.....' Lifting her swiftly, he laid her on the bed and joined her there, to cradle her tenderly in strong young arms.

Julie breathed in the male scent of his body, running her fingers hungrily through the mat of fine dark hair that arrowed down from his chest to his navel. Down, down, she trailed her fingers, teasing, stroking, almost driving him crazy with blatant desire, with excited anticipation.

He reached out and captured her wandering hand, and with a groan, leaned on his elbows, looking down into her face with a dark flame of pure lust in his grey eyes. And as Julie saw it, a seductive warmth curled through her, making her feel young and feminine and desirable and very capable of giving....

Later, as they lay, limbs entwined, satiated by the depths of their lovemaking, they kissed softly, gently, until they fell asleep.

It was still dark though the moon shed a subdued glow through the open curtains when she stirred sleepily. Her head was cradled close in the curve of his shoulder, and in the half light, she was just able to see his face. It looked young and vulnerable and defenceless, with nothing on it of the passionate man she had just known. Again the longing to touch him overwhelmed her and she trailed her fingers hesitatingly over his chest, her eyes soft with the memory of their union.

Suddenly his eyes flew open, thick lashes flickering.

'You look like a cat who's just finished a bowl of cream,' he murmured, his breath warm on her cheek.

'If you stroke me again, I'll purr,' she agreed huskily and snuggled closer.

'If I stroke you, we'll both start purring,' he warned softly. and once more, slowly this time, exploring every inch of each other's body, they made love. This time, he waited, taking her time and time again, to the edge of madness, only to pause, tormenting, teasing, until she cried out her need.

'Now – oh Mike, now....' she gasped as she writhed beneath him. Tiny beads of perspiration bedewed her brow, and she groaned softly at his deeper thrusts.

Then with a blaze, the world spun out of control and stars shot brightly behind her closed eyelids. Down, down again to earth they fell – to lie panting, struggling to quell the rapid beat of two thudding hearts.

'Cup of coffee, love? Come on, puss cat, stir yourself.'

Julie pulled herself up out of the depth of heavy slumber to find Mike shaking on bare shoulder, a mug of steaming coffee in his hand. 'I'll have to go, Julie. Don't know what the traffic will be like from here.' He reached down and kissed her thoroughly. 'Thanks, darling, be seeing you.'

And before she could ask him when, he disappeared and moments later she heard the front door slam. Bleary-eyed, aching all over, she gulped the coffee. Lord, she felt a mess and hoped Mike hadn't looked at her face too closely. There was the musky smell of copulation around her still, and she hurried through to take a hot shower. No time to wash and blow dry her hair this morning, she thought ruefully, hoping she didn't look too hung-over, too dark-eyed.

She saw Megan eyeing her with a knowing look on her round Welsh face.

'Heavy night, Julie?' she asked slyly with one black eyebrow raised enigmatically.

'You could say that. Sorry I'm a bit late. What's on, Megan?'

'I've got to leave you to it. We're a temp short today – off sick, so I'm having to stand in.' Megan didn't sound too pleased. 'I wanted to go for a fitting this afternoon – my wedding dress,' she reminded Julie.

'Oh dear! Don't worry, Megan, I'll ring round and see who I can come up with.'

Megan shrugged, 'It's all right, I've cancelled the fitting. See you.'

The phone rang. It was Peter Rogers.

'Can you meet me, Julie, tonight? Have dinner with me; I've lots to tell you.' For a moment she hesitated, wondering if Mike would be coming to see her. 'It's important,' Peter urged, so she agreed to meet him in the centre of Cardiff after she'd closed the office.

She had just replaced the receiver to start her letters, when the phone rang again.

'Hi, Julie! Awake now?' At the sound of Mike's deep voice, she forgot her letters, Peter Rogers, the missing temp, everything. All she saw in her mind's eyes was Mike lying beside her last night, his body lean and vitally alive, with a face that was a bit too handsome for her peace of mind.

'Just about. Were you late for work?' she asked.

'Not at all. I'm just ringing to ask about tonight?' An intense wave of disappointment swamped her then.

'I'm having dinner with Peter Rogers tonight, sorry.'

'Well, cancel. Old Pete won't mind,' he told her confidently.

'I'm sorry but it's business, I can't cancel, Mike. And I can't really suggest you come along too either. It's highly private.'

'Don't bother, Julie, I never did fancy three in a bed,' he replied tersely. His anger sparkled over the wires, filling her with dismay.

'I suggest you get in touch with Debra then; I'm sure she'll oblige.' Through the heat of her anger, she heard him catch his breath, and then came a faint chuckle.

'Sorry, darling, I'm being childish. It's just that I want to see you, be with you all the time. Of course you've got your business to run. I'm sorry,' he repeated apologetically. 'I'll give you a ring tomorrow, Julie. Bye, love.'

Julie was surprised to see that the hand replacing the receiver was shaking a little, and she cursed herself for being so affected by anything Mike could say. She sorted her post and then went through to the Exclusive Executives suite, to find Debra interviewing a prospective client. The tall blonde's manner was cool and courteous, obviously in full control. But Julie couldn't help notice that she used her incredibly long eyelashes frequently, giving the bemused man opposite her the full benefit of her lovely green cat's eyes.

Fifteen minutes later, Debra came through to speak to Julie, a complacent smile on her beautiful face.

'He's a computer expert. I'll have no trouble placing him, but I upped his fee, Julie. He'll earn it back in no time.'

Julie wasn't sure she approved, but decided not to disagree, so she smiled and said, 'I noticed he was falling for your eye-batting technique.'

'What I always say is – if you've got it, flaunt it!' The other girl patted a blonde curl, almost purring like a sleek Siamese cat, Julie thought.

'Since it's working in my favour, all I can say is – more power to your elbow, Debra.' Deep down she wanted to add, But don't try it on Mike; he's mine.

Back in her own office, she sat for a moment frowning at her thoughts. She was becoming too obsessed by Mike. He was getting to be like a drug; one that she was fast becoming addicted to. He was young; would probably pass on to someone younger than herself as soon as he tired of their lovemaking. At the moment, he seemed as crazy about her as she was about him. But then, he had nothing to lose, had he?

She was busy all day, but even as she worked, Mike's face kept coming between her and the files on her desk. All too often, she found herself day-dreaming; remembering how wonderful their loving had been the night before.

Wishing she had time to go home again to change, she made the best use she could of the ladies' room and then went to meet Peter Rogers. It was too early for the regular diners, so they had the full attention of the maitre d' and a small alcove to themselves.

'Nice to see you again, Julie,' Peter's eyes were full of admiration, telling her that he found her attractive. And in spite of her obsession with Mike, she couldn't help the little glow of pleasure that gave her.

He ordered their drinks and then consulted her carefully on her choice of the menu, so that she quickly relaxed. As they ate, they talked pleasantly and he took an interest in all she had to say. Julie was enjoying the well-cooked meal, finding that she really was hungry. She enjoyed too the warm admiration mirrored in the eyes of the fond-looking man opposite.

Over coffee, they talked business.

'It seems they're ready to go, Julie. My present employers are fighting every inch of the way. I can't work for three months; severence of pay; calling in my car and so on....'

'You're working with my legal friend, I hope?' Julie queried.

'Certainly.' Peter leaned back, his long fingers playing with a coffee spoon. 'They're working on the new people – to get three months' salary out of them, a firm's car, moving expenses and all legal costs.'

Dubiously, Julie asked, 'Will they do all that, do you think, Peter?'

He grinned confidently.

'I'm pretty sure they will. They want me and are willing to wait and pay. Meanwhile, I shall be working out an entirely new sales strategy. They need it. Their present sales force is being wasted.'

'So....' She let out a soft sigh.

'So, I thought I'd better put you in the picture, Julie. Also I want you to be there at the final signing of my new contract. You and the legal eagle!'

'Yes, I see. I'll be there, Peter.'

'Good practice for you. You'll know what to look for in any future contracts for your clients,' he told her.

'Thanks. You've been a nice first case to handle.' Her smile lit up her face.

'Hope you'll remember me.' He paused and then went on, 'In fact, I'd like to see you again, Julie, often. And not for business reasons.'

She bit her lip, not sure how to answer him.

'Well, you know I'm pretty busy, Peter. The new agency will take some getting off the ground. And I'm also still running the JP Agency.' She went on to tell him that only today she'd been without her assistant, Megan. 'So,' she put in quietly, 'I can't promise....'

'You're involved somewhat with Mike and the accountant chap, Alun Jones, aren't you?' Julie's lips tightened, and he hurriedly added, 'Sorry, I shouldn't have said that, but....'

'I'm not involved, as you put it, Peter, no commitment to

either.' Even as she spoke, she knew she was kidding herself. Her body, if not her heart and mind, was deeply committed to Mike.

'Well, I'll give you a ring; perhaps we can have a meal or something together, Julie.'

'I'd like that very much, Peter. Now I'm afraid I must go.' As their waiter bowed them out, she shook Peter's hand and thanked him.

'I'll be in touch,' he promised.

The rest of that week was busy – hectic at times. Like when an urgent call was put through to her desk.

'It's your doctor, Julie, for you.' She picked up her phone.

'Yes, Dr Simpson. Julie Prescott here.'

'Ah Julie – I need your help. My secretary's hurt her right wrist rather badly and I just can't manage without someone to replace her.' He sounded harassed, and she could picture the worry in his tired old eyes. But where on earth could she find him a medical secretary? They were a rare breed and hardly ever out of a job. Certainly those she'd had to deal with were all well placed.

'I'll have to give it some thought, Dr Simpson. I'll ring you back, shall I?'

'Thanks. And please, Julie, I'm desperate.' She made a soothing noise and then hung up, mentally running her mind's eye through the possibles.

'Megan, I wonder if Maisie would do me a favour? Her little boy's at school now.'

'I don't think her husband's too keen on her working, if I remember rightly,' Megan replied slowly.

'Get me her number,' Julie told her, not too confident of any success. She recognised Maisie's cheerful voice at once.

'It's Julie Prescott, Maisie; you know, the JP Agency. And

I'm in a jam and wondered if you could possibly help me? Dr Simpson, my doctor needs a medical secretary – just while his own gets over a bad wrist. Good pay – only a short spell. How about it?'

Even as she spoke, Julie felt doubtful. There was a pause and then, 'Julie, I'd love to help out. I'm going up the wall since the offspring started to school. Let me see – I'll check with my pal next door about collecting him at four, shall I? I'll ring you back.'

And in a very short time, she did. But the news wasn't so good.

'Rotten luck, Julie. You see, my neighbour's pregnant – half way there – and it's her monthly antenatal clinic tomorrow. She can't miss it; they're doing some tests. What a shame! Of course, it *would* just be tomorrow....' Maisie sounded regretful, and Julie put in quickly,

'Could I bring him from school? Keep him here until you, or she, are home?'

'Would you? Oh, that'll be fine. I'll let his teacher know you'll be collecting him.'

For a few more minutes, they exchanged instructions and finally Julie was able to let Dr Simpson know he'd have an experienced secretary (complete with her own medical dictionary) starting in the morning.

'Bless you, Julie my dear, you've been a great help.'

The following afternoon at four o'clock found her collecting a sturdy little boy from his fussy teacher. He stood, his crumpled school cap askew, looking up at her with dubious eyes.

'Will I see Mummy soon?' His bottom lip wobbled threateningly, and she crouched down to his level.

'Mummy's been helping out at my doctor's, Jamie. You know, writing his letters for him. She'll be home soon, but she asked me to collect you from school for her.'

Jamie still regarded her solemnly and she held out her hand.

'How about if we call in the shop and buy something for you to play with? A jigsaw puzzle maybe?'

'And a sweetie bar?' Young Jamie saw no reason why he shouldn't make the most of his opportunity. Julie smiled down at him and nodded.

'You can choose one – only one!'

Ten minutes later she steered a happy little boy clutching a large flat box and a bar of chocolate into her office.

'Oh, he's a pet!' Megan whispered as she took his blazer and cap and gave him a glass of orange. In no time, she and Julie and Jamie were all squatting down on the carpet trying to find the right pieces of the jigsaw she'd bought. Jamie wasn't much help and was inclined to get a bit cross when his piece didn't fit. But with a little guile and a great deal of patience, the two girls managed to amuse him and the time flew by.

'Can anyone join in down there?'

Three faces, three pairs of eyes looked up in surprise at the sound of the deep laughing voice coming from the doorway. Flushed and dishevelled, Julie sprang to her feet.

'Mike! I wasn't expecting you.' She glanced at her watch. 'Good grief, is that the time?'

Megan was trying to persuade Jamie to gather up the unfinished puzzle, while Julie hurriedly began to clear her desk.

'Aren't you going to say hello?' came a husky whisper in her ear as he kissed the nape of her neck. 'Thought we'd have a meal…' he began and she wailed, 'I've nothing in – I've been too busy.' This time he placed one long forefinger over her lips.

'Give me your key and leave the rest to me,' he demanded

and wouldn't brook a refusal.

Megan gave her boss a sympathetic grin. It wasn't often Julie lost her cool. The heated flush on her cheeks made her appear younger, and she couldn't help notice the look in her eyes as they followed the tall figure passing out of the office door.

'Come on, young man, your mother'll be wondering where you've got to.' Julie helped the little boy with his blazer and cap, fixed the box lid and gathered up her handbag and briefcase. 'Sorry I've kept you, Megan.' The Welsh girl chuckled.

'That work I liked, Julie. He's a poppet.' There was a tinge of maternal longing in Megan's voice that was strangely echoed in Julie's heart too.

When she finally got to Maisie's neat little semi-detatched, that hint of longing almost became one of envy. Some girls had everything!

But as she turned the car towards her flat, she pulled herself together. Domesticity wasn't for her. She had her businesses to run and she meant to climb as high as she could without any ties.

The lights were all blazing and there was a heavenly smell coming from the kitchen as Mike came through to greet her. He took her jacket and bags, and dropping them down carelessly, reached out long arms to gather her close.

'Long time, no see, boss lady,'' he complained.

'Yes, just what have you been going?' she queried.

'Dating all the luscious blondes in Cardiff, didn't you know?' he grinned. A shaft of jealousy pierced through her until she looked up and saw the wicked look in the laughing eyes watching for her reaction.

'You couldn't afford one!'

'Certainly won't be able to after this.' With a sweep of his arm he indicated the beautifully laid table in the dining-room. He had found her best table mats, lit two candles, and in the centre was one lovely slender red rose, perfect in the candle-light. She touched it with a delighted smile.

'It's what I call a token rose, Julie my love,' he told her, 'represents the whole bouquet I can't afford just yet.'

'Mike, it's lovely.' She swung round and reached up to kiss him passionately. So was the meal that followed. He had searched the supermarket and delicatessens and come up with a veritable feast; one that even his limited cooking skill could cope with.

They began with a delicately flavoured lobster bisque, followed by wafer-thin Wiener schnitzel and a selection of tiny new vegetables. He had defrosted a lovely bombe surprise that tasted heavenly and even remembered her favourite dark chocolate mints to serve with their coffee.

Slowly, with utter satisfaction, Julie ate her way through the meal, realizing she's eaten nothing all day. She replaced her empty coffee cup with a sigh of pure bliss.

'That was super, darling. And what a lovely surprise, too. Didn't think you....' She paused, not knowing quite how to go on.

'One day, when the cottage is finished, when I'm made a director, we'll eat every night like this,' he promised.

They both cleared away the dishes and tidied up the kitchen, for she knew she'd have no time in the morning to do so.

As they sat cuddled close in each other's arms on the settee, she thought wistfully of what he'd promised. But deep down, she knew that this lovely time couldn't last. Sooner or later, he would find someone – younger, nearer his own age.

As he reached over and found her lips, she dismissed her sombre thoughts and gave herself up to the moment. Why not take what Mike offered, enjoy today without worrying about the doubtful future?

They made love twice that night, and before they finally slept, Mike whispered, 'Julie love, I just hate the thought of going back to that awful place of mine after this. It seems worse every time....'

Once more she slipped out of bed first early the next morning, loath to let Mike see her until she'd done her face. She'd have to leave her usual morning chores to do tonight, she mused, glancing at the overflowing linen basket. Seeing Mike's shaving kit and toothbrush alongside her toiletries on the bathroom shelf, she wondered what it would be like to have them there permanently, or until such time as he found someone else...?

Six

At work the tempo increased as word began to get around about Exclusive Executives, and first one firm and then another recommended the use of the new agency. Julie found she needed to make more use of Alun and his sound advice. She knew he still hoped to persuade her to marry him and she tried hard to keep their relationship on a platonic basis.

When he rang up one day with some information she had been seeking, he ended up asking her out to dinner.

'No can do, Alun. I simply must catch up both here and at home. Besides all these working lunches and dinners with clients and propective employers is not good for my figure,' she told him with a laugh. Actually, it wasn't all a joke. She knew she had to watch her diet; couldn't afford to put on weight at her age.

'OK then, Julie my dear. How about a nice, long healthy day in the country? Let's go out on Sunday, you and I. Far from the madding crowd.' His soft lilting voice was coaxing and she found herself suddenly agreeing.

'Good,' Alun was pleased. 'I'll pick you up ten o'clock Sunday morning. And Julie – wear some stout shoes, mmm?'

'You mean I've actually got to walk?' she teased. 'See you then, Alun. Bye.'

It might not be wise to encourage him, but a day in the country sounded wonderful. But on Friday afternoon when Mike rang to arrange their weekend, he was coldly angry when she told him.

'Alun's taking me out on Sunday, Mike. Sorry, but I did promise him last Monday. It's instead of a meal out. He thinks I need some fresh air and exercise.'

'You could get both helping me over at the cottage.' He made no effort to disguise his disappointment. 'I thought we'd spend Saturday night together too.'

'We could still have Saturday together, Mike,' she pointed out quietly.

'That's not good enough!' His voice was thick with frustration. 'You'll soon have to decide who you want to be with, Julie, me or Alun Jones!' And with that he hung up, leaving her gazing hopelessly at the phone in her hand.

As she placed it on its cradle, she felt her temper start to rise. Mike was angry because he wouldn't be sharing her bed on Saturday night, wasn't he?

That meant, too, she would be on her own with no date for Saturday night. Damn Mike and his childish jealousy; he had no claim on her or her time. He wanted to come and go as he pleased and expected her to be hanging around 'on a sky hook' waiting for his calls.

When the phone rang again, she snatched it up ready to do battle if he'd rung to apologize. But it wasn't Mike, and she hat to swallow her angry retort.

'Hello, Julie, Peter Rogers here. I know it's er – cheek, short notice an all that, but I've got two tickets for that fantastic show on at Cardiff theatre for tomorrow night. I don't suppose there's any chance of your being free?' He paused anxiously.

'Oh, hello Peter. Nice to hear from you. Tomorrow night...?' She hated anyone to know she was dateless on a Saturday night. Then she decided on the truth and quickly explained how she came to be free to go with him.

'I can't be too late though, Peter. Alun's threatened a

healthy lot of walking all day Sunday.'

'Fair enough. Thanks, Julie. I'll pick you up…' He chatted amicably for a few moments before hanging up.

Well, thought Julie, rather smugly, that'll teach Mike and Alun not to consider me their exclusive property!

That evening, she did her shopping for the week, and on Saturday morning cleaned the flat and did some laundry. Raking through her wardrobe, she put out suitable clothes for the next day and decided to wear a new catsuit for her date with Peter.

Her hair gleamed, showing off the chestnut rinse she'd just used. Her face, flushed and shiny from her bath, soon took on a more sophisticated hue as she applied her make-up. Her eyeshadow matched the blue/green catsuit, and skilfully she applied a second coat of mascara to her long eyelashes.

She had bought nail varnish to match the eyeshadow and now she wondered if she'd the courage to use it. Why not? Recklessly she applied two coats and was still thinking it a little over the top when the door bell announced Peter's arrival.

'Hello, Julie. You look fantastic!' He looked rather dishy himself, she thought as she gave him a drink.

'I'm not too sure about my nails though.' She held out a slender hand for his inspection and he whistled softly.

'I like my women sophisticated,' he laughed, though privately he didn't really go for the blue/green nails bit.

The show was good, prior to its opening in the London West End. They had a drink in the crowded little bar during the interval and both Julie and Peter were hailed by several business acquaintances.

Altogether she found it a pleasant evening, with no stress or undercurrents. No one to get uptight or jealous, she told herself as she waited for Peter to claim his car.

'I've really enjoyed this evening, Julie. We must do it again some time.' He waited while she found her doorkey. Both knew that tonight had been a stop-gap date for both of them. Yet why not? Neither of them was attached or committed.

'Yes, we must. And thanks, Peter. Now I must go....'

'Yes, I know. Goodnight, Julie,' and he placed a friendly kiss on her lips and turned to go.

The early morning sun woke Julie, and she stretched luxuriously, looking forward to her day out. She had a leisurely breakfast and left everywhere tidy. A quick shower and shampoo refreshed her and she dressed quickly in denim jeans and cotton sweater. She planned to wear a lightweight blouson anorak – just in case of a spring shower.

As she finished her make-up she caught sight of her nails, but decided to leave the somewhat outlandish varnish. She ruffled through her drawer and came up with a matching blue/green silk square to knot around her throat. Her trainers were rather shabby but very comfortable. She checked her small shoulder bag and was giving her hair a final brush when Alun arrived.

His open face beamed a greeting and he looked almost young this morning with a colourful tee shirt under his suede jacket. His eyes lit up the sight of Julie waiting for him.

'Oh good, you're ready! Come on then, love.' As he handed her into his car, he put a small pile of brochures into her lap. 'Been doing my homework,' he told her.

She scanned the leaflets as he drove the car out of town and towards Chepstow.

'I never knew there was so much to the Forest of Dean, Alun.'

'According to that, they've created a new Culture Trail as well as the Nature one, etc. I've booked a table for lunch at the Speech House Hotel.'

'Yes, here it is,' Julie looked at the map with interest. 'Good lord, they still hold a Verderers' Court in the Speech House, did you know? It's been held there for hundreds of years.' She turned a page. 'And the miners still living in the Forest can mine for coal free.'

With a sigh of pleasure, she leaned back enjoying the warmth of the sun through the car window. She had always liked the quaint town of Chepstow with its old Castle ruins overlooking the muddy river; its lovely bridge and its narrow little main street, now peacefully by-passed by the wide new road.

This morning there was hardly any traffic about as they passed through sleepy villages and small country towns. Little groups were making their way to early church services; newsagents' shops were busily dispensing the Sunday papers. All quiet and serene and peaceful – away from the city's rat-race and rush, she thought pensively.

With Alun she could chat or keep quiet as the mood took her. Today he had set out to please her and so kept their conversation light and uncontroversial.

Gradually the countryside became more heavily wooded as the road wound between hills and valleys. Woodmen's cottages, stone-built and sturdy, showed here and there in the clearings. Alun drove slowly now, letting her admire the views. She caught glimpses of sun on water as they passed tiny ponds and smooth lakes.

'Look Alun, there … oh, it's gone. I saw a deer over there through the trees.'

'This forst used to be full of 'em,' he told her. 'In the old days a man was hanged for stealing one. Now there's venison on the menu sometimes at Speech House.'

There were dozens of smaller paths leading off the main road through the Forest. Here and there they saw convenient car-parks partially hidden by the shrubs and trees. Picnic areas with glorious views were scattered here and there, all well sign-posted.

'Come on – walkies!' Alun parked the car and they stretched their legs thankfully. With the aid of the guide book, they found the start of the Culture Trail. Beneath their feet the old bracken, dead twigs and leaves crackled. Round the boles of tall trees, Julie caught sight of the last of the spring wild flowers, clumps of primroses, sweet-smelling violets, bluebells and foxgloves. The trees were all green-leafed, bushes were bursting into blossom; on some, catkins hung, low and heavy with pollen. In some places, the tall trees arched high above their heads.

'Like a cathedral,' Julie breathed, her face first dappled with sunlight then shaded by leaves.

Then she suddenly caught her breath; ahead, the long shafts of sunlight had lit up a beautiful, hugh stained-glass window. Except it wasn't a window exactly, for the vast oblong was suspended by concealed wires to trees on either side of the path, so that it hung there above their heads, casting glorious multi-coloured beams of light over their faces.

'It's gorgeous, Alun,' she murmured, 'thank you for bringing me.' She stood enraptured, silently praising the artist whose concept this was. Reluctantly, she had to turn and follow Alun. Soon the sound of tinkling bells had led them down another path, and they came across several groups of hanging mobiles seemingly suspended in the air, giving off their soft chimes with every faint breeze.

On and on they walked, for the area was vast, and they

followed the flash-marked trees further and further, discovering new delightful surprises. They passed other people excitedly following the trail, but so dense were the woods, that it soon felt as if they were the only ones there. At last they came to the final showpiece. Situated high upon the pinnacle of a steep hill, they saw a giant-sized chair. Huge, like a throne, the legs, arms and every slat was made from a whole tree trunk. And as it stood there, silhouetted dark against the blue background of the sky, it looked like some monster king's throne.

'I don't think we'll climb up to the top, Julie. I reckon it looks better from here.'

She laughed. 'You mean you're pooped!'

'Not quite, but you *do* realize we've got a long walk back, don't you?' Indeed they had walked a long way without noticing the distance, but both enjoyed the leisurely stroll back to the car. The sun was getting quite warm, and there were more cars parked there now.

'Lord, I'm thirsty,' Alun mourned.

'So am I. We missed our coffee break, but it was worth it.' Julie took off her jacket and left it in the car when they drew up to the forecourt of the hotel. Inside all was quiet opulent comfort. They found a small table in the lounge overlooking the garden and Alun ordered drinks. Both asked for iced lagers to quench their thirsts, and Julie looked round, admiring the wealth of heavy oak beams, the ancient artefacts on the walls. Around them was the soft hum of voices, the smell of good food and flowers, the dark polished furniture invitingly comfortable.

But the highlight for Julie came with the sight of the big ancient hall that was now a dining-room. A raised balcony at the bottom end housed the heavy carved oak chairs and the mayoral seat used for the meetings of the Verderers' Court, going back to King Alfred's day so legend said. The wide open fireplace held logs and a collection of fine brass firedogs. Around the walls were shields, coats of arms, portraits and pictures of past visiting royalty.

'This is all rather grand,' Alun murmured. 'Hope the food matches it.' It did! Slowly, served by a soft-footed waitress, they ate through the haute cuisine meal, drank a bottle of good wine, and then returned to the sunny lounge for a tall pot of wonderful coffee.

Julie sighed contentedly; Alun certainly knew how to give a girl the best. And following the thought came one of Mike. How good it would have been if *he* had been the man at her side. Alun could afford all this, she thought ruefully, yet she would have gladly exchanged it for a day alone with Mike.

As if the sensual drift of her thinking had somehow transferred itself to Alun, she suddenly became aware of his arm along the back of the seat resting warmly on her shoulders. She refrained from moving away, not wanting to hurt him, wishing once move that he didn't love her. The utter waste of such caring love seered her heart.

Draining the last of the coffee, they rose to go. Alun paid the bill while she found the ladies' room – old-fashioned and genteel, with Victorian fittings and noisy plumbing.

Out again in the sunlight, he suggested they walk off the lunch. 'There's still a lot to see, mmm?' he queried. Quietly they strolled in and out of the leafy shadows and dappled sunlight, the air soft and warm with afternoon calm, disturbed only by the birds in the trees.

Once Julie felt Alun gently push back a lock of her hair and then later take her hand in his, linking their arms as they meandered along the pebbled tracks. They had been walking about an hour when they came to a quiet little dell away from the pathway.

'Let's have a breather,' he suggested, and before she could answer, he spread out his jacket over the crushed grass. With a sigh of satisfaction, he lowered himself to the ground, pulling her down beside him.

Julie's heart jerked; she didn't want this at all. She fancied she could hear his breathing quicken, or was it just the exertion? She knew she wasn't mistaken when she felt his arm encircle her waist, holding her closer. Before she could decide on her next move, he reached over, his bulk blotting out the sunlight and kissed her on the lips.

'Alun, don't....' She tried to push him away, hating herself, but knowing she had to stop him – now!

'Please, Julie, let me love you. If only you knew how I feel, darling....' His voice was ragged now, full of desire, wanting her, trying to force her to respond.

Her struggles only seemed to encourage and incite him, and for a few moments, she knew fear: startled and disgusted that she should come to know fear of Alun, dear devoted Alun. But just then as she tried to get free of his hold, his lips forcing hers apart with a fierceness that hurt, she *was* frightened. It was as if he had turned into someone else; someone she didn't know.

'Don't. Please, Alun, don't.....' Her words were forced from her dry throat as she struggled. Almost sobbing, she begged him to stop!

Then suddenly, he did stop and he let her go. She saw a dawning look of horror before he turned away, covering his face with his hands. Tears trickled slowly down her cheeks, and the lovely bright happiness of their day was shattered. And she knew that something good had been lost right then.

'Oh God, Julie, I'm sorry. How could I?' Alun's voice was raw with anguish and disgust at himself. 'Please, dearest, forgive me. I just lost my head.' His face was still cupped in his shaking hands, and pity made the tears flow down her cheeks.

'I … ' she began, her throat aching. 'I'm sorry too, but you frightened me, Alun.' Could a woman of her age and experience be scared of Alun, kind, gentle Alun?

But she *had* been frightened, and even then her heart was still throbbing against her ribcage, her pulse still pounding in her throat.

'Love can make a beast of a man, as well as a fool, I'm afraid, Julie. All I can say is – please forgive me. It – it won't happen again, I promise you.' At the depth of remorse in his voice, she swallowed convulsively, her words husky, 'I do forgive you, Alun. I made a fuss, panicked....'

'No, I came on too heavy and scared you. I'm sorry, Julie,' he repeated and then pulled himself to his feet. 'Shall we go?'

Dumbly she nodded and smoothed down her skirt and her hair as he picked up his jacket. There was an awkwardness between them now that was strange and had no part of their friendship. As if both were trying to gloss over that scene in the little copse.

But the memory of it hung there between them like a dark shadow, and Julie's heart ached for what had been lost perhaps for always.

'I won't come in, Julie.' He saw her to her door, his face tight shut, concealing his feelings.

'All right. Thanks for a grand day out. Hope my feet will recover.' She found herself babbling, trying to cover an awkward moment.

'Be seeing you.' With a sketchy lift of his hand, he went, leaving her watching his departure with sad eyes.

As spring moved into early summer, she didn't hear from

Mike all the following week. She made excuses to herself for him – he's working every night at the cottage, she told herself. She knew he was using all the spare time and the spare workmen he could find, doing most of the labouring, the fetching and carrying himself. The longer, lighter nights would be a godsend, she mused, longing to hear from him.

She couldn't really settle at work, wishing that every phone call was from him. At home, the quietness of her flat only emphasized the loneliness. It was at night, tossing and turning in her bed, that her thoughts gave her no peace, while her body burned for his touch. In the early hours of the morning, she would berate herself, calling herself a fool. She had behaved wantonly, practically seduced Mike, hadn't she? He wanted her, too, but not so desperately, she mourned, or he'd never be able to ignore her for days and days on end like this.

'You off colour, Julie?' Megan asked one morning, noticing the dark shadows beneath her boss's lovely eyes. 'Got a headache? I've got some tablets in my desk.'

'No, thanks, love. I couldn't sleep last night, that's all.'

Megan knew that things were going fairly well with Exclusive Executives, so she had her own views on what was bothering Julie, but she kept her thoughts to herself.

When the next day saw her employer looking more wan than ever, she said softly, 'Give him a ring, Julie. He might be sick or something.'

Julie's cheeks flushed, but Megan's voice had been kind, full of sympathy, so she answered gratefully, 'I think I will, Megan....'

It took several patient minutes to finally track Mike down at his workplace, and when she heard his voice she almost put down the receiver.

'Hello, who's there?'

At the faint exasperation in his tone, she took a deep breath and said, 'It's me, Julie. How are you, Mike? I thought you might be ill or something.'

'Julie! No, I'm OK – been busy.' His words were flat, giving nothing away, and she knew she had to make the first move.

'I – I'd like to see you, Mike. How about a meal at my place – tonight?' She tried hard to keep it light, but her voice sounded husky, almost pleading.

'What – no Alun tonight, Julie?'

'Mike, don't be like that. I want to see you, please.' Her voice cracked and Mike relented.

'OK, about seven, Must go, I'm wanted.'

'Yes, right. See you tonight.'

She leaned back in her seat, feeling drained; hating herself for her weakness. Then the thought of a night spent in Mike's arms cancelled out all else, and she was able to concentrate on her work until five o'clock.

She hurried round the shops, picking up food for their evening meal, adding a bottle of Mike's favourite wine and then drove home. By five to seven she was ready – make-up perfect, the table laid, savoury smells drifting in from the kitchen. Then the doorbell rang.

'Oh Mike.' She opened the door and gazed up at him, as if seeing him for the first time; not getting enough of the sight of him as he stood there. She looked up into his grey eyes, so intense beneath their fringe of dark lashes, and her throat ached with longing for the feel of him.

'Oh Julie,' he mimicked softly. 'I've missed you, boss lady.'

'Then why...?' she burst out angrily.

'I don't want to share you, Julie, with the affluent Mr Jones, that's all,' he replied flatly.

'You don't share me, but I need someone else in my life! I can't sit around her just waiting for you to put in an appearance or not, as the mood takes you, Mike.'

'All right, I'm sorry. Come here....' He held out his arms with a devastating smile and pulled her close. With a sigh, she reached up and his lips met hers, hovering, teasing, testing her reactions. For a while they kissed, both making up for lost time, both needing the other's nearness, reassurance.

Julie served up the meal, and as they ate, he asked, 'Well then, darling, how did your healthy Sunday go? Have a good time?'

She swallowed and then answered, trying not to remember how last Sunday had ended.

'Yes, it was great.' Something in her voice, or the look that shadowed her eyes, must have told Mike differently.

'So, what happened?' It was as if he could read her mind, she thought.

'I told you – we had a great time.'

'So ...?' Mike persisted, one dark eyebrow like a question mark.

'What do you mean – 'so'?' Her voice sharpened.

'Tell me what really happened. Did old Alun come on a bit strong?' The accuracy of his guess made her breath catch in her throat, and she swallowed hard, ready to deny it hotly. Mike was watching her, reading every nuance of expression on her give-away face. Damn him, she fumed. And then her anger drained away and she decided to tell him the truth.

'Yes, Mike, you're right. Alun lost his cool, and I got frightened.' His hands lying on the table tightened into hard fists.

'I see. I'll have to straighten him out.'

'No! Please Mike. He only lost control. It was my fault – being scared. I should have known Alun would never really hurt me.'

'All the same....' Mike's anger was still there as she went on 'I can't not see Alun, darling. He's got a financial interest in my business. Besides, I need him constantly. Need his help, his advice. I don't think it'll happen again. It was my fault; I've always known Alun fancies me, wants me to marry him.' She paused, trying hard to find the right words. 'In future, Mike, I'll make sure I don't get myself into a situation like Sunday's again. Now let's forget it.....'

'OK, as long as you remember – you're mine, Julie, and no one else's.'

How could he say that, she asked herself hotly as she washed the dishes? *He* wasn't ready to make a commitment; he never offered her marriage or a future of any kind. Dear heavens, why did she allow this to go on; why had she this foolish obsession for a man almost a decade younger, who offered her nothing at a time but a night of sex and lust? Her bitter thoughts kept pace with her angry movements as she scrubbed at the sink.

Yet she knew she couldn't go through another arid desert of time she'd just gone through – not seeing him at all; knew she would take whatever he was prepared to give and be grateful for it!

The depth of her need was all too apparent later that night as they made love with a sensuousness that had her body responding to him while her mind told her she shouldn't. Her whole being was racked with desire and she was appalled by her own wantonness.

Mike, jubilant in his triumph, laughed softly and whispered in her ear, 'Hey, lover, take it easy. You're such an intense little lady, aren't you?' He kissed her passionately. 'But as long as it's all for me....'

He was fierce and gentle by turns, taking her to heights

she'd never known before.

'Darling, how could we ever risk losing what we have between us?' he asked, nuzzling her neck, dropping little kisses all over her face, her eyes; gently soothing her into her first real sleep for ages.

In the following weeks he spent more and more time at her flat. He left spare clothes alongside hers in the wardrobe; dropped dirty shirts and socks into her linen basket in the bathroom.

Megan noticed the bloom on Julie's face, the look of contentment that lit up her hazel eyes in the days that followed.

'Glad to see you happy, Julie, but be careful! I don't want to see you get hurt again. And – well, nothing can come of it really, can it?' For once she sounded older than her boss.

'So – I'll burn the candle at both ends,' Julie laughed at the other girl's fears.

'Just mind you don't get burned, that's all.'

'Makes a lovely flame though, while it lasts!' Julie retorted. *While it lasts!* For a second, those words sent a shiver through her. Somehow, she vowed, she'd keep up with Mike; be young again with him and let the future go hang!

With the promise of summer, Julie found that her JP Agency list began to include senior school leavers, college graduates, all wanting jobs during the coming holiday period. With the increase of applicants came more and more urgent requests from firms needing temporary staff, extra employees for the tourist and holiday trade. To offset this, there was a lull in activity at the Exclusive Executives Agency. It wasn't the time of year when high tech firms sought new top men, or the whizz-kids of commerce looked for a change of position.

Megan's wedding date had been set for June 6th, and Mike

had promised to accompany Julie to the reception. Tactfully, Megan hadn't invited Alun.

The week before the wedding, Mike told Julie, 'I'm going to London this weekend, darling. Must see my parents; they're off to France for the summer.' The grandmother who had left him his cottage, had also willed to his parents a tiny holiday place in the south of France. So one night she helped him sort through his clothes. He also had a suit to go to the cleaner's in time for Megan's wedding.

Julie looked round the dark and dismal apartment, disgusted by the poor amenities he had there. He tried to laugh it off by telling her about his landlady.

'I've never seen her really sober, or without a cigarette dangling out of the corner of her mouth.'

Putting her arms round his waist, she hugged him close. 'Poor old Mike.'

'And do you know what she says when I complain?' He struck a truculent pose. 'An' what d'you expect for the money, boyo,' he mimicked, his eyes full of mischief. But Julie couldn't bear it for him and was glad to get out of there as quickly as possible.

Julie missed Mike that weekend and was too restless to do anything constructive, thankful that he would only be away for a short time.

Megan's wedding day dawned bright and fair, and the church was overflowing with friends and relatives. As the organ struck up 'Here comes the Bride' Julie turned to watch her walk slowly down the aisle on her nervous father's arm. Megan looked radiantly beautiful in her lace gown, her dark hair threaded with tiny white flowers.

A lump tightened in Julie's throat and memories of her own wedding day came flooding back. Please God, let Megan's marriage be a happier one, she prayed, as the tears pricked behind her eyelids.

'Here.' Quietly Mike passed her a clean hankie, his eyes full of tender understanding.

The reception was noisy, happy, with ribald advice flying back and forth to the new husband's embarassment. Julie couldn't help notice that Debra Deane was doing her utmost to monopolize Mike's attention. The blonde girl's beauty did its best to outshine the bride's, and Julie was dismayed by the surge of pure jealousy that rose in her breast as she watched Mike laughing down into Debra's upturned face.

She understood then how he felt when she had dates with Alun. Whether it was that thought, or the lovely sentimentality of the wedding she didn't know, but she did know she wanted more than the nebulous attachment at present between herself and Mike.

The bride changed out of her bridal finery and left amidst showers of rice, confetti and good wishes, leaving Julie with a turbulence of mixed feelings churning inside her.

'Come on, sweetheart, we're joining a crowd and going on to a night-club later.' Not caring who saw him, he cupped her face in his hands and placed a long and fervent kiss on her parted lips.

'You still look all weepy. But you look beautiful, boss lady, tears and all,' he told her and the look in his eyes made her heart contract with happiness.

And for the rest of the evening, he never left her side. They danced near together or linked close in each other's arms, laughing, drinking, kissing and loving. She felt like a young girl again and she enjoyed every moment of it. She and Mike ought to get out more, she thought drowsily on the way home in the early dawn.

It was very late when she awoke and slipped quietly out of

bed, leaving Mike sprawled there taking up two thirds of the
space.

In the bathroom, she regarded the reflection in the mirror
critically. Her smudged stale make-up, the late night of
smoke and wine had left their mark. She hastily washed her
face, touched her lip slightly with a soft lipstick and brushed
her hair. Still not satisfied at the way she looked, she
shrugged and went to make some coffee. Then carrying a
small tray and the Sunday papers, she went back to the
bedroom.

'Wake up time, Mike, my lad.'

'Go away,' came the groan in answer. With a grin, she
wafted a mug of coffee near to his nose. He rolled over,
peering hazily up at her through thick tangled lashes. 'I might
just survive with that.' He reached over, grabbed the coffee
and gulped gratefully.

'You've got your priorities right, woman. That's number
one. And now number two.' He replaced the mug and pulled
her down across his chest to kiss her long and deeply, his
hands in her hair holding her tightly. 'Mmm,' he murmured
against her lips, 'I could settle for waking like this every
morning.'

Struggling free, she raised herself on her elbows and
looked down at his face. Apart from a dark-shadowed chin,
he showed no signs of last night's capers.

'Oh no, you've got your priorities in the wrong order.
You'd need to reverse number one and two, I'm afraid.'

At that, he started to kiss her with vigour, at the same time
tickling and teasing her. Of course she had to retaliate, and for
a few lovely moments they romped and wrangled like children.

The bedclothes all askew, Julie lay back, her arms at the
side on her head, laughing up at him.

'Enough!' she gasped. 'I give in – no more!' His chest heaving, a wide grin on his flushed face, Mike laughed triumphantly. Then as they rested there, his eyes grew darker, the desire shadowing them as he watched her.

'Julie....' His voice husky, he began to kiss her passionately, and her pulse started to race. She reached up, trailing exploring fingers across his chest, round the back of his broad shoulders and down his straight, hard spine.

His lips left hers to explore the curve of her neck and into the deep cleavage between breasts already swelling at his touch. With a devilish glitter in his eyes, he surveyed first one proud pink peak and then the other, teasing each in turn with soft nips of strong white teeth.

Beneath him, she moaned, softly, her body undulating urgently from side to side, then arching her pelvis, inviting his plunder. Then with little gasps of yearning, she trailed moist lips down his skin, savouring, tasting the slightly salty taste of him. Then with a deep thrust he was inside her, filling the aching void that was crying out for him. Slowly, forcefully, they began the old and ancient ritual-like blending of two eager bodies. Her legs wrapped round his waist, begging for more of him. For a long time they were locked in heated passion that threatened to burn them completely. And then, with one glorious last hard thrust, he filled her with his warmth as they both reached a wonderful climax together – the most fantastic timing of all!

With a deep sigh, Mike rolled away, his body glistening with perspiration, his chest heaving. At his side, Julie felt that she had never known such absolute satisfaction before. He drew her close again and they kissed gently, almost as if giving each other thanks, and then fell swiftly and silently into sleep.

When they awoke again it was past lunch-time.

'No wonder I'm hungry, I'll have to eat you.' Mike made to grab her but she dodged him and picked up her bathrobe.

'I'll have to get up, I need a shower,' she laughed. He reached out again.

'Have a shower and then come back here; let's have a lazy day in bed.' It sounded heavenly!

'I'll shower. And then make us brunch while you shower. First one back gets choice of the papers,' she suggested. A quick shower, swift sprays of her body lotion, quick brushing of her hair, and she hurried through to the kitchen. While she cooked scrambled eggs on toast, she could hear Mike singing loudly and off-key under the shower. Adding extra toast and a pot of marmalade, she filled a coffee pot and carried the loaded tray to the bedroom.

Peacefully, contentedly, they demolished all the food, drained all the coffee, and soon the bed was strewn with newspapers. Taking surreptitious glances at Mike's face, she envied him his vitality. Several parts of her body ached from their energetic lovemaking; her head still felt a bit muzzy from the previous day's indulgence, but he looked as fresh and sparkling as ever!

He glanced up from his paper and caught her watching him.

'Nothing in your paper?' he asked, 'Here, swop.'

She shook her head. 'No, I think I'm still tired.'

'Poor old gel, let me kiss you better,' he coaxed.

'No, don't.' Just the one word – 'old' – but it cut like a knife and she pushed him away. She saw faint bewilderment shadow his eyes and added softly, 'I'll have another doze; don't rustle the papers too much, or I'll push you out of bed.' She turned over and felt him drop a kiss on her bare shoulder. And gradually she fell asleep again.

When she woke, the bed was empty and a note was propped up against the clock on the bedside table.

Darling sleepy head,
Gone to the cottage. See you later,
M.

Julie stretched and then got up, longing for the time when the cottage was finished. Of course Mike needed to take advantage of the long days of light, but she hated sharing his attention with a heap of stone and wood!

Her head felt clearer, so she began to tidy up the flat, put some clothes into the washer, pressed and prepared her office clothes for the coming week. As she ironed one of Mike's shirts along with her blouses, she thought again of his awful rooms. As she worked, an idea kept coming back in her mind – why couldn't he move in with her? There was a small spare room, holding suitcases and so on at present. He would need to buy a new bed for his cottage. Why not now?

Later she was peeling potatoes, nibbling her bottom lip, her hazel eyes pensive, when she heard the doorbell.

'Hi,' she began and then looking closer exclaimed, 'Good grief, Mike, you're filthy!'

'I know. Sorry, darling, I need another shower.'

'And I'll need more bath towels at this rate,' she grumbled.

'Just one kiss first,' he insisted.

When they had finished eating the meal she had prepared, she began tentatively, 'Mike, can I suggest something? Something we'll need to talk through properly?'

'Sounds ominous, darling. What is it?' Slowly, watching his good-looking face closely, she told him what she had been considering earlier.

'If you buy a bed you can use it for the cottage.'

His eyebrows rose a mile! 'Why do we need another bed?'

She held up her hand. 'That's just it, Mike. You'll have

your own room; look after yourself; keep yourself.' As he made to interrupt, she hastened on, 'I'm a busy woman and I'm not looking for someone else to take care of. We can share lots of things....' She mentally cursed the flush that heated her cheeks, but he caught her drift. 'It's just that I hate those awful digs of yours, and there's heaps of room here, But,' she emphasized the word, 'we're both free agents, to come and go as we please.' She waited and he sat there with a creased brow, deep in thought.

'Think it'll work, Julie?'

'If we both stick to the rules,' she told him firmly. 'As long as it doesn't stop you getting on with the cottage. Just why are you so keen to get it all done so much?' she put in. 'Couldn't you move in and finish it as you go along?'

'No, I couldn't do that!' His voice was surprisingly adamant. 'I have my reasons; I mean to stick to them. And I must get it done as soon as I possibly can.'

'Oh, I see,' Julie murmured, but she didn't and she was to remember his words in the coming months, but right then she put it down to masculine pig-headedness!

'But if you think it'll work, I'd love to move in, darling. What about the rent?'

'Just a token sum towards light, phone and so on – no rent as such. The place is my own – well nearly,' she smiled. 'Should work out better for you anyway than that grotty place.'

'To say nothing of a gorgeous landlady who's fantastic in bed.'

His grin was pure devilry and she said, 'Down boy! Dishes to wash right now. And the landlady's bed is by invitation only. 'No entry' on my door means just that!'

'To show what a good lodger I am, I'll do the dishes all by myself while you sit there.' And Julie let him, although she still had plenty to clear up later after him in the kitchen.

With Megan away on honeymoon, she had little time to help Mike move in. As he was busy too both at work and at the cottage, it was accomplished in dribs and drabs, after he'd spent two nights clearing out the spare room. Waiting delivery of the bed he'd ordered and with the rest of his belongings in suitcases and boxes, he either had to sleep at his own lodgings or in Julie's bed.

Anxious not to set a precedent, but mostly because they were both too tired and too busy, she saw little of him during the two weeks Megan was away from the office.

The bed, when it finally arrived, was what Mike called 'queen-sized' and he looked peeved at Julie's fit of giggles. Nothing of a queen about him, she laughed. It was old-fashioned, in dark wood, but the mattress was new. He had also found a tallboy chest of drawers to match.

'These'll do nicely for the second bedroom at the cottage,' he told her and she was rather surprised at how knowledgeable he was about such things. He certainly knew exactly what he wanted for his damned cottage, she told herself, as she helped him polish the tallboy to a glowing patina.

'Will you give me a hand choosing stuff – carpets and curtains and so on? That is, when the time comes?' She nodded, her thoughts on the meal cooking itself in the kitchen.

A week later, Megan was back, looking radiantly tanned and happy. There was a contented look about her that Julie envied. Things seemed so simple and straightforward in her Welsh friend's life, she sighed. But that night was to be Mike's first real night as a lodger. He had at last said goodbye to his awful landlady, and was duly installed in Julie's second bedroom. A single wardrobe in dark linenfold oak to match the bed and tallboy had been delivered and she had her own wardrobe to herself.

That night, after a mad scramble to rustle up a meal for two, they drank a toast to the new arrangement.

'I'll have to provide some meals too, love. Don't know about wine though.' Mike raised his glass and clinked it with hers. 'To Mike and Julie – under one roof!'

And as she sipped her wine, she hoped fervently that it would work out....

Seven

Life suddenly became more and more hectic, but fun. Even when Mike was busy with his DIY labouring, she still could feel his presence in the flat. The smell of his aftershave in the bathroom, muddy wellies behind the kitchen door, all reminded her that she wasn't lonely any more.

She had qualms about telling her folks that she now was sharing her flat with Mike. Weakly she decided to wait for a suitable opportunity to break the news to them. And she just hoped Mike would not answer the phone when her mother made one of her 'long chat' calls.

She shopped hurriedly in her lunch-hour, dashing home as early as she could to start a meal at night. Sometimes she went back to the flat at lunch-time, ate a quick sandwich, and did some chores before hurrying back to the office.

Once, she had barely begun to tidy up when she heard Mike's key in the door.

'What are you doing here at lunch-time?'

'No, that's not what you should say.' His face had lightened when he saw her there. 'You should say – "love I've come home specially to see you"' He hugged her close and kissed her protesting lips. 'Actually, I came to pick up some measurements I want for tonight, but now you're here, I can think of something better.....'

'Stop it, Mike, I want to clean up a bit – the place's a tip.'

'It'll keep; I won't. Come on, darling.' Kissing her, making her knees turn to water with his persistence, he gradually edged her near to the bed.

'Good grief, Mike, you can't ... we can't.....' She struggled to get out the words, to evade his seeking hands.

'We can, my love.' And they did!

It was crazy coming back to the flat, both of them, to make love at lunch-time. But the sheer heady bliss of it all made her feel like a young girl again. She was carried along ecstatically on his wave of passion, unable to deny him anything.

She found herself avoiding Megan's eyes when she got back late to the office, still breathless and flushed.

But Megan had no such inhibitions!

'I've an idea you've been doing exactly what I've been doing with my lunch-hour, mm?'

'Cleaning my flat,' Julie retorted, as Megan hooted derisively, and then changed the subject hurriedly. 'How is it this firm's asking for another temp – the third this month?' She held out a form in a back to business gesture.

'Could be the boss has wandering hands,' Megan suggested.

'Well, find out and if that's true, take them off our books. Might just be some other trouble though.'

Mike didn't come in that evening until she had gone to bed, but she had left him a ham salad and a lemon mousse in the fridge. As she undressed, she chided herself for worrying whether he ate or not. She ought to begin as she meant to go on....

She overslept the next morning and he had already left for work. He had also left behind last night's dishes as well as that morning's. In the bathroom she found a dirty shirt half in the linen basket and an odd sock on the floor. She bit her lip, and pushed the offending items out of sight. After all, she didn't mind doing the odd shirt along with hers, did she?

For once she had to skimp her make-up and dash out to the

car to join the traffic jam heading townwards. She had two important interviews facing her.

Mike phoned during the morning at a busy time.

'I've got two pass tickets to a HTV show tonight. Shall I pick you up, or will you meet me there? It's for ...' He named a famous chat show. 'At Culverhouse Cross studios.'

'But I've got heaps to do ...' she began.

'Hey, come on, boss lady – it's for free! Tickets are hard to get, and who knows, that business brain of yours might get some ideas from watching a TV show made.' That was true. Besides they had few nights out, and she didn't want to sound fuddy-duddy giving housework as an excuse.

'All right, Mike. I'll need my car for morning, so I'll see you there.'

She wished she had something more dressy to wear, for she was determined the he would always see her looking at her best. She did what she could with her face, and was waiting in the car-park when he arrived there. He gave her a swift hug and they joined the queue going in. Mike was as curious as a small boy, peering behind screens, trying to inspect all the equipment and scenery before they were allocated their seats. A one-time comedian acted as a warm-up man, and she enjoyed watching the amusement on Mike's face, hearing his deep chuckles of laughter. It was fascinating to see how the show was put together, clapping when the board said Applaud. She watched the cameras, the adverts, never knowing when such knowledge could be put to use. They had a drink in the crowded bar and then drove back home, with Julie following the tail-light of Mike's car.

'Made a change from a restaurant or pub, didn't it?'

'And it was for free!' As soon as the words were said, Julie regretted them. She caught a dark shadow in his eyes. 'I'm sorry, Mike, I didn't mean.....'

'I know, Julie. But just hang in there until I've finished the cottage and I'll take you to all the expensive places your greedy little heart desires.' The cold expression on his face made a chill shiver along her spine.

'I'm not greedy. Anyway, I can afford to buy whatever I want myself. If I couldn't, I would quite happily go without.' She picked up her mug of coffee, leaving his on the draining-board. 'I'm going to bed. Goodnight, Mike.'

Deep in thought, she sipped her drink, listening for the sound of Mike finishing with the bathroom. Tonight she meant to cleanse and cream her face without his seeing her do it. Anxiously she peered into the mirror, looking for signs of age, touching the faint lines round her mouth and in the corners of her eyes.

She couldn't get off to sleep, longing for the feel of Mike's body beside hers, wondering if she had done right in letting him come to live in the flat.

The next morning she slipped out of bed early and went into the bathroom, loath to let him see her until she'd done her face. In the clear light of morning she knew she would do everything in her power to keep him by her side; to feed the longing for him that racked her body constantly. Making his breakfast along with her own, she called, 'You'll be late, Mike....' Still damp from the shower, he looked at the table and then hugged her close.

'Morning, darling. How about a kiss first?'

'Kiss all your landladies, do you, Mike?' She lifted her face and responded to the pressure of his lips with a lift of her heart. His bear hug almost lifted her clear off the floor.

'You're a whole lot of woman, Julie, my love.' And as he began to eat, she wondered – did he mean she was getting fat? She poured out another coffee. You're pathetic, Julie my girl, she told herself in disgust. The phone rang and Mike, who was nearest, grabbed it, a piece of toast in the other hand.

'Hello ...' he called, paused, and then replaced the receiver. 'Must've been a wrong number. Shall I see you at lunch-time?'

'Can't, Mike. I've a hairdresser's appointment.'

'It looks all right to me, pet,' he raked a plundering hand through her hair and dropped a kiss on the nape of her neck. She couldn't tell him she needed a colour tint to enrich the chestnut tones. Instead, she pushed him away.

'Scoot. I need to put the cleaner round before I go to work.' She paused and looked up in query, 'That is unless you're going to do it for me?'

'Oh, you've got a wicked tongue, boss lady. See you.' And he scooted, leaving Julie to dash round trying to do a few chores before she too had to leave for the office.

Later that morning, Alun came in to see her. Surprised, she saw his face had a shut tight look about it.

'Hello, Alun, I wasn't expecting you.' He usually rang first.

'I did ring your flat this morning but....' Then she remembered, Mike had picked up the phone.

'Why did you hang up?' There was a white line round his mouth, a bleak look in his eyes.

'It was Mike Stephens, wasn't it, Julie? There – at your flat this morning at a quarter to eight....' His words jerked with pain.

'Sit down, Alun,' she said quietly, pity for the man opposite softening her voice.

'I suppose he'd stayed the night?' Reluctant to meet the unhappiness in his brown eyes, Julie fumbled with the pen in her hand.

'Yes, Alun, he did. And really it's none of your business, is it?' she asked quietly.

'You must be mad, Julie!' His anger exploded as he flung himself down into the chair. 'He's younger than you; he'll take all he can get and then leave you for some little ...' The words choked in his throat. 'I can't bear to see you get hurt, my dearest.' The hoarse words were full of love.

'Oh Alun.' Pity shadowed her tawny eyes as she watched him struggle with the emotion that was hurting him just then. 'I'm so sorry, but I've never pretended to love you – to be more than a friend.' She paused, her heart aching for him. 'I can't help what I feel for Mike. It's something I can't deny. I know he could well leave me one day, but until he does, I'm going to be with him as much as I can.' She took a deep breath and then said softly, 'Mike moved into my flat, into the spare room. His place was awful. He needs every penny he can get to put his cottage right. So until he's done that, he's staying with me, as a tenant.'

'Sharing your bed, I suppose,' Alun put in bitterly. Julie's soft lip tightened. She knew she had to leave Alun in no doubt – leave him no hope.

'That's my business, Alun, I'm sorry, but I wish you'd be happy for me – be my friend.' For even as she said it, she knew she'd be lost without his help, his friendship.

For a long moment, he sat there slumped forlornly in his chair, his arms hung loosely between his knees, his hands clenched and white-knuckled. At last, he sighed and looked up.

'All right Julie. All I can do is stand by, waiting to pick up the pieces. But don't expect me to wish you and Mike luck. I hate his guts for taking you from me.'

She could have pointed out that she had never been his, but pity made her hold back the words.

'Thank you anyway for staying my friend, Alun. Please don't be too bitter.' Her tentative smile begged his forgiveness, and as he rose, he gave her a sad smile in response.

'I'll be seeing you, cariad. I'll always be here for you.' She went round the desk and reaching up, kissed his cheek.

She had managed to pull herself together when Debra came in to see her about one or two queries. When they had finished, the blonde girl said nonchalantly, 'I haven't seen anything of the gorgeous Mike Stephens. Is he still around?'

Startled and with a little surge of jealousy, Julie answered, 'Oh yes, he's around, but he's rather busy on his DIY cottage project.' And with that she abruptly changed the subject. All the same as Debra closed the door behind her, she realized she would have to tell Megan that she now had someone sharing her flat.

'I rather thought that's what would happen.' Megan wasn't at all surprised and said so. 'Best of luck, Julie. I think you and he will be very happy together,' she added. Julie smiled her thanks.

'And if not?' she asked, betraying her uncertainty.

'So who gets a guarantee?' Megan shrugged. 'Grab your happiness today and let tomorrow take care of itself. Anyway, he's good for you, and what's the use of saving yourself – living like a nun?'

As each day passed, Julie found that life got more frantically busy. She found herself dashing around at lunch-time, shopping for their evening meal, fitting in an hairdressing appointment, buying new clothes, extra drinks for the sideboard, extra toiletries for the bathroom. If she found herself using her bank cards more and more to pay for the extra expenses, she didn't mind one bit. She was far too happy then. Too alive, as if every nerve in her body pulsed with renewed youth and vigour.

It was hard work keeping up with Mike. *His* job hadn't the responsibilities of hers. He didn't have the worry of having to find salaries, mortgage repayments and the running costs of two companies, two offices, to say nothing of the flat. He hadn't brought up the question of rent again, and she was loath to spoil the happy atmosphere by mentioning it.

The nights were getting longer, and Mike spent all the time he could over at his cottage, arriving back late and tired and dirty. In between, Julie spent all the time working; doing the cleaning, and everlasting washing and ironing. Some nights, too, she was obliged to bring work home from the office to make up for her extra long lunch hours. Trying to fit in being both a competent business woman and a housewife took some doing. But the nights when Mike was beside her in bed, loving her, making her feel young and beloved, more than made up for the scramble her life had become.

He would come home to a cooked meal, the breakfast dishes cleared and the flat all tidy, his clothes washed along with hers. If she grumbled, he would come into the kitchen and slip his hands around her waist and she would melt against his long, lithe body and count it all worth while.

Occasionally he would coax, 'Let's eat out, Julie, honey. Give the cook a rest...?' And she would go and make herself look as glamourous as possible and they'd go out to dine and dance. Mostly it was *her* credit card that settled the bill, with Mike paying for the drinks at the bar beforehand. They would come back late to a night of loving – and another mad rush to work the next morning!

'I hope he's doing his share of the chores?' Megan warned when she needed strong, black coffee to get her started that morning. Julie grinned a trifle wearily.

'I reckon he thinks the fairies do it, Megan.'

'They all do! You have to disillusion 'em!' Megan advised. Which was all right for Megan, Julie mused wryly. She had youth on her side; didn't have to worry constantly whether she was beginning to show her age. Megan didn't have to worry about nagging or not, did she? She was married....

And as spring was left behind and summer deepened, those thoughts haunted Julie. She began to feel her energy sap in the heat of the day, the constant rush around. She sometimes longed for a quiet evening with her feet up, no housework to do and her face free of its careful make-up for once. But somehow she couldn't, she daren't, not when Mike seemed so young and full of energy. She was always reminded of the difference in their ages, and it drove her on like a spur, making her determined never to let him see her looking tired or unkempt – old!

Constantly too, she worried about what her folks would say about Mike's living with her and kept putting off telling them. So that when he passed the phone, saying, 'It's your mother, Julie,' her heart skipped a beat.

'Hello Mum, how are you?'

'Julie,' came the well-known voice, 'who was that answering your phone?'

'A – a friend, Mum. I'm just doing us a meal.' She hated the tremble in her voice, the implied lie.

'Oh!' Her mother sounded doubtful, wanting to ask more. She went on, 'Your father's retirement time has arrived, love. We're having a lovely big party next weekend and want you to come for it. Will you?'

'Of course, darling, how lovely.'

'Bring that friend with you, Julie. Make up the numbers. He sounded nice....' Again her mother was seeking more information and Julie knew it.

'Yes, he is. I'll ask him and let you know, mmm?' For a while longer they chatted, discussing the present the family would be giving her father. All the time, she was conscious of Mike standing at her shoulder, listening intently.

'That was my mother.' Trying to collect her thoughts, she went on, 'It's my father's retirement party next Saturday. Mum wants me to go for the weekend. You, too. What do you say, Mike? Fancy a family get-together?' Deliberately, she kept her tone casual, not pressing him, giving him a chance to refuse. Watching her give-away face, he asked,

'Do they know about us? That I'm living here, I mean?'

'No. I haven't told them yet. Perhaps I will next weekend.' She waited for his answer.

'Yes, darling, I'd love to come with you. Time I got to see your folks anyway.' So Julie duly sent off a little note of acceptance, telling her mother to expect the two of them, enclosing her cheque towards the family present. She would get a little present for Mike to give to her father separately, she decided. She wanted him to create a good impression.

The following Saturday morning, they drove across the border, along the motorway towards Sutton Coldfield and the old rambling place that had been her family home all her life. Immediately they were in the midst of a bustling, busy horde of relatives filling every corner of the house.

'So this is Mike?' Was all her mother said as Julie introduced him, but the pale blue eyes were watching him keenly. 'How are you, darling, it's ages since we saw you last? How's the new business going? Is Megan settling down to married life all right?' Julie laughed and hugged her mother close. She hadn't changed a bit. As usual, she asked a dozen questions at once, never waiting for an answer to one! Her father raised one quizzical eyebrow and grinned.

'Hello, Julie, my love.'

'Hi Dad. And congratulations and all that.' They kissed warmly, hardly needing words between them, these two. Mike was introduced all round – to her sister, Helen, husband and two children; to numerous cousins, aunts and friends.

And Julie watched happily, loving the way he charmed them all at first glance.

'Come on, darling. You're sharing your old room with Aunt Eunice. And I've put Mike on the top floor with Uncle Sydney. Will that be all right?' Just in time she caught Mike's startled glance and grimaced behind her mother's back.

'That's fine, Mum. Where's my case, Mike, still in the car?' Left alone in her old room, she saw that nothing had been changed, except for the single camp bed set up in the furthest corner. Hearing the clatter of Mike's feet along the landing, she looked out and pulled him in hurriedly.

'I'm sorry about this, love, but for this weekend....' She paused apologetically.

'It's all right, darling, but I promise we'll make up on Sunday night when we get back home.' His kiss sent a shiver of excitement through her and she whispered, 'I'll keep you to that. Now it's upstairs to Uncle Sydney for you.' He grinned and placed another fierce kiss on her upturned mouth.

'Hope he doesn't snore!'

'You'll survive.' She laughed heartlessly. From then on, everything was chaos, laughter and fun. She had brought a new dress to wear for that evening's special party. It was made of a heavy-grained silk in a deep midnight blue and it fitted her beautifully. She touched her eyelids with blue shadow, her pulses with fragrant perfume and knew she looked her best. In his dark grey suit and pale blue shirt, Mike looked more handsome than ever, and she was pleased to see that he was as nice to her elderly relatives as to the young flirtatious ones. The long dining-table was loaded with food and drinks and the talk was noisy and friendly. And when the time came to toast her father, Julie saw that his eyes were moist with happiness. The family had decided to get him the new heated greenhouse he'd been wanting for ages, so he was given a glossy brochure and the key, with the promise of installation next week. Julie had bought a box of small garden tools, gloves, etc., and gift-wrapped it was a present from Mike.

'Good girl,' he said, squeezing her knee under the table.

No mention of paying me back – the sour thought crossed her mind and immediately she hated herself for it! It was later in the kitchen as she was helping her mother put away the food and dishes that her mother began to gently pump her about Mike.

'He's a good-looking chap – bit young though I should have thought for you, pet?' Julie, her back to her mother as she reached into a cupboard, stiffened.

'He doesn't think so, Mum.'

'He certainly seems to be in love with you, Julie. How do you feel about him?' Her mother hardly needed to ask; her daughter's face had made it plain all day how she felt about the tall young man she'd brought home with her. 'I can't help worrying about you, darling, after Jeff....' Her voice tailed off, afraid to say too much. Julie had always been a private sort of person to her, being much closer to her father.

'Pretty crazy about him, Mum. But not so crazy I'll make the same mistake again. I – I might as well tell you now, darling,' Julie took a deep breath and then rushed on, 'Mike's staying at my place – in the second bedroom. He's doing up a lovely little cottage and needs all the spare cash in the meantime, so....'

Her mother was no fool; she got the picture. But all she said was, 'You're more than old enough to know what you're doing, Julie. Just don't let him break your heart. And whatever happens, we're always here for you.'

'Thanks, Mum. And don't worry, I'll be careful.'

'I told Mum about having you share the flat.' They had left the high flyover behind them, the car eating up the miles of motorway going westwards, and Julie broke the comfortable silence. They had talked about the weekend, the party and meeting her relatives. And then the hum of the engine had almost lulled her into a light doze.

'What did she say to that?' For a second, Mike took his gaze from the road ahead and glanced down at her closely.

'What everyone says – don't let him break your heart, Julie, not again.'

'And what did you say to that?' There was a note in his voice that warned her to be careful how she answered him.

'That it is my – our business and that I don't intend getting my heart even slightly dented, let alone broken.'

'But you're happy, aren't you, Julie? We're good together, you and I?' The touch of anxiety in his voice somehow gave her a little thrill of pleasure. She snuggled up closer to him.

'Very happy, darling. But a bit fed up at times at the extra slog I'm getting....'

For a moment he tensed beside her and then said regretfully, 'Sorry, pet, I'm a thoughtless devil. I should help out, sorry. My head's full of plumbers and carpenters and so on these days.'

She reached across and kissed his cheek. 'I'll let you off for now.'

The following morning, he washed the few breakfast dishes, getting in Julie's way, delaying her more than his help was worth. And that evening when he began to help with the meal, she almost lost her cool. He silenced her protests with his lips, and then with a final passionate kiss, placed one finger on her mouth.

'Just marking the place; don't go away.' And he dashed out of the kitchen to return with a huge, satin-bowed box of chocolates.

'Oh Mike.' She shook her head ruefully, but how could she reproach him? Or tell him how strictly she had to diet! Or that something towards their living expenses would be far more acceptable than an extravagant present?

They had few mutual friends, and on the nights they weren't working they had been content just to be alone together. But as time went on, she was afraid Mike would be getting restless, long for company. His enthusiasm for housework had died the death in a very short time. Then came the day when he announced, 'I'm going to the firm's Social Club do on Wednesday night, darling. It's hardly your scene – a disco.'

'But it *is* yours, Mike?' She couldn't keep the hurt out of her voice.

'Hardly, but I'll have to show up, won't I? I shan't stay long though,' he looked at her face. 'Hey, boss lady, afraid of all those lovely little dolly-birds grabbing me?' he teased. The shadow that passed over her face betrayed her thoughts.

Was he ashamed of being seen with her – an older woman amongst the young girls there? Did he really want to go alone, leaving her at home like an old Cinderella?

That night after Mike, dressed in tight jeans, a polo sweater under his suede jacket, had left for the Social Club, she told herself that it was good to have a quiet night to herself, so she curled up in the chair with a magazine she hadn't found time to read before. She realized just how tired she'd become lately, but she was determined to keep up with Mike's youthful zest.

All the same, she found that all the rushing around, doing two jobs at the same time was beginning to tell on her, and gradually, it took all her skill to disguise the tiredness in her face.

'You look tired, love.' Peering over her shoulder into the bathroom mirror, she saw the concern in Mike's eyes and she knew why he'd asked. She looked awful!

'Too many late nights, too much work.' She shrugged off-handedly, and then as she turned, she saw yet another heap of soiled shirts on the floor in the corner. 'And too many of those to wash and iron.'

She saw a dismayed frown crease his brow.

'You sound just like a wife, Julie, my love.' And as the anger at his reply registered on her face, he pulled her close, stroking the back of her head with a gentle hand. 'I'm sorry, darling, just teasing. You're tired. How about spending the day over at the cottage on Saturday with me?'

As she made to demur, he added quickly, 'No, not to do anything; just to look round and see what's been done. You can sit in the sun and relax. What do you say, pet?' The love and care in his words, the hint of worry in his dark eyes made her feel ashamed then of her tired outburst.

'I'll pack us a picnic ...' she began.

'Lunch only, Julie. At night, we'll eat out. I'll book a table. Now, shall I shove this lot in the washer and leave it to grind away till tonight?' He looked so anxious, trying to be helpful, that her heart lightened.

That Saturday was a glorious golden, sunny day, and she felt her spirits lift as they set out early for the cottage. She had closed the flat door on everything that needed doing, determined to enjoy the day with Mike. He was dressed in his disreputable working gear, and Julie had put on her oldest pair of jeans and a brief sun-top.

'Mike, I can hardly believe it!' She stood and gazed open-mouthed at the cottage. 'It looks so ... it's absolutely lovely.'

Indeed the little cottage – no longer so little – had changed enormously. The new slate roof gleamed, window frames no longer sagged. The stonework of the double garage added on one side already seemed to match the rest, as did the room built above it. New doors, new guttering, everything carefully restored, made it all look wonderful to her bemused eyes.

'There's a lot to do inside yet, but – well, come in and see.' Mike was almost bursting with pride and Julie was feeling ashamed. Ashamed of all the times she'd resented his being at the cottage and not with her; resented all the money it had cost him.

'But, Mike, it's been so worth it.'

'I think so,' he sounded positively smug. 'It's been hard work and hard cash too. And I'll still owe the bank when it's all done!' Inside smelled of new wood and he flung open windows as they went from room to room. In the front living-room there was still a huge hole in the chimney breast.

'I'm having an open fireplace there; slate hearth, ironwork fire basket for burning logs.' Eagerly he pointed out all that was still to be done. The extended kitchen, bright and airy in the sunlight, was still bare, awaiting all its fixtures. Upstairs there were two light bedrooms, with piles of timber ready for making the built-in cupboards and wardrobes. The bathroom was rather tiny, but every inch had been cleverly used.

'Still a lot to do, but my part's practically done. I'm handing over to the experts, the plasterers and tilers, the carpenters. All the labouring's done.' Mike turned to her as she stood gazing around in pleased amazement. 'I need some ideas, Julie, for curtains, kitchen fitments and so on. Like to help? Any suggestions?'

So they sat, scribble pads on their knees, in the sun, tossing ideas back and forth.

'That living-room calls out for an old oak settee in the inglenook, Mike. And heavy chintz covers and curtains; good dark oak furniture, real or reproduction.' Sitting there, soaking up the sun, she felt herself relax; business worries forgotten, enjoying the sight of Mike's happy, animated face as they agreed on first one idea and then another.

'Pine and copper for the kitchen? I'm all for mod cons in there otherwise. Can't beat a good cooker and micro, washing machine, dryer, etc.'

They ate their picnic lunch outside with nothing but the drone of the fat bees flitting from flower to heavily-laden flower to disturb them. No traffic, no noise or fumes.

'Simply heavenly.' Julie stretched idly, her lovely face already pink from the sun. 'Mike, you've got a winner here, but this garden's a mess.'

'Right then, boss lady, get cracking.' He rose and stretched, his body taut and fit. And the sight of it brought a frisson of longing through Julie's as she looked up at him. He watched her face and to her it seemed that he had the ability to touch her with a glance. Reluctantly, trying to ignore the invitation in her hazel eyes, he went on, 'I'll start clearing up the rubbish inside ready for the chaps on Monday. You, madam, can start battling with those weeds.'

'Worst job for me, as usual,' she grumbled mockingly. He kissed her hard and then went indoors before he capitulated altogether. She found an old chopper in the garage and began hacking away at the waist high weeds. In one corner there was a bed of lovely rose bushes, almost hidden by the weeds. Deciding to take some back to the flat, she looked for some secateurs, but only found a rusty old knife.

'This'll do,' she murmured to herself, but it wasn't much good. She hacked away, holding the rose stems away from the weeds. 'Ouch!' she gasped aloud, wincing at the pain in her hand. She had caught herself on a thick thorn. Dropping the knife, she sucked hard and finally managed to pull it out with her teeth. 'Damn.' She cleansed the wound with her lips, spat out, and then tied her hanky round the afflicted place. 'Damn,' she repeated, 'it's sore. Time to knock off, Julie my girl.'

Eight

By Monday morning, Julie's finger was red and swollen and painful to touch. It didn't help that they both overslept and in the rush to get to work, all the discord returned, yesterday's peace forgotten. For once Mike's easy going phlegm was missing, and as she scrambled round, annoyed if he got in her way, grumbling at all the jobs that had to be left, he lost his temper too.

'Stop nagging, Julie my love. Now you're sounding like a wife again. An old wife,' he added this time sarcastically. Shock caught her then in her throat, and fear clutched like a giant hand. It was the first time Mike had ever referred to her age.

Anger at what she considered his selfishness boiled over, and for the first time, they quarrelled. Fiercely and bitterly, suddenly all the things she'd been bottling up inside her, but trying to ignore, spilled out. His casual expectation of meals ready and waiting whenever he walked in the door, all the extras she'd had to pay for, and all the washing and cleaning up she did for him as well as holding down her own busy job. In her tired state, she forgot to hold her tongue, to consider her words.

'Oh yes, Mike, you're on to a good thing, aren't you?' she accused bitterly. 'All the privileges of marriage and none of the drawbacks.' On and on she went, her voice shrill with anger and dismay. It seemed that she couldn't stop herself. And Mike's scathing retorts were equally bitter. She shouldn't

141

have suggested he came to live with her in the first place – she wasn't the type to share her life with anyone else – her business came first! His face looked tight and drawn, his eyes bleak at what they were doing to each other.

He slammed the door on his way out, and she slumped into her chair, tears streaming down her face, her temper spent, wishing with all her heart she could take back the bitter words she'd thrown at him.

During the day, the ache in her heart was matched by that in her throbbing finger. It had swollen more than ever and the pain was almost unbearable.

'It's no use, Megan, I'll have to see someone with this. I think it's turned septic. Will you cope?'

'Of course, Julie. You look awful. I should go home afterwards, if I were you.'

'Thanks, I will.' At the hospital, she had to wait ages to see the overworked young doctor in Casualty.

'Mmm, nasty, Mrs Prescott. I'll have to open that up I'm afraid – get rid of the poison.' The relief was enormous, and with a prescription for an antibiotic and a large dressing on her hand, she went shopping for food for their evening meal, not knowing if Mike would be in or not.

All day the memory of their quarrel had been tormenting her, and she vowed to do her best to patch things up between them. The thought of losing him was unbearable.

What did Mike really feel, she wondered? He had never ever said he loved her. Wanted her – yes, often. As she wanted him, with a fever that burned her up at times. Since her divorce from Jeff, she had refused to consider being in love; lust was nearer the mark – this obsessive hunger for a man much younger. No – not love, she told herself, but even as she did, she knew she didn't ever want to be without Mike.

Awkwardly, one-handed, she was laying the table when

the door opened, and in came Mike's briefcase. A moment later, his head appeared round the door, and then a hand waving an enormous bouquet of roses.

'Is it safe to come in?'

'Oh Mike, I'm so sorry.' With a cry of relief, she flew into his arms and held him close. 'I'm so sorry for all those awful things I said this morning.'

'Me, too, darling. A truce, eh?' His kiss was hungry and passionate. It was as if they had been on the edge of a precipice and then pulled back just in time.

Both were rather subdued during the meal; both being careful not to upset the delicate state of reconciliation. Julie hated herself for putting that worried look on his face, remembering her accusation of selfishness. Both were deeply thoughtful, knowing that a turning point in their relationship had been reached.

That night they made love more passionately then ever, as if it would heal any wound left by their quarrel. He kissed her with a deep, raw hunger, and she felt his heart thudding wildly beneath her splayed fingers, only a drum beat faster than her own. And she knew she didn't ever want to try going on without him.

During the next couple of weeks, Mike was obviously doing his best to please her. He helped with the chores, bought her silly little expensive presents, and on the surface things seemed happy enough. He still spent some evenings at the cottage, then he took to staying there odd nights, leaving a sleeping bag and some toilet kit there to use. To Julie, it seemed as if they were waiting for something....

She still felt overtired and wretched. Her finger had healed and she blamed her weepy state on the antibiotic tablets she'd taken. Summer holiday fortnight had brought a lull in both the offices. She found that Debra Deane managed the Exclusive Executives side of things extremely well. Behind her cold green eyes was an equally cool and calculating mind so eminently suited to her job.

During the long hot days, Julie blamed her low state on the heat and tried to spend more time at home to give herself a breathing space.

She was folding some clean undies, one eye on the TV news when she heard the name of Mike's firm mentioned.

' ... alleging that there has been an obvious leak of information to the French. Figures and costings of their new tender have somehow found their way across the Channel, and they say the matter is extremely serious....'

It was Mike's department that was involved, wasn't it? Did that explain his worried look lately? Just for a brief second, she wondered if he had anything to do with it, and then immediately felt a wretched sense of guilt. Her trust in him went deeper than that surely?

'Switch on the news, darling. There was something on earlier about your firm – your department, I think.'

To her consternation she saw him give her a dark glance, a shadow in his eyes. Had he guessed about her momentary doubt? Had it shown on her face, in her voice?

They listened closely to the later bulletin which gave fuller details.

'I see.' Mike switched off. 'And that got you to thinking I'd sold out for cash, did it, Julie?'

'No! No, of course not.' But even to her own ears, her denial sounded weak. He shrugged his broad shoulders, his anger dying.

'Wouldn't blame you. I need the money, but it wasn't me. In fact, they've got a good idea who it was. Actually Julie, I think this is a good time to tell you.' He paused not meeting her eyes as he went on, 'They're sending me to the States next week.'

She felt her heart contract with the sudden shock.

'Next week? For how long?'

'Three months exactly. I'm not keen to go, but it's a challenge. Besides ... ' he rose to his feet and went to stand looking out of the window, 'I reckon it'll give us a break – a chance to stand back and take stock – to realize what we mean to each other – what we both want.' Quite a long speech from Mike; he must have been giving it some deep thought, she told herself desperately.

To Julie's ears it sounded like a death knell; he was leaving her; she was losing him! A cold chill swept through her veins, freezing her with fear.

'Do you want us to finish – is that it, Mike?' She hardly recognized her own voice; her lips felt stiff, her brain numb.

'Of course not, Julie! But I think we both need a breathing space, a time to stand back a while.' His shoulders slumped, somehow he seemed to have aged these last few minutes.

'All right, darling, I understand. I – I'll miss you terribly.' She took a deep breath, refusing to give way to the tears that threatened to overwhelm her. She would have to let him go.

She had always despised a clinging woman who didn't know how to end an affair gracefully. In the past she'd pitied those who had tried to breath life into ashes along after the embers had died.

'You haven't got much time to get ready, but I'll help you. Got your passport, your visa?' He nodded.

'I had the necessary jabs today,' he told her.

So he must have known about this for some time? It seemed to Julie that she died a little death each passing day as the time for Mike's departure grew nearer.

'How about the cottage?' she asked him.

'The carpenter chap I've got – he works for himself. Well,

his wife is going in every day. To clear up, put up curtains, let in the other workmen and so on. I'm paying her – not much, but she's glad of the little job. I've left them a key and a long list of instructions.'

'So, I've no need to go over?' She strove hard to conceal her growing dismay. It all seemed so final, as if she was never going to see him again.

She took him to the station to catch the train to Reading for the Heathrow connection. And her face felt stiff with the effort of keeping back her tears as they stood on the crowded platform.

'I'm not going to promise to write, Julie....' As she began to protest, Mike went on, 'No, I'll be on the move and you'll be busy. Besides, I meant what I said – we *both* need breathing space, time to think. So – no letters, but ... ' He paused and reached out to cup her face between his hands. His eyes looking at her with a kind of hunger, implanted the sight of it on his memory for the days to come. 'Take care of yourself, boss lady,' he said huskily. She nodded, swallowing hard.

'You, too. I'll miss you, Mike.'

Sounds of departure made them draw apart, and then cling tightly for one last lingering kiss. She felt the hot tears spring up behind her eyelids. He leaned out of the window, and caught her hand, kissing it even as the train began to pick up speed.

'Bye, Julie darling, think of me....'

As in a trance, hardly believing he'd gone, she watched the end of the train finally disappear down the line. She was losing him! He was going away for three long months, but would he come back to her?

She was losing him – and she loved him! Loved him as she'd never loved Jeff. She stood there a lonely, forlorn figure as it came to her like a clear light – she loved him! And with the revelation came the knowledge that she would always love him, for ever. If she had lost him, how could she face the long bleak days without him?

He had never actually said he loved her; she hadn't wanted him to. No commitment, no ties, she'd told him and he'd gone along with that. And there; on the now empty platform, she knew that she loved and wanted him by her side for always. Beside her, to share everything, to live and laugh and grow old along with her. He'd gone and his going had left her so lonely and bereft; a solid lump of ice where her heart had been.

As she turned to go, the platform seemed to rise to hit her in the face. Swaying on her feet, she found a seat and sat down, struggling to regain her balance.

'You all right, miss? Missed the train, did you?' At the sound of the friendly voice, Julie glanced up at the elderly porter.

'No – er, yes. I'm all right, thanks. Just going.' Her face drawn and pale, she tried to smile as she rose to go.

Somehow she found her car and drove home, the sense of loss so deep that she felt dead inside. She made herself a sandwich and a mug of coffee, but the food stuck in her throat and she couldn't swallow it. The flat seemed so quiet, so lonely, and she wondered how she could go on. Was it always going to be like this for her, she wondered? She couldn't bear the thought that she would be alone for ever, without seeing Mike, being loved by him.

Was it her fault? Had she tried to alter him too much? Subconsciously tried to make him seem older and herself younger? Had she driven him away with her constant harping on their age difference? With her nagging about the running of the flat?

As she sat there, her elbows on the table, her hands cupping her chin, the coffee grew cold, but her heart was colder, like a dead thing inside her. Why had she been so adamant that love wasn't for her after Jeff? She could see now that what had started out as a sexy, physical attraction had gradually turned to love. But she, poor fool, hadn't recognized it, had she?

She had made no allowances for Mike's being younger; hadn't taken in his tenderness, his faithfulness. Seeing him only as a young man on the make – "on to a good thing" she had riled him.

Sick at heart, she went back to the office after lunch.

'God, you look awful, Julie,' Megan couldn't hold back the concern as she looked at her employer. 'He's gone then. Three months will soon go by; keep busy, that's the thing.' Even as she chattered on, Megan knew Julie wasn't taking in her words.

That night, Julie sank into her own private hell. She missed Mike already, needed him. She wanted him to be here beside her, to call her name. She found herself crying slow, hopeless tears that trickled down her cheeks and dripped on to the surface of the kitchen table.

In bed later, lying bleakly wide-eyed, she wanted him and his love-making; knew she's miss that pleasurable ache next morning when he'd made love to her.

Instead, she was shocked by the sight of her reflection in the bathroom mirror. Her cheeks were wan, her lips drawn in an unhappy droop. Her eyes were deep and hollow with pain – a pain that would always be there now – a look of pain that no amount of tears would ever wash away. Back in the kitchen, the thought of food sickened her, but she swallowed her coffee, hoping the feeling of nausea would go away.

Megan had to go out on a temp call, and Julie was glad of

the extra work this left her with. Nothing she did could keep the thoughts of Mike away. He would be in New York now. Was he missing her, she wondered? Surely he hadn't meant what he said – no letters, no news for three months?

At lunch-time she didn't even consider going out to eat. Even the sight of the packet of sandwiches Debra brought in sickened her, but she forced one down, trying her best to get rid of the nausea.

As the days dragged by, things didn't improve. In spite of working hard, she still couldn't sleep, although during the day her eyelids felt heavy with fatigue and she had difficulty in staying awake at her desk. And always inside there was this quiet drone of sadness and wanting. She despaired of ever feeling happiness again, unable to face up to the lonely time ahead without Mike.

What a fool she had been! She had thought she would take the end of their affair calmly, but she'd been wrong. Some women could take a love affair in their stride, walk into it with a smile and walk out with a shrug, but it seemed that she wasn't one of them! She had fallen in love and all she faced now was a bleak and lonely future if Mike didn't come back to her.

Then came the morning when she passed out at work. She had risen quickly to reach over to a file when the room suddenly heaved and the floor came up to meet her, and then blackness enfolded her like a dark blanket. When she came round, she was on the settee and Megan's frightened face was peering down at her.

'Sorry, Megan.' She struggled to sit up. 'I've not been sleeping well, or eating lately.' There was an enigmatic look in the Welsh girl's eyes.

'I think it's more than that, Julie, I think you're pregnant!'

Pregnant! The word reverberated around in Julie's head.

She couldn't be! She was turned thirty-six and on the Pill; she couldn't be pregnant.

Unaware that she said the words aloud, she stared, shocked and dazed, up into her assistant's anxious face.

'Those antibiotic tablets....?' Megan began. 'You know, when you had that septic finger. I've heard that sometimes they cancel out the protection of the Pill.'

Julie was trying to do a count in her head; why on earth hadn't she noticed before? But lately all her waking thoughts had been on Mike, and how much she was missing him. And now it seemed that she was going to have his child!

Suddenly, as the realization hit her, her heart leapt joyously. Mike's baby – she would have something of his to cherish and keep. She had never hoped to have her own baby, and the watching Megan saw her face light up with a radiance she'd never seen there before.

'You want the baby?' she asked. 'You'll keep it?'

'Of course!' There was firm conviction, not a shred of doubt in Julie's answer.

'What about Mike? What do you think he'll say?'

'I shan't tell him. If he doesn't come back, Megan, I shan't tell him.'

'But he has a right to know whatever ...' Megan put in.

'Don't you see, I can't hold him like that; can't use the baby to make him stay with me, can I?'

'No, I suppose not,' Megan was not so sure. 'I'll help you all I can, Julie. First, you'd better see your doctor – soon.'

Julie stood up slowly and put her arms round the other girl and held her close. 'Bless you, pet.' The words were husky and Megan's eyes glistened with tears.

'Think this through, love,' she begged. 'It's such an important decision to make – to have the baby, to keep it, to tell Mike' She paused and then went on sincerely, 'Only you can answer all those questions, Julie. But whatever, I'm here for you.'

Julie hugged her again and then sat down with a calm and serene glow on her face.

The doctor confirmed her pregnancy the next morning.

'About six weeks at least, Mrs Prescott, I'd say. And yes, you're right, those tablets could have upset your protection. Now I want you to attend my antenatal clinic regularly and later I'll need to make some tests.'

Tests...?' Her voice rose sharply.

'Just a precaution we take these days with – er, more mature mothers-to-be. Nothing to worry about.' And he went on to tell her about her diet and the care she should take to ensure a healthy baby.

'Yes,' he answered her query, 'you can still work, but don't get overtired, you're a healthy girl, so don't worry.'

Clutching her prescription for vitamins and iron tablets, she went out into the sunlight. She felt as if she was walking on air, and she found her hand straying to touch her stomach gently in wonderment. Mike's child was there, growing beneath her heart! In a dream she walked slowly back to the office, seeing in her mind's eye a little dark-haired boy with his laughing eyes, or a tiny girl with his mischievous grin.

September brought the early promise of autumn, with early morning mists and cooler days. The flower beds were a riot of colour, with dahlias, gladioli and early chrysanthemums; some of the trees began to show hints of yellow and gold among their green leaves. Workers hurrying to work seemed brighter, fresher with the end of summer's heat.

But day after day, with no news from Mike, Julie felt as if she was only half alive. Most mornings she rose to the awful feeling of nausea, and her face was wan and peaky looking, her normally bright hair lank and dull. If Mike saw her now, he'd certainly think her old and drab, wouldn't he?

But eventually the bad mornings passed, and gradually she took on the bloom of pregnancy that makes expectant mothers look more beautiful. She ate good, nourishing food, careful to keep to her diet and not put on too much weight. She walked whenever she could and did much of her paperwork resting on the settee in her office.

She grew closer to Megan, finding the young Welsh girl her staunch ally at all times. Together they often discussed her feelings for Mike.

'You must tell him about the baby, Julie. I'm sure he loves you, and he'll be pleased. He has a right to know.' Megan insisted.

But Julie was adamant.

'If and when he comes back to me – if he wants to be with me – then I'll tell him, but only after....' Stubbornly she kept to her decision. No way was she binding Mike to her side because of the baby, and as the three months passed and the day of his return grew nearer the fear that he wouldn't come back to her persisted.

'I'm sure he loves you, Julie,' Megan told her repeatedly. 'I could tell by the way he looked at you.'

Dear God, I hope she's right, Julie prayed. She scanned the mirror for signs of the growing baby, but apart from the feeling of heaviness in her breasts and a slight increase in her waistband size, there was only a small sign of a bulge in her tummy. And she didn't know whether she was pleased or not about that. She didn't want Mike to suspect, to know before he had made his decision. She would have to be patient, though she longed to see him, to tell him about the baby, that she loved him.

Without telling Julie, Megan rang Mike's office to discover exactly when he was expected back, and when they told her the date, she told Julie.

'He gets back on the 12th. What say we go out and buy you a new outfit?'

Big baggy tops were in fashion, and though not her usual style, they found a smart skirt with a loosely-pleated top that completely hid her increasing size.

When the 12th came and went without any word from Mike, Julie's heart sank further. It looked as if her worst fears were to be confirmed!

'Perhaps he's held up over there,' Megan suggested. She hated to see Julie looking so unhappy, for no matter how she tried nothing could disguise the lost bleak look in her hazel eyes.

When another week passed without news, she gave up hope. She knew that somehow she had to be strong, to face up to the future alone for her baby's sake.

But unable to watch her misery any longer, Megan rang Mike's office again, pretending it was a business call.

'Mr Stephens? Hold on, I'll check.' The girl at the other end seemed friendly enough and Megan hoped she wasn't going to cause trouble by interfering, but somebody just had to get some news for Julie!

'Are you there? Mr Stephens is not in work – someone reported him sick. Can I take a message?'

'Er – no. No thanks, I'll try his home.' With a frown she replaced the receiver. His home? It was no use, she'd have to tell Julie what she had found out and hope she wasn't too cross with her.

'Ill? But where is he? Why didn't he contact me?'

'Perhaps he can't.' As she spoke, Megan regretted the words. Julie's pale face grew paler still, and for a moment she looked about to faint. 'It's no use, love, you'll have to try to see him. You can't go on like this. See him – settle things one way or another. You're killing yourself.' Pity for her employer choked her. She looked dreadful! 'Go over to the cottage, Julie, today. He's perhaps there –ill. He might need you.'

It was those last few words that rang through Julie's head. 'He might need you'. And she knew – pride or not – she had to find out for herself.

'Yes, I'll go, Megan. Thanks for everything.'

She cleared the work on her desk while Megan made her a hot drink. Refusing the biscuits, she changed into the new two-piece and then spent precious time trying to disguise the pallor of her face. It took all her skill with make-up, and still her eyes were shadowed darkly, her mouth lined with un-happiness.

'You'll do, love. Your baby doesn't show yet, so don't worry. You look fine,' Megan lied sturdily.

It was four o'clock when she set out for the cottage. What if Mike wasn't there? Above all, what if he didn't really want to see her? Sick desolation ate into her very soul, but Megan was right – she had to know!

The faint autumnal mist drifted over the fields, and all around the beautiful tints of bronze and yellow were lost on Julie's distraught eyes. She longed to see Mike; it seemed so long since he went away. Just the sight of him could ease some of this pain....

The cottage looked lovely and peaceful in the fading light; fully restored now, it stood sturdy and snug, just as Mike had predicted it. There was no sign of life at the front, and she hesitated for a moment and then went slowly round to the rear and knocked on the back door.

It was opened at once by a pleasant, middle-aged woman wearing a bright overall and with a teatowel in her hand.

'I'm sorry, but ...' Julie could hardly get out the words, her heart seemed to be beating in her throat, 'I came to see Mike – Mr Stephens. Is he in?'

'Why surely,' the woman beamed a friendly smile. 'Come away in.' Inside, the kitchen was bright and clean – again all as Mike had planned it to be. 'He's been so poorly. Would you be his Julie?'

Julie nodded.

'Oh dear, then it's all spoiled – the surprise....' The older woman paused; she'd already said too much. 'I've been looking after things, and Mike, since he came home. Actually, he was just about to get up for the first time. I've lit the fire ready.' Flustered, the lilt in her voice became more pronounced. 'Come away through, miss. I'll tell him.' And leaving Julie to go through to the living-room, she hurried upstairs.

Looking round, Julie fell in love with the charming room. The glow from the log fire shone on the polished furniture; the chintz covers and curtains were perfect. Nervously she went over to the easy chair on the far side of the hearth as she heard sounds from above.

'Julie!' Mike stood there before her, in a dark dressing-gown, his face looking terribly pale. There were lines round his mouth, and the skin stretched taut over his cheek bones.

Shocked, she saw that he looked – not older – but somehow more *mature*. The young man had gone forever; he was now a man.

'Oh Julie.' He went to take her in his arms, his eyes hungry for the sight of her.

'No Mike.' Striving to still the thud of her heart, she stepped back. 'Please, sit down, we've so much to say. Don't hold me or kiss me, I must think clearly.' Her voice broke.

'Why...?' Mike's lips tightened, and then, as if in agreement, he took the easy chair opposite her.

As the daylight faded, the flickering flames cast darker shadows in the corners; cast shadows too on his face. He had been ill, that was all too clear to see.

'Oh Julie, it's all spoiled,' he began jerkily. 'I – we'd planned it all. A lovely meal here ...' he spread his hand wide, everything all nice and cosy; all finished, with me telling you everything. And then the delay – the plane held up in Heathrow to return us a day late. Several of us picked up a bug and what with jet lag and feeling lousy, all I could do was come here – my plans all upset!'

'Why didn't you let me know?' Her voice was accusing.

'I was too bad, passed out. But Mrs Thomas has been looking after me. I still wanted to see you *here*, in this little place I've made specially for us. My gift to you, Julie.' He paused, staring into the fire as if seeing pictures in the flames. 'You see, darling, I couldn't go on as we were.'

As she made to interrupt, he held up his hand.

'Hear me out first, Julie.' He swallowed convulsively and then calmly, quietly, he went on, 'At first it was fine. You laid down the rules and they suited me. I wanted to spend all my money on this. I fully intend to pay you back, by the way.' Again he paused and then went on, 'But it wasn't working out, Julie. You see, I began to love you. No, not "fall in love" but really love you. I wanted to break your damned rules, to have that commitment, to have you here, in my home, with me taking the reins. But all you were interested in was your business, wanting sex without any strings attached. And day after day I had to watch you worrying about that blasted age difference! Oh yes, Julie, I know how hard you tried, worrying, never letting me see you without make-up. Don't you know that beauty's in the eye of the beholder? That to me, you'll always be young and beautiful?'

As he went on, Julie thought her heart would burst with

happiness, but Mike was still looking deep into the flames.

'So when the States job came up, I took the risk, hoping you'd miss me, come to want me as a permanent fixture in your life. I planned to meet you here – to tell you how much I love you – to ask you to marry me – to put my gift of love at your feet. To tell you that I can't give you a written guarantee that it's going to last for ever. I can't give you that; I don't suppose anyone could. But that I knew we could make it if we really wanted to.'

He glanced across at her then, his smile rueful.

'And then I blew it all by picking up a lousy bug on top of jet lag. Sick as a dog, I had to put it all off – longing to see you, to hold you....'

'Oh Mike.....' With a little cry of understanding, Julie went across the hearth, to throw herself at his knees. He reached out and pulled her into his arms and found her willing lips. There was such a fierce hunger burning between them – so much time to make-up.

'I did miss you, darling. As – as your train pulled out, it seemed to take my heart with it, and I knew then – that I loved you as I'd never loved anyone before. I love you, Mike, with every kind of love there is. It's part of my soul and I can't get it out. It's there for ever, my dearest, and it's only for you.'

'So, you'll marry me then and live here?' Ages later, they drew apart long enough for Mike to ask her anxiously.

And Julie knew it was time to tell him.

'Is that little bedroom big enough for a nursery?' She watched him as the words sank in and the happiness on her face was like a light that touched every corner of it.

'A nursery?'

'Yes, my love, we're expecting a baby in about four and a half months' time.' His face was radiant with wonder, still half-believing.

'Julie! Oh Julie, you clever girl!' The pride and delight rang through his voice, and then he asked, 'Are you pleased; do you want it? Have you seen a doctor? Get up from there – the chair's more comfortable....'

He half-lifted her across to the other easy chair as if she was something fragile and precious; smothering her face with kisses, holding her close, almost delirious with joy.

Then, like a miracle of good timing, Julie felt a sudden little flutter in her stomach, like a feather moving – a gentle tiny flutter.

'Oh it moved! Mike, I felt the baby move.' Her face shone with awe and wonderment.

'Are you all right, love?'

'On top of the world, but I'm starving.'

At that Mike's laugh rang out, and as if on cue, Mrs Thomas gave a gentle rap on the door and came in bearing a loaded tray.

'Soup, sandwiches and coffee. That suit you both?' One look at their faces told her all she wanted to know. 'I've made your bed afresh, so I'll be getting back to my man now. 'Night.'

'You'll stay, Julie?' Mike asked.

'Try turning me away,' she laughed. 'Us away, I mean,' she added as she gently touched the roundness of her tummy. 'Just you try!'